DEADLY COVE

DEADLY COVE

BRENDAN DuBOIS

MINOTAUR BOOKS

A THOMAS DUNNE BOOK

New York   **3 1336 08885 9146**

A THOMAS DUNNE BOOK FOR MINOTAUR BOOKS.
An imprint of St. Martin's Publishing Group.

DEADLY COVE. Copyright © 2011 by Brendan DuBois. All rights reserved. Printed in the United States of America. For information, address St. Martin's Press, 175 Fifth Avenue, New York, N.Y. 10010.

www.thomasdunnebooks.com
www.minotaurbooks.com

Library of Congress Cataloging-in-Publication Data

DuBois, Brendan.
    Deadly cove : a Lewis Cole mystery / Brendan DuBois. — 1st hardcover ed.
        p. cm.
    ISBN 978-0-312-56634-0
    1. Cole, Lewis (Fictitious character)—Fiction.   2. Journalists—Fiction.   3. New Hampshire—Fiction.   I. Title.
    PS3554.U2564D44 2011
    813'.54—dc22

                                                                    2011007074

First Edition: July 2011

10   9   8   7   6   5   4   3   2   1

THIS NOVEL IS FOR MY SISTERS-IN-LAW:

Beth, Bernie, Liz, Cindy, and Lara—strong women, all.

ACKNOWLEDGMENTS

In addition to his wife, Mona, the author wishes to thank the following for their assistance in the years of research it took to research this novel: David Barr, Dave Conti, Sarah Cloutman, Joe Grillo, Brad Jacobson, Greg Kann, John Kyte, Jim Martin, Dick Messina, Pam Morse, Sue Perkins, Larry Rau, Dave Scanzoni, David Schwab, Bruce Seymour, Ron Sher, John Tefft, Patti Torr, Brenda Tringali, Rob Williams, and Dick Winn.

Thanks as well to Toni Plummer and India Cooper of St. Martin's Press and my skilled and devoted agent, Nat Sobel.

And a special debt of gratitude to the late Ruth Cavin, my editor at St. Martin's Press for more than ten years, who gave Lewis Cole such a supportive and productive home.

DEADLY COVE

CHAPTER ONE

I'm sure the events that autumn at the Falconer nuclear power plant will eventually spawn magazine articles, documentaries, and books about the demonstrations, the unsuccessful fight to keep the peace, the violence, and the tragic and unnecessary deaths, but all I know is the little corner of what I saw during those cold and gray days, and that corner was depressing enough.

For me and thousands of others, it began on a Thursday afternoon in October when I was standing on a piece of land owned by a New England consortium of ten utilities, which was home to the only nuclear power plant in New Hampshire. Placed in Falconer, at the southernmost end of New Hampshire's eighteen-mile shoreline, the property contained hundreds of acres with fields, marshes, and boxy concrete buildings that looked like they belonged in a 1950s science fiction film, complete with transmission lines heading out to the rest of New England, generating nearly twelve hundred megawatts of electricity and lots of controversy.

The particular piece of land on which I stood jutted out onto the wide salt marsh, and on either side of me were members of the news media, including Paula Quinn, assistant editor and reporter for the Tyler *Chronicle,* and one of the two best writers in this part of the state. She's a number of years younger than me, slim, and blond, and she was wearing jeans and a black wool coat. She had a digital Canon camera slung over one arm, and her small hands held a reporter's notebook.

With us there were also reporters from every major newspaper in New England, as well as the *New York Times,* and a host of television crews. We members of the alleged elite news media were looking out over a fence about fifty yards away, ringed on the top by three strands of barbed wire, with most of us shivering from the cold breeze coming off the ocean.

Paula leaned into me. "The natives are restless."

I followed her look out to the salt marsh. "Most aren't natives, but they're restless enough."

Out beyond the fence a rocky outcropping fell to the flatlands of the salt marsh, a large expanse of grassland that flooded every high tide and was furrowed by creeks and old drainage ditches. Beyond the salt marshes toward the left and a couple of miles away was a thin strip of land with buildings that marked the beaches of Tyler and Falconer. To the right and much closer, a thick stream of people was emerging from wooded areas bordering the marsh, coming out onto the grasslands.

They marched in ragged lines, chanting and yelling, waving banners and flags, a few beating drums. Some of the banners were huge, carried by a host of people, and even at this distance, I could make them out: NO NUKES. PEOPLE BEFORE PROFITS. SUN POWER, NOT NUKE POWER. Balloons on strings bounced and rippled above the demonstrators, and there were a couple of huge papier-mâché puppets. A few banners announced the name of the group supposedly in charge of the protesters: the Coalition for a Livable Future. The mass of people kept on streaming out and out, and Paula gave a nervous laugh. "You know, you look at those protesters . . . maybe they'll do it this time. They might actually do it."

I did know, and though I knew the demonstrators were mostly peaceful, there was a little gnawing sense of unease that grew at the base of my skull. I thought of the outnumbered defenders of the Alamo watching the Mexican army march before them, and tried to push the thoughts away. These people weren't violent, but they were certainly direct and enthusiastic. The protesters wanted to do more than demonstrate, as did their predecessors when the plant was being constructed; their goal was to occupy the Falconer nuclear power plant, shut it down, and prevent further construction of another reactor unit on the property.

Near this group of news media was a temporary trailer where a couple of construction workers in blue jeans, heavy boots, sweatshirts, and hard hats stood on a wooden porch, arms folded glumly, staring out at the marchers. For the trade union workers in New England, the thought of new construction at the Falconer nuclear power plant was the proverbial shot in the arm, said arm representing hundreds of union workers who had seen most large construction projects in New England disappear. A few years ago, the owners of Falconer Station had announced plans to construct a second reactor to help power the growing demand for electricity in the region. Their plans had gone forward with as much speed as one could expect from the federal bureaucracy, and except for a handful of arguments posted by some antinuclear groups, it had looked like concrete was going to be poured soon for the first buildings of Falconer Unit 2.

Then, half a world away, an obscure power station that had been built in the days of the Soviet Union and of the same design as the Chernobyl nuclear power plant had an explosion and fire. One would think that decades after Chernobyl, some important lessons would have been learned, but such was not the case for the Kursk nuclear power station. After the explosion, fire, and initial and clumsy cover-up by the Russian government, it became front-page news for over a month as a radioactive cloud spread across Eastern Europe. In a matter of ill-considered timing, that was when the announcement came from the utility consortium that construction would begin soon for Falconer Unit 2, which was then blocked by the federal government wanting to take one more look at the unit's licensing and design.

Hence the revitalization of the local antinuclear movement, but there was more than one movement out there, which Paula now pointed out to me.

"Look," she said. "More people to the party."

The first group of protesters had a festive air to go with their anger and determination, but the second group was just angry and more direct, and I could sense something change in the air when they emerged from another copse of trees. These protesters wore face masks or bandannas, some had hockey helmets on their heads, and most held wooden shields in front of them, which they banged on with wooden clubs. The shields bore a logo, a radiation trefoil symbol with a slash mark across it, bordered by the letters *NFF*, which stood for Nuclear Freedom Front. While the mainstay of the protesters out there were peaceful and wanted to overrun the power plant and occupy it in a nonviolent manner, these marchers were more direct and had assumed the motto of another protest organization: No Compromise in Defense of Mother Earth. Their plan was to come onto the plant site, tear down enough equipment or buildings to shut down Falconer Unit 1, and violently confront anyone—police, National Guard, or plant security—who got in their way.

Paula said, "You know, sometimes we reporters have to sniff around to look for stories. Nice for a change to have one fall in your lap . . . but something about this one is creeping me out."

I offered her a smile. "Me, too."

Looking to another collection of people, Paula folded her arms and said, "Just makes you wonder . . . what happens when that group meets this group." Standing in two lines about a dozen yards away were policemen and policewomen from a variety of public safety agencies in New England, and behind them, as some sort of reserve, were groups of National Guardsmen. The police and the Guardsmen wore riot helmets with raised visors, and while all of them had on different uniforms, they also all had gas-mask bags holstered at their sides.

"Whatever happens, it won't be pretty," I said.

Paula said, "With that, my friend, you're now the front-runner for understatement of the month."

"Nice to be in the run for something."

She eyed me with a bit of curiosity. In addition to her blond hair, Paula has fair skin, a pug nose, and ears that stick out too too much for her, but which I've always thought was quite cute and attractive. Some time ago we had a relationship that for a number of reasons never worked out, but we've remained friends ever since. The last I knew, she was still involved—if that term was still being used—with the town counsel for the town of Tyler.

Paula said, "I still don't know why you're here. I mean, everybody else has got hourly or daily deadlines. But you? I didn't think your monthly column meant you'd have to be slogging around here with the rest of us ink-stained wretches."

I shrugged. "There's a new managing editor at *Shoreline*. She wants more bang for her payroll buck, so I was asked to do a feature article about the demonstration for an upcoming issue."

"Asked, or ordered?"

"You're now part of management," I said. "You tell me."

She laughed, and we both went back to looking at the advancing line of demonstrators, the larger group on the left marching in ragged bunches and lines, and the smaller group on the right marching in good, disciplined order. It was like watching a miniature Roman legion being accompanied by a larger undisciplined ally, both coming at the target with different goals and objectives.

The smaller group then halted. No raggedy lines, no bunching up. Very sharp, very disciplined. Then the group split in the middle, and a tall man came out, wearing khaki pants, an old military jacket, a black watch cap, and a red bandanna around his face. Next to him were two younger men, dressed similarly, holding a portable sound system. The man who marched forward held out an arm, producing a brief moment of cheering from the smaller group and a couple of yells and catcalls from the larger group of protesters.

"Our mystery man approaches," Paula said, a touch of wonder in her voice. "I heard rumors that he wasn't going to show up, that he was afraid of being arrested."

"A leader has to lead, or he isn't much of a leader," I said.

One of the young men held a microphone up to the hidden face of the tall man, and he started speaking, his voice booming out. "My name is Curt Chesak, and I am the coordinator for the NFF, the Nuclear Freedom Front!"

More cheers from his followers. "I won't talk for long, for unlike some of our so-called allies, my people and I believe in action, not talk talk talk."

More jeers and catcalls from the larger group, echoed by cheers from the NFF crowd. Chesak held up a hand and said, "I've put everything on the line by being here. I know there are police and federal officials who would like to seize me, question me, and ar-

6

rest me. Perhaps even declare me an enemy combatant, and make me disappear. But I'm here for the greater good, to occupy, seize, and destroy this facility of death!"

The cheers came louder. I said to Paula, "Certainly doesn't mince any words, does he."

She picked up her camera, snapped off a couple of shots. "Conspiracy, incitement to riot, felony vandalism . . . lots of law enforcement types would like to be down there, put him in cuffs."

I pointed to the line of police officers nearby. "Then how come nobody's moving?"

"How come you don't remember your history, pal? Think of the charge of the Light Brigade; those cops wouldn't stand a chance."

I nudged her. "Nicely done, Madam Editor."

Out on the marsh, Chesak called out, "We won't quit until we win . . . and we won't talk talk talk, but fight fight fight!"

He dropped the microphone and melted back into his crowd of fellow protesters, and I said, "He sure speaks purty, doesn't he."

"Yeah, he does."

"Maybe he should run for president," I said. "Easy enough to get your name on the ballot here."

Paula laughed. "Speaking of presidential primaries—how's your fair companion, Miss Annie Wynn?"

"Still trying to elect Senator Jackson Hale to the Oval Office."

"Good for her," she said. "What does she plan to do after the election in November?"

"Sleep for a month," I said. "Or so she's said."

"Hah," Paula said back to me. "Do you plan to keep her company then?"

I smiled at Paula. "I plan to do my very best to show that sacrifices for our great democracy don't go unnoticed—and speaking of democracies, how's your male friend?"

"Mark? Still the lawyer for the town of Tyler, but you know what I know. He's thinking of running for the state senate next year. Gah, politics. Sometimes I think there should be a plague on both their houses, you know?"

I looked at the row of cops and National Guardsmen, and one of the cops looked familiar. I said to Paula, "Yeah, I know. Look, I'm off to visit the law enforcement side of the house. If anything newsworthy happens while I'm over there, you'll let me know, won't you?"

That got me another smile from Paula. "Since you're from a magazine and not a direct competitor, deal. Of course, if you were the Porter *Herald*, I'd politely tell you to go to hell."

I walked away from the newspeople and watched as a Boston television crew did a stand-up live broadcast, bracketing the shot so the intrepid correspondent had a line of barbed-wire fence and armed cops behind her. I moved on and went up to the line of cops, and I was eyed with suspicion, since I was wearing a bright black and yellow PRESS tag around my neck, identifying myself—at least to cops—as one of many enemies out there.

Save for one, who gave me a welcoming look as I got closer. She had on a black jumpsuit that had a dull gray and black patch on the sleeve, indicating she was a member of the Tyler Police Department, and she turned to me, and I said, "Detective Sergeant Diane Woods, so nice to see you in such a newsworthy place."

Her light brown hair was covered by the riot helmet, but her smile and a small scar on her chin—received from a drunk in the booking room who was one of the few people in this world who ever got the drop on her—were evident, and she said, "Thought this would be something you'd be able to cover from your living room, not out in the mud and dirt."

"Every now and then, I need to get off my butt and see things close-up."

Diane—my oldest and dearest friend—smiled and said, "That sounds fine, but don't get too close to this one, Lewis."

"Why's that?"

She looked around her, and then I joined her as she walked away from the line of cops, leaving us out of earshot. She said in a low voice, "What I mean is that there's been bunches of demonstrations here over the years, beginning when the first construction permit was issued, decades ago. We've never had anything like that, though." With that last phrase, she gestured to the straight lines of the Nuclear Freedom Front.

"The previous demonstrators," she went on, "we've seen them before. They come here, wave their banners, bang their drums, make a few halfhearted attempts to climb over the fence, and then they go home, telling each other how brave and committed they were. It's like one of those dances from Japan . . . what do you call them?"

"Kabuki dance," I said.

"Yeah, Kabuki. Very formal, very ritualized, everyone knows his or her roles. They played the part of the oppressed minority, getting their voices heard, and we played the role of the corporate lackey, arresting them. They went home happy that they'd made their point, and us cops went home, happy with the overtime pay. This time it's different. The direct action guys, the ones led by that fugitive, Chesak, they're itching for a fight, and they've made it very clear what they want to do. The other demonstrators— they want to occupy the site, shut it down, and plant trees and build windmills here. The direct action guys—they want to crack some skulls, burn some things, and tear down what they can."

"Looks like they're outnumbered," I said.

"Oh, yeah, they are, but that doesn't mean some people aren't going to get hurt. And don't forget the other folks in the mix."

"The union guys?"

She nodded. "Oh, yeah, the union guys. For the past few years, there's been a lack of big-ticket construction projects here in New England. Then, with the demand for more electricity, and more people thinking nuclear is a green option, the plans for Falconer Unit Two get pushed through. Suddenly, all the unions and trade organizations see thousands of good-paying jobs lasting for years coming down the highway, and they're practically drooling in anticipation. Then . . . the Kursk disaster. The anti-nuke groups get reenergized. And if you're a union guy, what are you going to do if you think a bunch of out-of-state tree huggers are standing between you and your jobs?"

I said, "You sound very well informed, Detective Sergeant."

She grimaced. "I have my sources of information."

Remembering something from a lunch conversation we had last month, as the protests started being planned, I said, "Tell me, is your Kara out there?"

She looked around, to see if anyone could overhear us; seemingly reassured that we were isolated, she said quietly, "Oh yeah, she's out there. In an affinity group associated with the peaceful demonstrators, thank God. I didn't want her to go out there, but no matter what I said, I lost the argument."

"I find that unusual."

"Why's that?" she asked. "You find it unusual that I'd lose an argument?"

"No," I said. "I find it unusual that your Kara, your computer whiz-girl Kara, who can make a laptop sit up and beg, who's comfortable with all sorts of technology, who's been in a number of successful software start-ups, I'm just surprised she's out there."

"That so?"

"Sure," I said. "The power plant that exploded in Kursk—there's nothing like it in the United States. Or France. Or Japan. That kind of accident can't happen here."

"Very observant," she said. "You're repeating the same arguments I was trying to use, and they didn't work. In her head, Kara knows that technologically speaking, Kursk and Falconer don't compare, but her heart is ruling now, Lewis. She's seen the television footage of scared mothers standing in long lines in Poland and Ukraine, desperately getting liquid iodine treatments for their children—and pictures of scared mothers and crying children will always outweigh cool debates about risks and containment buildings."

From both lines of demonstrators, the chanting and the beating of the drums increased, and Diane said, "I suppose I should get back to work, such as it is. What's on the schedule for the Fourth Estate?"

"In general, I have no idea," I said. "In particular, I'm going to attend two rallies this afternoon."

"Lucky you," she said. "What kind of rallies?"

"First one is a union rally, down at the co-op fishing building. Sort of an anti-antinuke rally, led by the head of the local union council, trying to drum up support for Falconer Unit Two. A guy named Joe Manzi."

Diane nodded. "Sure. Joe Manzi. Union organizer from Massachusetts who likes the high life. What's the other rally?"

"That one takes place a couple of hours later, at a campground in Falconer being used for the antinukers as a staging area, featuring Bronson Toles."

Diane laughed. "Bronson. Yeah. I'm sure he'll be walking across the marshlands at high tide. All right, my friend, take care of yourself."

"You, too," I said.

Back with Paula, she checked her watch. "We should get going soon if we plan to see both rallies up close."

"Will our minder let us leave?"

"Let's check."

Standing apart from the crowd of cops and National Guardsmen, a slim man with eyeglasses, wearing khaki slacks, a dark blue windbreaker, and a light blue hard hat emblazoned with the Falconer power plant logo was being interviewed by two camera crews. Paula and I walked up to him. He was talking calmly about the thousands of protesters nearby.

"We have full faith that local law enforcement will protect the plant and property," the man said, smiling at both camera crews. He was Ron Shelton, spokesman for the power plant, and our escort while on plant property. There was another question tossed his way, which I didn't make out, and he answered, "No, the operation of the power plant continues. We continue to produce enough power for one million New England homes, and we hope that the majority of the demonstrators honor their pledge to protest peacefully."

After a couple more questions, he was able to move away gracefully and approach Paula. She said, "Ron, any chance my friend and I can slip out?"

"If security says you can, I don't see why not. Come on, let's find out."

I followed Paula as she fell in with Ron, and I kept to one side as she peppered him with questions about upcoming events. We came up off the rough terrain onto a large paved area. Among the blocky buildings of concrete—including the hundred-foot-tall egg-shaped reactor containment building—other workers moved along, all sporting hard hats and wearing identification badges on their coats. On the pavement were yellow lines outlining paths to walk, and Paula and I stayed with Ron as we came out into a parking area, where there was a pair of light blue pickup trucks with spotlights mounted on the side doors. Men in dark gray jumpsuits and black boots and with semiautomatic weapons over their shoulders stood by a yellow concrete post that had a gray telephone communications box mounted on it.

Ron went up to the security officers and talked to them for a moment. One of them came back with him. "Where's your vehicle parked?" he asked me.

"Over there," I said, pointing. "The dark blue Ford Explorer."

The officer said, "Sir, just get into your vehicle and follow me. We'll slip you out of the Stony Creek Road gate."

"Thanks," I said, and Paula said to Ron, "Any chance for one last interview tonight, before deadline?"

The plant spokesman looked friendly but tired. "Sure. You know how we operate, Paula. Twenty-four/seven. Just call me, or have security page me. We'll get back to you."

We walked over to my Ford and got in. I started her up and followed the security pickup truck, which left the main parking area near the security building, a concrete cube surrounded by razor wire. Instead of going out one of the two main access roads that led to Route 1, the truck went down a bumpy dirt road that went underneath some of the huge transmission lines overhead that fed the plant's electricity to the regional power grid.

As we drove, I switched on the heat, and Paula said, "Thanks for being my taxi driver today."

"Not a problem," I said, the steering wheel vibrating in my hands as we made our way down the dirt road. "Let me know tomorrow if you need another ride, if your car is still in the shop."

"Deal, friend, deal."

Up ahead the security truck made a left turn, and we followed. We went down a narrow dirt lane that came to a tall chain-link fence with a gate in the center. The truck pulled to the side, and one security officer jumped out, went to the gate, and, after unlocking it, waved us through.

I sped up the Explorer, and there was a bump as we went onto paved road, and in the rearview mirror I caught the officers swinging the gate shut and locking it. Up ahead were a couple of cottages and small Cape Cod houses, and the road widened a bit as we approached Route 1, the main two-lane road running north and south from Massachusetts to Maine, also known as Lafayette Road.

Paula said, "Looks like the circus is pretty widespread."

"Sure is," I said.

Where the road met Route 1, lines of people were walking by, some of them carrying the same kinds of signs and banners as their brethren at the salt marshes. I pulled up and waited for a break in the foot traffic, as well as the vehicle traffic. Cars and trucks moved by slowly, accompanied by a couple of National Guard Humvees.

A noise on my side window startled me. I looked over and saw a young woman standing there, smiling, gently tapping on the glass. I lowered the window. She was in her twenties, with long brown hair parted in the middle and wearing a gray sweatshirt, a long red peasant skirt, and sneakers. She handed over a leaflet to me.

"There's a rally tonight, at the Seaside Campground," she said. "My name is Haleigh. Will I see you there?"

I smiled. "Sure. We'll be there."

I raised the window, and Paula said, "That wasn't nice."

"What wasn't nice?" I asked, and, finally finding a break in the traffic, I eased out onto Route 1 and started heading north.

"You told her that we'd be at the rally tonight," she said. "I bet she thought that meant you'd be there as a supporter, and not a reporter."

"Not my fault if she thought that," I said.

"You getting crusty in your old age?"

"Maybe," I said, "but I don't feel old."

That earned me a laugh as we went up Route 1, the traffic finally thinning out, the sun shining brightly, and the foliage on the trees on both sides of the road burning a bright red and orange. It looked nice, it looked quiet, and this would prove to be the last peaceful day in Falconer for some time to come.

CHAPTER TWO

It took about twenty minutes of driving to get where we wanted to go, as we took Route 51 down to Tyler Beach and then looped our way back to Falconer, traveling on Route 1-A, also known as Atlantic Avenue. Here there were cottages and lots of motels and shops, most them closed down for the cold fall and winter that was coming our way, and off to our left, the endless moving gray waters of the Atlantic Ocean. We crossed over the Felch Memorial Drawbridge that spanned the channel leading from the Falconer and Tyler harbors to the ocean, and to the right, lobster boats and stern draggers were moored as a sharp wind made whitecaps dance on the waters.

"Tell me again about your new boss," Paula said.

"Do I have to?"

She laughed. "A real mouthful, isn't she. Denise Pichette-Volk, right?"

"Good memory," I said.

Paula added, "Also known as 'Denise the Dastardly.' Known for coming into newspapers and magazines that are struggling, cutting costs, squeezing more personnel, getting, quote, more efficiencies, unquote, from staffers. You getting squeezed there, Lewis?"

Up ahead I saw lines of people marching along both sides of the road. There were chain-link fences on the right, and beyond that, a flat parking lot and a large white building with a peaked black shingle roof that was the fishing cooperative for most of the fishermen working out of Falconer and Tyler harbors.

"Usually I like being squeezed by women," I said. "Not this time."

"Any juicy details?"

I thought for a moment, slowing the Explorer some as I reached the open gate of the cooperative. "Not a one."

She smiled, but there was a hint of frustration in her face. "Some days your secretive past and lack of conversation can be charming, but not today. I feel sorry for your lady friend, if this is the kind of face you show her, day after day."

She turned and pretended to be interested in the line of marchers clustered around the gate to the parking lot. As Paula looked out the window, I did, too, and remembered.

About a month ago I had been summoned to appear at the offices of *Shoreline* magazine, located in a renovated mill building in South Boston. The monthly magazine covers the history and happenings of the New England coastline from the upper reaches of Maine to the lower depths of Connecticut, and I have a monthly column called "Granite Shores," which covers the New Hampshire seacoast. I became a magazine columnist after an unfortunate series of events when I was a Department of Defense employee that led to the death of some friends and co-workers, including a dear woman who might have become Mrs. Lewis Cole one day—but that wasn't meant to be, like JFK's second term.

Being told to appear in South Boston had been a shock, and

was going to be one of many that day. In the brick-lined and comfortable offices of the magazine, the biggest shock was seeing someone different sitting behind the desk of the magazine's editor, retired U.S. Navy Admiral Seamus Anthony Holbrook. His office had mementos of his navy past and a great view of Boston Harbor, but the woman sitting at his desk was out of place. She was much younger than me, had long black hair, and wore a stunning black and red dress. All in all, she looked like one of those women devoted to fashion magazines that have an ad-to-copy ratio of about ninety to ten.

She stood up, gave me a brief shake of the hand, and got right to it. "My name is Denise Pichette-Volk. I'm now in charge here at *Shoreline*."

I sat down, nearly missing the chair. "What happened to the admiral?"

She shrugged. "Off on medical leave. For something."

"Where? For what?"

"I don't know." She looked down at some papers. "What I do know is that the publishers have taken me aboard to make some changes, and your name is on the top of the list."

"Just what kind of list is that?"

She turned a sheet of paper. "The list of those who get paid extraordinarily well for doing extraordinarily little. Mr. Cole, your sole responsibility to *Shoreline* is producing one column per month, for which you get paid at a higher rate than more than ninety-five percent of the staff. Doesn't sound particularly efficient, now, does it."

I cleared my throat. "My arrangements here with *Shoreline* were made with the full knowledge and cooperation of Admiral Holbrook, and—"

Denise held up a manicured hand. "I know all about the arrangements. I know some about your service with the Department

17

of Defense. I know that your job here was initially a gift to you, for your faithful service to our country, blah-blah-blah."

Something cold tickled at the backs of my hands. "I'm sorry, what do you mean, 'initially'?"

She looked at me with her cold brown eyes. "Initially the Department of Defense paid for your salary and benefits through a rather . . . unusual accounting arrangement, but that arrangement ended a few years ago. Cost-cutting, you realize, on the behalf of the federal government. Ever since then, *Shoreline* has been paying your full freight. Through the intercession of Admiral Holbrook."

My hands and the back of my neck were now quite chilled. "I never knew that."

"From what I understand, that was the admiral's decision. He has some old-fashioned concept about promises made and loyalty to subordinates. Now that decision has been overruled."

"I see."

"Um, no, I don't think you see. The decision of the admiral to keep you on and pay you was based on your performance as a columnist, but you're going to do more for the magazine now, Mr. Cole. An additional article in each issue, from a story idea that will be assigned to you by the editorial staff here. Copy editing from home on some of our less-talented freelancers' contributions. Perhaps even some sales work, going to businesses along the New Hampshire seacoast, convincing them to advertise with the magazine."

I shook my head. "Not going to happen. Look, you should know that my agreement with the government meant that—"

She dropped her fountain pen, smiled, and leaned back in the admiral's chair. "Yes, your agreement with the government. I don't know the details of your agreement, but I do know that in exchange for keeping your mouth shut about some past embarrassing incident, you got this comfy job. Fine. Take it up with the government if you have a problem with the way you're being treated. Although, trust me, that won't get you far. Considering all the dirty laundry that's been aired this past decade about what our government has been up to, do you really think you can convince them to return to your original agreement if you threaten to go public? Over some past embarrassment?"

My hands were clenched. *Past embarrassment,* I thought. A long time ago, I worked as a research analyst for an obscure section of the Department of Defense, and on a training mission in the high Nevada desert, we were all killed—save for me—after being exposed to a nasty biowarfare agent that didn't officially exist. All those co-workers, my dear Cissy Manning, all dead and gone and forgotten . . . except they were now considered an embarrassment.

I said, "You seemed to have thought this through."

Her face had a triumphant little smile. "I certainly have. That's why I'm here. So what's it going to be, Mr. Cole? Your new arrangement, or unemployment, in this economy and at your age?"

"I'd like to take some time to think about it."

She leaned forward in the admiral's chair. "Take all the time you want. Just make sure it's in the next thirty seconds. I'm a very busy woman."

I took a breath, and then another one. "Then I suppose my answer is yes."

The triumphant smile on her face widened. "I never had any doubt."

I drove up to the open gate to the fishing co-op, then stopped and touched Paula on her shoulder. Surprised, she turned to me, and I said, "Many years ago, I worked at the Pentagon. One day I was part of something that got a lot of friends of mine killed. I was the sole survivor. I got paid off, and to keep my mouth shut, I was given the job at *Shoreline*. I've kept my mouth shut ever since then."

Paula looked shocked. "But . . . you've just opened your mouth."

"I guess I did."

"Why?"

Behind me horns blared. I didn't move. "Because I kept up my end of the bargain, while other people didn't."

She looked at me, and her smile this time was genuine, no frustration mixed in. "Well, you certainly are full of surprises, even at this late date—but, Lewis?"

"Yes?"

"Get your butt in gear. We're going to be late for speechifying."

Through some intercession of the parking gods we found an empty space, though we had to walk across what seemed to be a couple of acres of parking lot to get to the co-op building. There were a lot of pickup trucks and SUVs, and not a single hybrid in sight. The wind was sharper off the harbor, and Paula stayed close to me as we walked. The co-op was built like a large white barn, with doors set in the front, and there was a knot of people by the doors.

Paula said, "Still not sure why the union people are meeting here."

"Biggest hall in the area," I said, "and guys and gals who work with their hands—they tend to look out for each other."

We got closer to the knot of people, some with windbreakers and jeans, others fellow members of the news media. There was a gatekeeper up forward, standing there, burly-looking, arms crossed, wearing a gray sweatshirt with a hood and soiled jeans, face red and belligerent. As I moved up I heard him say, ". . . and that's it, nobody else gets to go in."

I went up to him, held up my press pass. "Just the two of us, all right?"

He looked and said, "Damn out-of-staters, coming in to stir things up. Nope, the hall is full."

I said, "I live in Tyler, and so does she, so we're not from out of state. So how about stepping by?"

A firm shake of the head. "Nope. I got my orders. Room is full. Nobody else gets in."

Paula said something, but I couldn't make it out because of the other people talking. I said, "Look, we need to do our job, we'll get in and stand in the back, and—"

The gatekeeper said, "Hey, I'm fucking tired of talking to you, so get out of my face, all right?"

"I don't think your face is worth getting into, and—"

He unfolded his arms and stepped toward me, and I let my reporter's notebook drop to the ground, and I felt that quick warm tingling that tells you things are going bad, very quickly, and just as quickly, it calmed right down when I felt a soft touch on my shoulder and heard a familiar male voice say, "Everything all right here?"

I turned in relief and then bent down to scoop up my notebook. Felix Tinios stood there, dressed sharply in black shoes, black trousers, and a light tan jacket that was partially zipped shut. The jacket fit snugly around his well-built shoulders and arms, his dark-skinned face was shaved smooth, and his black hair was well coiffed, as always. He was smiling, and his eyes were merry, but there was a sense of energy about him, like a man who would graciously allow you to cut ahead of him in traffic but would cause you grievous bodily harm if you ever crossed him in private or public.

I suppose he was my friend, though what passed for a relationship was much more complicated than that. In any event, I said,

21

"No, everything is not all right here. Paula Quinn and I are trying to cover Joe Manzi's press conference, and this character won't let us in."

Felix nodded crisply and went up to our nameless gatekeeper and said, "Hey, they're going in, okay?"

The guy said, "My orders are that the room is full and—"

Felix put his hand on the man's shoulder, gave it a firm squeeze. "I'll take full responsibility. The name is Tinios, and I'm in charge of Mr. Manzi's personal security."

The guy opened his mouth, and then not a word came out. Whether he was struck speechless by Felix's logic or by Felix's hard grasp on his shoulder, he closed his mouth, swallowed, and moved aside. Paula ducked between us and got inside, and I looked to Felix and said, "Thanks."

He looked unfazed. "It's what I do."

"So you're now working for a union? I mean, come on. That's a cliché and you know it. Next thing, you'll be telling me that you're doing consult work in Las Vegas."

That got a laugh. "Cliché or not, the money is still green, it's steady, and usually I'm home every night at a good time. As for providing security—it's good work for little effort."

"Thanks again," I said, moving now into the meeting hall, and then a wall of sound and smell came at me. I spotted Paula, standing against the rear wall, being jostled by some guys in dungarees and sweatshirts, and I elbowed my way in next to her. Near us was a wooden platform that allowed the television cameras to shoot over the heads of the seated audience.

The hall looked like it was designed to hold about a hundred people, and I'd guess there was nearly twice that number in there. The smell was of old cigarette smoke, stale beer, sweat, and anger. Those who weren't standing were sitting on folding chairs, and up on the other side of the room was a raised stage, only a couple of feet high, with another row of chairs and a lectern. An American flag and a New Hampshire state flag flanked the speaker, who was leaning so far over the lectern, punching the air with a closed fist, that it made him look like a drunk attacking shadows.

". . . and another thing," he bellowed, "those who are out there keep on yapping to us about green jobs this, and green jobs that, and you know and I know that all this talk about green jobs is so much horseshit. Windmills are okay, unless you're rich and don't want them spoiling your view. Hydro is fine, unless they might harm some small snail nobody's ever heard of. And solar, yeah, solar is great, except nobody wants them in their backyard or in some endangered desert."

That got a burst of laughter and some cheers, and the man, his face almost as red as the gatekeeper's outside, nodded with satisfaction as the cheers went on for a bit. He was short and solid, with wide shoulders that would have suited a hockey goalkeeper, and his dark brown hair was slicked back. He had on a blue windbreaker with the logo of some union organization over his chest.

Paula raised herself up on her toes and talked into my ear. "Joe Manzi, champion of the working class, head of the New England Trade Union Council, and owner of a nice condo in Aruba."

"Looks like a real man of the people," I said as I started scribbling in my own notebook.

That earned me a dirty look from a couple of the nearest guys, so I kept my mouth shut as Joe went on. "Believe it or not, we know what are green jobs. Green jobs are the ones that give us good jobs at good wages, that allow you and you and you"—and with each "you," he pointed to someone in the audience—"to own a house, to get a car, save some money for your kids to go to college. And what's wrong with that? Not a goddamn thing!"

More cheers, more applause, and Joe stepped back from the lectern, nodding, and then applauding as well, and when the noise died down he went back to the lectern and said, "Those kind of green jobs worked for my dad, and his dad before him, and by God, they'll work for you! And right now, the best green job for all of us is across that marsh, at Falconer Unit Two. Ironworkers, pipefitters, painters, electricians, carpenters—we can all have a part of that project and part of something that's gonna provide power for this region and our country, and we're gonna see that it gets built!"

Now the audience was on its feet, cheering and applauding, and I looked around at them all, sensing the desperation in their cheers and applause. They had bought into what was once the American dream, and now they were scared and angry and they were listening to someone who was promising to make it all better. I understood them, and with what had been going on with *Shoreline* magazine and me, I also felt that chill of having the unknown out there threaten your livelihood.

Another raise of the hand from Joe, and they quieted down. "Look," he said, again draping himself over the lectern. "Let's be real, all right? The protesters, the tree huggers, the Volvo drivers, they're upset about a power plant in Russia that couldn't even be designed over here, it's so freakin' dangerous. So just because the Russians don't know how to do something well, does that mean we have to pay the price for it? No, it doesn't. Let me tell you, when push comes to shove, when it comes to choosing between some sixties leftovers and good jobs for all of you, I know what's going to be done. We're not going let some tree huggers stand between us and good jobs. Whatever it takes, my friends, whatever it takes. My brothers and sisters, we cannot—"

Near the front of the row of seats, two young men and an older woman suddenly stepped up, and from underneath one young man's jacket, they quickly unfurled a banner that read NO NUKES NO FALCONER 2, and they started chanting the same words painted on the piece of cloth.

The reaction was immediate. The television cameras swiveled as one to take in the breaking news, and Paula raised her camera, snapped off a couple of shots, and then the booing and yelling started, some men got up and tore down the banner, chairs were overturned, more yelling, and two uniformed Falconer cops waded into the fracas, and there were more shouts and screams, and I grabbed Paula's arm and said, "Let's get out of here."

She shook off my grasp. "In a second. I want to get another shot." She climbed up on the wooden platform where the television cameras were placed and brought the camera up to her face. My skin tingled. I didn't want to be here, not at all, and on the opposite side of the room, Felix Tinios walked over, took Joe Manzi by the elbow, and then Joe left, joined by the others. A chair was thrown, and then Paula got off and came to me, grinning. "Got a great shot, somebody getting punched out."

"That's sweet," I said. "Looks like Joe has left the building. Can we leave now?"

Outside there were sirens, and inside, more shouts and a scrum of bodies up where the protesters had stood up to make their stand, and Paula said, "All right, we can leave now."

When we stepped out, the air was cold and sharp, and Paula said, "One of these days, Lewis, you'll get the bones of a journalist. Wanting to leave just when the story got interesting."

I said, "Only bones I'm interested in are mine and yours, and keeping them in one piece. Let's go see what the other side's press conference has to offer," and Paula laughed and slipped her arm into mine as we walked over to my Ford Explorer.

That was one of the last times I was to see the Paula Quinn I knew and had once loved.

CHAPTER THREE

Fifteen minutes later, parking was a problem yet again, and I had to abandon my Ford on a dirt road that led into a camping area on the north end of Falconer. A dark brown wooden sign with white paint read SEASIDE CAMPGROUND, and there was a little cottage along the way that served as the campground's office, but it was closed and the lights were off. There were cars and trucks and a couple of news vans pulled to the side of the dirt road, and there was room only for walkers. Brush and pine trees were on both sides, rising up into the cold sky.

Paula joined me as we heard singing in the distance. The people walking with us were mostly young, laughing and talking to each other. The dress code here was more casual than at the fishermen's co-op: lots of jeans, flannel shirts, long skirts, hair done up in braids, body piercings, and tattoos, plus the usual anti-nuclear signs and banners were carried along as well.

Paula said, "Well, that certainly was exciting back there."

"Exciting?" I said. "Seeing people beat the crap out of each other doesn't seem that exciting."

She smiled. "Still, it makes for great photos and great copy, doesn't it."

"Maybe you're right," I said softly. "Maybe I don't have the bones for your line of work."

She said, "Oh, don't be so hard on yourself. I mean, you hang around with that North End character, Felix Tinios."

"What do you know about Felix?"

26

"From Boston originally. Connected to the mob, but supposedly freelance." She then laughed. "Hard to believe he was working at the union rally, providing security."

"Believe it," I said. "One April, a few years back, he showed
me his tax return. It said his occupation was security consultant."

Another laugh. "I still don't believe it."

"If it's good enough for the federal government, who am I to
say otherwise?"

Paula muttered something about the federal government's
competency, and as we made distance along the narrow pathway,
more and more people joined us. Paula said, "Seems like a much
happier group."

"Of course," I said. "They're unmarried, with no car payments,
no mortgages, no kids looking to them to keep them clothed and
fed and healthy, no sick parents or college bills. They can afford
to be happy."

"Cynic, aren't you."

"Happens when you get older."

"Then don't get old."

"I've tried," I said. "Odds are stacked against me."

The road ended in a large open area of grassland surrounded
by trees, with picnic tables and chairs scattered underneath like
large wooden toys. Music boomed out from loudspeakers, and
tents were set up, and there were fires burning merrily along, and
some of the more enthusiastic participants were dancing in circles,
laughing. A wooden stage was set up with a banner flapping
beneath it, the words reading A NUCLEAR-FREE FALCONER. On
the stage was a huddle of people, and one man stood to the side,
arms folded, nodding as an intense woman talked to him. He had
on blue jeans and a dungaree jacket and wore big black-rimmed

27

glasses. His beard was thick and gray, making up, it looked like, for the sparse cover on his head.

The intense woman seemed about twenty years younger and wore a long skirt and a thick sweater. Her black hair was in a pony-tail, and she had a clipboard in hand. Paula said, "There they are. The couple of the day . . . or week."

"I didn't realize Bronson Toles was married," I said. "I know he runs the Stone Chapel, but wasn't he a widower?"

Paula took a picture of the stage and people. "Yep. Until a number of years ago. Gotta keep up with the news, Lewis. That's Laura Glynn Toles—or as some would say, the Mary Magdalene to the antinuker's Jesus of Nazareth."

I turned to her. "Who's being cynical now?"

Another smile. "The Stone Chapel has always been a quiet little folk music place, a good place for those up-and-comers to earn their chops before they go on to bigger and better things. Story I heard once is that Laura likes the extra publicity her hubby's activities bring to the Stone Chapel. Before they got mar-ried, the place was always about a week or two away from having its power cut off. Now they make enough money so they can hire a cook to sling hash, instead of making Laura and her son do double or triple duty. Even do some catering work for the de-voted ones who are getting married or who throw a party to raise money for the latest cause."

A plump older woman with lots of bracelets on her wrists stepped up to a microphone, and there was a burst of feedback that almost made me grab at my ears. She looked chastened and said, "Sorry . . . sorry, folks . . . I know we're running late, but we'll start as soon as we can. I know all of us want to hear our own Bronson Toles tell us about our challenges and what faces all of us here, not only tonight, but for the years to come."

Some applause and a few cheers, but most of the people

28

there seemed interested in the music, although there were lines of people still streaming in from the woods. From beyond the stage, the flat marshland stretched out all the way to the utility's fence line and the lights of the Falconer nuclear power plant.

"Enemy in sight," I said, pointing out the view. Paula laughed, and there was a sharp voice: "What's so funny?"

There was a tall, skinny guy behind us, wearing cargo pants, a multicolored T-shirt, and some sort of woven wool hat that had the colors of the Jamaican flag. He had a stringy beard that went down midchest, and both eyebrows were pierced.

"I'm sorry," I said. "What did you say?"

"I said, What's so funny?" he demanded, stepping closer. "That plant over there is spewing death on a daily basis, is a ticking time bomb ready to kill us all, and you think that's funny?"

Paula began to speak, but I interrupted her. "What I think or she thinks really isn't your business, is it."

He stepped closer, flipped a finger on my press pass. "Hah. Member of the press. Paid corporate shill. Not reporting the real news. Covering up for your corporate masters."

Another flip of my press pass by his dirty hand, and I said, "Touch it again, friend, and you and I will be making some news, right here."

Paula touched my arm, and then another woman spoke up. "Henry, go away and leave them alone. They don't get paid to listen to your lectures."

I recognized our new friend: the young woman from earlier in the day, the one passing out the leaflets on Route 1. Henry snorted and walked away, and Paula said, "Thanks. Do you know him?"

"Sure," she said. "We both go to UNH. We hooked up for a bit, until I realized he thought hooking up meant sitting in his dorm room and listening to the latest conspiracies."

Paula smiled, offered her hand. "Paula Quinn. And this is Lewis Cole."

The woman returned the smile. "Haleigh Miller. From UNH Students for Safe Energy. Glad you could make it."

I was going to say something, but there was another squeal of feedback as the same woman started speaking again at the microphone. By now the area around the stage and the campgrounds were crowded with people, mostly demonstrators and a few other members of the news media. In my mind's eye, I was already working through what the article would eventually look like for my new boss at *Shoreline*. Something about this whole demonstration having its roots in the history of protest in an area that's always had revolutionary fervor, and that this was another attempt by the informed and enraged citizenry to make their points in a public and peaceful way, and wasn't that a nice thing in this increasingly computerized and Internet-connected age.

Ick, I thought. I'd have to come up with something better.

As has been said by so many people, be careful for what you wish for.

The squeal came back again, and then the sound boomed out. "Welcome, welcome, welcome to the place where a change is a-going to come," the plump woman said. "I know you haven't come to hear me speak—so I shan't waste any more of your time. Fellow lovers of our Mother Earth, I'm so proud to present our own Bronson Toles of Tyler, Bronson Toles of the Stone Chapel, and Bronson Toles, our guide in making Falconer and the rest of the world a nuclear-free zone."

Around us there were cheers and applause, and some of the women started trilling their tongues, making sounds like Middle Eastern tribeswomen. Bronson Toles ambled over to the microphone, and he joined in the applause as well, holding out his arms as if cheering on his supporters. Paula started moving toward the stage, camera in hand, and I followed her until we got right to the front.

Bronson leaned into the microphone and said in a mellow, quiet voice, "With so many here in our quest to save our coast and save our planet, I have no doubt we will overcome . . . and we will succeed."

More cheers, more applause, and I took some notes as he spoke up. "For decades, I and so many others have resisted that tempting siren call of joining what passes for civilization, to be better consumers, better rapists of our Mother Earth, better cogs for the machine that serves to control us all. Instead I made a choice, years ago, to do something small, something beautiful, something that would work toward healing communities, not breaking them apart. From our humble beginnings at the Stone Chapel, where we fed the hungry, sheltered the homeless, and gave many a struggling artist their first step on their way to well-deserved fame, we were always here for you."

Over the applause Paula raised her voice. "At least he didn't talk about loaves and fishes. Even for Bronson Toles, that would be too much."

Bronson waited again for the cheers to subside. "Other people, at almost the same time as me, had choices to make, and they made the wrong ones. So many years ago, we chose the wrong path when it came to producing the electricity for our homes and businesses. You see, after the atomic bomb was first used against civilians at the end of the Second World War, the military-industrial complex had built a system of engineers and uranium processing, and a support system that needed to be used. It couldn't be allowed to wither away. So that's how that . . . place over there on our coast got built. Because the military-industrial complex needed to continue their monopoly on power, on secrecy, on inserting themselves into our life . . . such that the Falconer plant was built, a plant that will disease and kill this living cove behind us, turning it into a place of sickness, of death, a deadly cove."

The cheers, applause, and trilling returned, and Bronson nodded again, applauded again, and when the noises subsided again, came forward and said, "Together, though, working together, being together, we can change the destiny, can protect ourselves and our future, and—"

Two young men scrambled onto the stage, holding up their right arms, fists clenched, and started yelling, "No compromise! No compromise! No compromise! Bronson's too weak! Bronson's too weak! Bronson's too weak!"

They turned and tore off their jackets, revealing the logo of the Nuclear Freedom Front. There was chaos up on the stage as a couple of women tried to hustle off the two young men, and there were yells and screams next to me, and Paula spoke in my ear and said, "This is good stuff. Civil war breaks out in the antinuclear ranks. Help me up, will you? This'll be a great photo."

I said, "I don't think that's a good idea," but I don't think she heard me, and Paula glared, and I hoisted her up by grabbing her slim hips, and she stood up on the stage, held out her camera.

Lucky me, from where I stood, I saw and heard the whole thing.

Heard: a loud, flat *crack*.

Saw: Bronson Toles's head shatter open in a pink flower of blood, brain, and bone, falling, Paula next to him, falling as well.

Heard and saw: screaming and terror seizing everyone around me.

CHAPTER FOUR

The crowd pushed me against the wooden stage, nearly breaking my ribs, and there was a sharper scream, and Haleigh Miller was next to me, shoved up against the edge of the stage as well, her throat being crushed. I elbowed someone out of the way, pushed again, moved to Haleigh. More screams and shouts. The earsplitting pitch of feedback burst over us all, and then a frantic male voice: "Is there a doctor here? Is there a doctor here? Please, calm down . . . please . . . calm down! We need a doctor up here, right away!"

I pushed again, grabbed Haleigh's arm, was able to spin her so that she wasn't being strangled, and then the crowd pushed us again, slamming my back against the wood. I kicked back and found the thin wood covering the bottom of the stage was loose. I kicked and kicked again, and then pulled Haleigh down with me, going under the stage as a thin slab of plywood broke free.

"Do you . . . do you think a doctor will get there in time?" she cried out to me.

In my mind's ear and eye, I heard the crack of the rifle shot, saw how the top of Bronson's head was blown apart, and—

Paula.

She had fallen as well.

"No, it's too late," I said. "Head shot. Instantly dead."

She put her hand up to her mouth.

"Hold on," I said. "I need to check something."

I pushed my way through the legs of the people around the stage, thankful that the crowd was thinning out. Sirens were sounding in the distance, and there were two forms on the stage that I barely could make out through the men and women kneeling next to them. I saw one set of feet that belonged to the very dead Bronson Toles, and another set of feet that belonged to Paula Quinn.

"What . . . what's going on?" Haleigh asked, now standing next to me.

"My friend is down," I said. "I've got to see her."

"But I only heard one shot," she said. "Only one. Maybe she just fainted. I'm sure she's fine."

I started to say something, shut up. The curse of being well-read, and of being a student of history, for I was about to tell Haleigh that in every war, a certain number of casualties are wounded by the bone fragments of their comrades shot or blown up while huddling next to each other while under fire.

"I'm still going to check," I said. I spared a glance. Still a fair number of people but not as many as before. "Stay here. It's relatively safe."

The sirens grew louder, and I saw the flashing lights of police cruisers and ambulances bouncing down the dirt road. I put my hands on the rough stage, pulled myself up, and got up on my knees. It was crowded, and there were shouts and more yells, and I tried to push my way in, and then I was blocked by a red-faced, sweaty patrolman from the Falconer Police Department.

"You a doctor?" he demanded.

"No, that woman, she's a friend and—"

"Off the stage, now," he said. "Too many people up here already."

"I want to check on her—"

"Off, now," he said, pushing a hand into my chest, and I stepped back, stepped back, and the third time, my feet found only air and I fell back onto the dirt lot.

34

Lots of things were hurting. I tried to catch my breath, didn't quite succeed. I was on my back, which was throbbing, and my ribs ached as well, from having been pushed into the edge of the stage earlier. I coughed and rolled over, got up. More flashing lights. The stage was nearly empty. Three ambulances were parked up close to the stage, and there was a line of Falconer cops and state police keeping everyone away. There were knots of people standing around, craning their heads, trying to see what was going on, and then one ambulance, and then another, pulled away, with a state police cruiser leading the way, siren whooping, lights flashing.

My jaw hurt, too. I rubbed at my jaw and then went over to the stage, bent down, and looked at my hidey-hole.

Haleigh Miller was gone.

I stood up. Who could blame her?

The stage was now a conclave of cops, investigators, and other men and women in serious suits with serious attitudes. Crime scene tape had quickly been strung, and little yellow and black plastic folding signs designating evidence sites were placed on the floor, and there were brief bursts of light, like sudden lightning, as photographers did their job.

I reached into my coat pockets, found my reporter's notebook, my cell phone, and the keys to my Ford. A real reporter, I suppose, would stay behind and try to get the story here, at the actual crime scene, where a prominent antinuclear and peace activist had been gunned down. That's where the story was. News vans from the Boston television stations and the sole New Hampshire television station were already racing down the dirt road, nearly ramming into each other to find a parking spot.

I pulled out my car keys.

Never said I was a real reporter.

I started jogging back up to where my Explorer was parked.

Where Paula and the corpse of Bronson Toles had gone was no big mystery. The nearest hospital was about two towns over from Falconer and an easy drive from Route 1 to the interstate to Route 101, heading west. It's usually a twenty-minute drive. I did it in under fifteen, and I would have gotten there quicker save for a moment when I had to pull over, when I saw Paula's purse sitting on the floor, in front of the passenger seat, like a forgotten pet. I didn't like seeing her purse on the floor. It didn't belong here by itself. I picked it up and put it back on the passenger seat and resumed driving.

Exonia Hospital is a sprawling campus of brick buildings in the charming town of Exonia, home to a famed prep school and a bunch of authors, most of them laboring in deserved obscurity. From past experience and visits, I pulled into the emergency room parking lot, which was already nearly full. I moved quickly through a set of automatic sliding glass doors, and inside, the waiting area of the emergency room was a miniature of the chaos I'd left behind in Falconer. Hospital security officers were trying to keep some sense of order, and men and women and even some children argued, yelled, and cried as others pushed up against the admissions desk. There was some low chanting from a group that sat on the carpeted floor holding hands, praying for whatever was worth praying for.

I pushed and shoved my way up to the admissions desk, and a thin, harried woman in a blue smock looked at me and quickly said, "No statement from us. You'll have to wait for our community relations rep to get down here."

I realized she had looked at my press badge. I tore the badge off my jacket and shoved it into a pocket. "I don't give a hoot for Bronson Toles and his condition. There was a young woman who was transported here as well. Paula Quinn. What's her condition?"

The woman's eyes narrowed in suspicion. "Are you a relative?"

"Co-workers," I said, and then, not sure if that was going to do it, "She's also my fiancée."

That seemed to get to her. "Oh, okay." She looked at a couple of sheets of paper. Her hands were shaking, and I thought what it must be like, to be working in an ER on an otherwise quiet night, and then to have the place flooded with angry and upset people and an instant news event. "Paula Quinn . . . she's still being examined in Room Four. You can see her in a few minutes. Why don't you take a seat and we'll call you when she's up to seeing a visitor."

I looked back at the groups of people, voices raised, demands being made, the security officers and now a couple of Exonia cops trying to maintain order. I said, "All the same to you, I'd like to stay right here. I might get lost if I join that crazy bunch."

Not a nice statement on my part, but it had the desired effect. She gave me a quick, tired smile and said, "Stand over there, by the elevator. I promise I'll get back to you when it's time."

"Thanks a lot," I said.

Surprisingly enough, it didn't take that long, and in about ten minutes I was led back into the examining rooms, off to Room 4, and at the other end of the polished corridor, past gurneys and chairs and medical equipment on casters, there was a knot of cops standing outside another room, and from that room, I heard the great, racking sobs of a woman.

I turned back and went into Room 4, where I hoped I could do something.

. . .

The attending ER physician was a Dutchman, a nice guy in blue scrubs with bad teeth and a two-day-old growth of beard, and a last name that had about two consonants and fifteen vowels. He started talking, and for a few minutes I ignored him. Paula was on a medical bed, curved on her side, wearing the standard-issue hospital jammie top. It was light green. Her blond hair was a tangled mess. There were flecks of dried blood along one cheek and her neck. Her eyes fluttered open and closed, and she was breathing shallowly, as if her lungs had been damaged. There was an oxygen tube looped under her pug nose and an IV tube inserted in one hand, and I held the other hand, the flesh cool and clammy.

Finally I looked up at the doctor. "Excuse me, what did you say?"

He paused and then resumed. "I said, there are no apparent physical injuries, though from what I understand, she was standing right next to the other victim when he was shot. She has no wounds or fractures, but it appears that she may have sustained a slight concussion when she fell upon the stage."

I looked back at Paula. "Why is she like this? She's unconscious . . . breathing hard . . . like she's having lots of bad dreams."

"Ah," the doctor said, making a notation on her chart. "When she arrived here, she was quite frantic, upset. She was struggling, crying . . . we had to give her a sedative to calm her down before we could examine her."

I squeezed her hand, hoping for a response. A machine over her head on a stainless steel stand beeped twice, and that was it.

"How long do you plan to keep her?"

"Overnight, of course—but perhaps longer. We shall see."

I kept on looking at the pale face, the brown spots of blood on her fair skin, blood that had belonged to a man that had been breathing, living, and applauding not more than an hour ago. "Why longer, Doc? What's going on?"

He put his pen down. "Years ago . . . I was working for Doctors Without Borders . . . assigned to refugee camps in the Sudan, yes? I saw many, many things among the refugees . . . especially those who had received sudden and unexpected violent trauma, or had witnessed same. Your fiancée here . . . she was only a couple of feet away from a man who was violently killed. She was sprayed with his blood and brain matter. She has gone into shock. A night of bed rest, some sedatives, should bring her out of it in a day or two."

I rubbed Paula's hand. "Should?"

"All of us are different, are we not? Your fiancée, perhaps she will bounce back quickly, but she may not. She may need help . . . therapy . . . she may emerge from this dreadful experience a different person. All we can do now is wait."

I looked back at Paula. While the doctor bustled around and a friendly nurse came in to check Paula's vitals, I took a moment and wet down a paper towel, and I spent a few minutes gently washing her cheek and neck, getting Bronson Toles's blood off of her, and then I sat back down, watched her breathe, watched her eyelids flutter. When I didn't think anyone was paying me attention, I got up and bent over and whispered in her ear, "Paula . . . you take care, tonight, okay? You can beat this . . . honest, you can."

Then I sat back down.

More minutes passed.

The friendly nurse from before came over and said, "Is there anyone else we can contact on her behalf? Other family members, perhaps?"

I thought for a second and said, "Mark Spencer. He lives in Tyler. He's the town counsel."

She wrote down what I had told her. "Is he a relative?"

"No," I said. "He's her boyfriend."

The friendly nurse now looked not so friendly and confused. "I'm sorry," she said. "I . . . I thought she was your fiancée."

"I'm sorry, too," I said. "I lied."

Later the nurse came back and said that calls had been placed to Mark Spencer, and that it was time to move Paula Quinn to a regular hospital room, and unfortunately visiting hours were wrapping up, but I could come back tomorrow after 9:00 A.M. and see how she was doing then.

I said that was fine, and shook her hand, and the hand of the Dutch doctor, and bent down and kissed Paula's forehead, and then left Paula's room. The scrum of cops and investigators at the other end of the hallway was as large as ever, and I made my way back to the waiting area of the ER, where it was quieter, with some sobs and low conversation about Bronson Toles.

Outside it was pouring rain, but it didn't stop everyone from doing their job, performing their roles. Satellite trucks from the Boston television stations had set up shop, camera lights harshly illuminating the parking lot and the emergency room entrance. Behind hastily erected wooden police barricades, followers of Bronson Toles had gathered, some of them carrying the same antinuclear and safe-energy signs as before, others trying to keep sputtering candles alit in the downpour.

I got to my Ford Explorer, climbed in, and started it up. Paula Quinn's purse was still on the passenger seat. I wondered if I should go back and try to give it to someone to place in her room, but I felt queasy at the thought of having to navigate that mourning crowd out there and the sharp journalists who were busily recording every shout, slogan, or tear.

Tomorrow, I thought. *Tomorrow.*

I backed the Explorer up, and in navigating out of the parking lot, I stopped at an intersection. Underneath a maple tree, lit up by a nearby streetlight, a young woman stood there, alone, arms crossed, as the rain came down. I looked at her twice and recognized her. Haleigh Miller, the demonstrator from the nearby University of New Hampshire campus.

I stayed at the stop sign.

It looked like she was shivering.

I powered down the Explorer's window. "Haleigh! Haleigh Miller!"

She looked up, hesitated, and then walked across to me, running a hand through her wet hair, pulling it out of her face. "Oh . . . it's you . . . the writer . . . ah, Lewis, right?"

"Right," I said. "Lewis Cole. Look, it's late, you're getting soaked. Can I give you a ride somewhere?"

She said, "Oh . . . that'd be nice . . . I'm staying with some friends back at the campground . . . the campground where . . . well, you know . . ." and then she started weeping, her arms clasped tight around her chest.

From behind me a car was approaching, the headlights coming at me fast. "Get in," I said. "I'll give you a ride."

She skirted around the front of the Explorer, and then I gently took Paula's purse and deposited it in the rear. Haleigh got in, and I drove off, leaving the lights and the protests and the cries behind.

CHAPTER FIVE

After a couple of quiet minutes, Haleigh said, "This isn't the way back to the campground."

"I know," I said.

Her voice grew stronger. "What's going on, then?"

I said, "Haleigh . . . the weather report says it's going to rain all night tonight, and into tomorrow morning. So I'm offering you options. I can drop you off in Tyler, put you up for the night in a motel, or you can come back to my place, bunk out on a couch. You're sopping wet, and to climb into a damp sleeping bag, in a damp tent . . . well, I didn't think you'd have a good night."

She stayed quiet as I made my way through the wet streets, then said, "Thanks for the offers."

"You're welcome."

"You could have told me earlier."

"I could," I admitted, "but I didn't want to get into an involved discussion at a stop sign while you were getting more drenched."

I sensed a smile from her side of the Explorer. "All right. I accept your offer."

"Which one?"

"The one where I spend the night on your couch. I don't want you spending any money on me."

"That's a deal, then."

"Oh, and just so we're clear. . ."

"Haleigh, I've just come from the hospital, where an old friend of mine is in shock and is being admitted. That's all I have on my mind right now. I promise you a comfortable, warm, and safe night. That's all."

"Oh," she said again. "I'm sorry . . . is she going to be all right?"

"I hope so," I said.

She folded her arms, then unfolded them, then ran her hands over her wet peasant skirt. "Bronson . . . I can't believe Bronson is dead. I just can't believe it."

Then she started crying again as I sped up the Explorer.

My small house is on Tyler Beach, directly across the street from the Lafayette House, an old Victorian-style hotel that's been on Atlantic Avenue for more than a hundred years. I went through the hotel's parking lot—situated on my side of the street—to the lot's northern end, where some rocks had been moved away to allow a small dirt lane that leads down to my home. It's two stories tall, weather-beaten, with a scraggly lawn and a sagging shed off to the right that serves as a garage. I pulled into the garage, and we both got out and sprinted to the front door. I got the door unlocked, we got inside, and I took our wet coats and hung them in the near closet.

Next to the closet was a closed door that led to the small cellar, and over both doors were wooden stairs that went up to the second floor. To the left was a small living room and sliding glass doors for the rear deck, overlooking a rocky portion of the coastline and the Atlantic Ocean. Adjacent to the sliding glass doors was a tiny kitchen, and everything was small and cozy, because at one time, more than a century ago, my house had been a lifeboat station to rescue mariners out on the ocean.

I went into the living room, turned on a couple of lights and kicked up the oil furnace, and in a few moments, warm air started cascading into the room. Haleigh rubbed at her arms and said, "Nice place."

43

"Thanks," I said. "It works for me."

She stepped up to the glass doors and said, "I bet when it's sunny outside, you get a wonderful view out there."

"I surely do."

She looked through the glass, out at the rain-swept darkness. Her voice was quiet now, almost melancholy. "A view like this is a dream for most people, do you know that, Mr. Cole?"

"Mr. Cole is what people called my father. Please call me Lewis."

She gave me a quick smile. There was a dimple in one cheek. "All right, Lewis . . . a dream, that's what it is . . . and for Bronson, a way of offering a view of a clean, healthy environment, no matter where you went in this world was a dream worth pursuing, a dream worth keeping—and now he's dead." Haleigh wiped at her eyes. "Who do you think did it?"

I went over to the refrigerator and opened it up, just seeing what I had to offer my unexpected houseguest. "These are passionate times, you know. The economy is staggering, jobs are hard to get, energy is expensive. Then you have something like the Falconer Unit Two project, which promises jobs and more power down the road . . . and you have Bronson opposing it . . . people's passions rise up."

Another wipe to the eyes. "You think somebody who supports the power plant did it?"

I closed the refrigerator door. "Or somebody who thinks Bronson didn't do enough, maybe one of those Nuclear Freedom Front folks—or something else. I just don't know. What I do know is that you're soaked to the skin, and even with the heat on, you can't be comfortable."

She said nothing, just looked at me calmly. I went on. "So why don't you go upstairs, and at the top of the stairs is a bathroom. Duck in and take a shower. In the bathroom is a washer and dryer. Toss your clothes in the dryer, they'll probably be dried by the time you're done—and, Haleigh?"

"Yes?"

I stayed in the kitchen, behind a waist-high counter that separated us. "I'll stay down here, and the bathroom door locks from the inside. So no worries, okay?"

She nodded, then went upstairs, and I heard the door close, and I listened, but I didn't hear the snap of the lock. In a few minutes I heard the humming of the dryer in action and the rush of water into the shower.

I switched on the television, checked the time, saw that I could probably catch a top-of-the-hour newscast in a few minutes, and then looked at my telephone and nearby answering machine, which was blinking a green numeral 2 at me. Two messages. I hit the PLAY button, and there was a *whir-whir* as the tape rewound, and then the messages started.

Beep. "Lewis? Denise Pichette-Volk here. I heard about the shooting at the rally this afternoon. I trust you were there. I want some details. Call me."

Click, followed by another *beep.* "Hey, writer man," came the low, female voice, and I smiled and the room instantly felt warmer. "Annie calling, from the campaign trail. Give me a ring, no matter the time. I doubt I'll be sleeping . . . Ta."

I erased both messages, got the phone, and dialed a number from memory. It rang three times, and then a woman's whisper answered. "Yes?"

"It's writer man," I said. "Remember me?"

A slight giggle. "Hold on. I need to leave this meeting."

In the background I could make out a slight babble of voices, and then Annie's voice came in clear and sharp. "Whew, nice timing," she said. "You got me out of a meeting discussing the best ways to allocate our resources to certain congressional districts and vital precincts and so forth and so on."

"Where are you?"

She sighed. "If this is Thursday, then it must be Virginia—and tomorrow will be Kentucky, and the day after that . . . Indiana. I think."

"Days like these, bet you miss the quiet life of New Hampshire."

"Hah," she said. "My last couple of months in New Hampshire were anything but quiet, thanks to you and the senior senator from Georgia."

"How's Senator Hale doing?"

A breath from her. "All right. The race is tightening, which is good, because that usually means it breaks for the challenger, and he's holding up well, with all the airplane food, banquet chicken, and fourteen-hour days—as is his gorgeous and efficient staff."

I paused, then said, "How about the senator's wife?"

Annie said, "In Alaska. Then Nevada. About as far west as possible."

"Good."

"I agree," she said. "So what have you been up to, my friend?"

I switched the phone receiver from one ear to the other. "I was out covering an antinuke rally in Falconer earlier today. There was a shooting."

"God, anybody hurt?"

"Killed. A guy named Bronson Toles. Antinuke activist and owner of a local club and restaurant."

"Any arrests?"

"Not yet," I said. "Looked like a shooter hiding in the woods . . . and another thing. You remember Paula Quinn?"

46

"Sure," she said. "The reporter that you had a brief thing with few years back."

"She was standing right next to Bronson when he got hit. She got sprayed by blood, brain, and bone from the poor guy. She's at the hospital in Exonia being treated for shock. Among other things."

"Sweet Jesus, Lewis, is there anything else you want to tell me?"

Upstairs I heard the shower switch off. "Well . . ."

"Go on. You're definitely breaking up a long workday."

"Well, there's this college coed. Name of Haleigh Miller. She's upstairs taking a shower."

"Any particular reason why?"

"She got caught in a rainstorm and was soaked to the skin."

"You peek in on her while she was showering?"

"Gave that up a while ago," I said. "Not enough of a challenge."

That brought forth a laugh, and I said, "She was next to me at the shooting and got caught up in the chaos afterward. Almost got hurt. She's pretty shook up about the killing, and instead of sending her off to spend the night in a wet tent with the rest of her antinuke friends, I offered her my couch."

"My noble writer man," Annie said. "How sweet—but it had better be just the couch, or I'm going to go medieval on your ass at some time."

"How would you know?"

"I'm a woman, with appropriate and magical powers," she said, "and after Indiana—I'm begging for at least a twelve-hour pass to New Hampshire, where you will have the distinct privilege of wining, dining, and bedding me, not necessarily in that order."

My heart rate picked up a bit. "For real?"

"For real. How does Monday sound?"

"Sounds like a date," I said. "No matter what nonsense is going on down in Falconer."

She paused, and I could hear the murmur of voices in the background, and there was a sigh and she said, "The demands of democracy are chomping at my ankles, wanting me back in the conference room. I'll let you know later the particulars of my trip to your fair state. Deal?"

"Deal."

"Sweet," she said. "Miss you."

I said the same in return, but by then, she had switched off.

I hung up the phone, thought about the first message of the night, and decided one phone call to a female per night was going to be enough.

It being the top of the hour, I turned on the television and got an update from the local cable all-news channel. Not surprisingly, Toles's death was the lead story of the hour, and there wasn't much footage of the actual shooting. The television cameras were under the burden of taking their footage from ground level, so what one saw on the screen was a mass of people, heads and shoulders mostly blocking everything, and the upper torso and head of Bronson Toles, speaking as he did, and then the first chaos when the NFF youths jumped up and hijacked the proceedings, and then I made out Paula Quinn coming into view, followed by—

Gunshot. The camera tilted and there was lots of movement, shouts, and cries, and then a stand-up from a reporter outside the Exonia Hospital, stating the obvious, that Bronson Toles had died from a single gunshot wound to the head. Then that was followed by a quick interview with a bulky detective from the New Hampshire State Police, who didn't have much to say, and then by a couple of antinuke protesters, who promised to redouble their efforts to close down Falconer Unit 1 and prevent the construction of Falconer Unit 2.

No report was made of an assistant editor from the Tyler *Chronicle* who had also been injured during the shooting.

There were footsteps coming down from upstairs. I switched the television to the History Channel and got up to greet my guest.

Haleigh Miller came down, smiling shyly, looking about five years younger than when she went upstairs. I got up and headed to the kitchen, and she intercepted me, and after a few moments of polite give-and-take, I let her take charge in my kitchen. About a half hour later, we were eating an egg-and-cheese dish that had a number of vegetables in it and was pretty good, considering most vegetables and I aren't on speaking terms.

Eventually she said, "I haven't properly thanked you, you know."

"For what? Shelter and a shower were pretty easy, and though I supplied the ingredients, you made the meal."

"That's not what I meant. Back at the campground, after the shooting . . . I was trapped, Lewis. Trapped against the stage when all those people were pressing in against us, and I thought for sure that my throat was going to be crushed. You saved me."

"Easy enough to do."

She shook her head. "No . . . no, it wasn't. I get the feeling that some of my buds from UNH, if they were there, would've stood there, shocked, but you didn't. You moved. You took action. So thank you."

"You're welcome," I said, "and it's my turn to thank you. Where did you learn to cook so well?"

She dabbed at her lips with a paper napkin. "The Stone Chapel. I started working there a couple of years ago as a waitress, when I was in high school in Dover, and then I learned to do some short-order cooking, and then became sort of an assistant manager, helping out where I could. That's when I got to know

Bronson Toles, and later, his wife and his stepson, Victor. It's . . . it's a special place. Hard to believe it'll be the same with Bronson gone."

"What made it so special?"

A gust of rain hammered at the sliding glass doors that led to the rear deck. "Oh, it was a job, but it was more than that. Bronson made it feel like you were part of a family, part of a movement. I mean, we worked hard, especially when we had group nights, when musicians came in to play. We even had a softball team that played restaurants in the area during the summer. When we worked, it could get very, very busy . . . but other times, Bronson would just talk and we'd listen, and argue, and learn from each other."

"What kind of things did you learn?"

She smiled. "It sounds strange, telling you here, and not at the Stone Chapel. It just sounds . . . pretentious, I suppose, to say such things in your house, but not at the chapel. Anyway, we learned about resistance, nonviolent disobedience, the teachings of Gandhi, Martin Luther King, and Mandela—and Bronson made the connection, you know? That small, safe, renewable energy is the key to changing our society. Once we're not held hostage to large corporations, large utilities, large government, we can take control of our lives and our communities, and, well, I guess I've talked too much, hunh?"

I finished off the last bit of our dinner. "No, not at all. So opposing Falconer and the new reactor—what do you hope to achieve?"

A shy smile. "By taking over Falconer, by doing what we can to convert it to something else safer and more reliable, we hope to start a change, a revolution in the way we think and the way we make electricity. Something so simple but so right."

I took a sip of ice water and said, "So no nukes, right?"

A firm nod. "Right."

"What, then?"

"Mmm?"

With my fork I pointed to the lights overhead. "Those lights, that stove, and the hot water you just used for your shower, that's all powered by electricity, and that electricity comes from the power plant in Falconer. So does about twenty percent of this country's electricity, produced by the splitting of atoms. So you shut down Falconer, what then? I'm sure you're not in favor of oil, natural gas, or coal. All produce greenhouse gases."

"There are other sources . . . like wind, solar, hydro." Her voice was hesitant.

"Absolutely," I said, "but there was a proposal to build a wind farm off of Cape Cod, wasn't there? Give the Cape about two-thirds of its electricity, but the local landowners and politicians didn't want the windmills spoiling their view—and it's still being challenged in court. Solar is fine in some parts of the country, but look at the weather out there—not much solar can do if you have this kind of rainy and cloudy weather off and on. As for hydro, that means dams, and do you think anybody will be building any more dams down the road, disrupting the free flow of rivers?"

Her face seemed a bit flushed. "So nuclear is the answer, then?"

I wiped my hands with a napkin. "Depends on the question, I guess. On the plus side, the safety record in the States is pretty good, it doesn't contribute any greenhouse gases to the environ-ment, and—"

She leaned over the counter. "That's just the surface, Lewis! There's the destruction of the ecosystem when the nuclear power plants get built, the degradation when uranium is mined and milled and processed, the cost of the steel, iron, and concrete, the fuel from all the construction vehicles . . . you've got to look below the surface, Lewis. That's one of the things Bronson taught all of us, that there's more to what goes on than what we see.

51

And—" Haleigh suddenly got quiet. "I get the feeling you're mocking me."

"Not at all."

"You think you have all the answers, do you?"

"Not for a second. I know I just have most of the questions."

She said, "I know I'm young, I know I think I know it all—but when you were my age, weren't you committed to something? Didn't something worry you so much that you devoted your time and life to it? Something that you were passionate about?"

Something cold and tasteless seemed to tickle at the back of my throat. "It was a long time ago."

"Okay, but it was something, wasn't it? What was it?"

I sighed. "Something that was in this world for just over seventy years. A place that some called the evil empire."

Her face was a mix of curiosity and puzzlement. I went on. "The Soviet Union."

"Oh. So, what did you do, then?"

"Right after college I went to work for the Man, otherwise known as the Department of Defense. As a research analyst."

Then she smirked, and I suppose I shouldn't have taken offense, but I did.

"Something funny?"

She shook her head. "No, no, no. It's just that the Soviet Union . . . for me and everyone else I know, that's just ancient history, that's all. It's just that it's hard to believe that so much energy and billions of dollars were spent on a threat that turned out to be no threat at all. Bronson once spent an evening telling us the truth about that, how the threat from the Russians was just made up by the military-industrial complex to seek bigger budgets for the Defense Department and defense companies. No offense."

"None taken." There was a pause, and then I said, "You ever read *The Great Terror* by Robert Conquest?"

"No."

"*The Gulag Archipelago* by Solzhenitsyn?"

"No."

"*Darkness at Noon* by Arthur Koestler? *1984* by Orwell? Have you even heard of any of those books, Haleigh?"

Her face was red, and she looked like she was about to step away from the counter, and I shook my head. "Sorry. My turn to apologize. It's just that . . . well, for decades, no matter what the Bronson Toleses of the world have to say in their coffee shops and music halls, there was a group of hard, dangerous men who killed millions and spread an ideology devoted to tyranny and murder—and to this day, we're still dealing with the toxicity of what they stood for."

"But Russia's evolved, it's—"

"They're still an imperial power threatening to turn off natural gas supplies to the Europeans if they don't vote the right way in the UN—and when the, quote, evil empire, unquote, was at its height, it spent billions spreading hate and discontent among a number of ethnic groups and terrorist organizations, some of which are still raising merry hell. Including the merry hell that came from their 1979 invasion of Afghanistan."

I got up and picked up both of our plates. "My apologies again. I was lecturing. Not a good habit for a host, especially when the guest attends the local university. I'd guess you get lectured there enough without having it shoved at you after dinner."

She smiled, picking up the glassware and silverware. "No problem. I think you'd like my dad. He's in the air force." I started washing, and she started drying. "Oh, he's not a pilot or anything. A senior master sergeant in maintenance."

"What does he think of his counterculture daughter?"

She placed one dry plate upon another. "He tells me to keep on raising hell. That maybe whatever hell me and the others raise

53

will cause people to change their minds and the way they do business. Because the status quo won't work."

I rinsed off the glassware. "What status quo is that?"

She sighed. "The one that keeps him on deployments, year after year, from Iraq to Afghanistan and points in between. One of the reasons why my mom and him broke up."

"Oh. Sorry to hear that."

Haleigh focused on drying off the silverware. "It happens, Lewis. It happens."

Later the rain was coming down even harder, with the wind whipping off the ocean, splattering rain against the windows and the sliding glass doors. I made a small fire in the fireplace to lighten up the living room and cut some of the dampness, and I opened up the couch, put down some sheets and blankets, and came back from upstairs with a simple blue-and-white-checked cotton nightgown.

"For you, if you'd like," I said.

"Thanks," she said, and then she teased me. "You always have women's clothing stashed away for unexpected visitors?"

"Only for one," I said.

"Your girlfriend?"

"I suppose so, although saying that makes me feel like I'm back in high school."

Haleigh said, "I take it you've been out of high school for a while."

"College, too," I said. "If you must know, I'm ancient."

"How ancient is that?"

I said, "I only wear baseball caps with the bill facing forward."

She smiled at what I said, unfolded the nightgown, and laid it out on the couch. "Where is she?"

"In Virginia."

"Doing what?"

"Working on the presidential campaign of one Senator Jackson Hale."

Haleigh yawned. "You know, the next time you talk to your woman friend, maybe you could tell her that the senator should really change his position on high-level nuclear waste disposal and—"

I gently touched the side of her cheek, just for a moment. "The time for debate, protests, and counterpoints is over, Miss Miller. Time to go to bed."

She blushed, and I went upstairs.

I slid into my own bed, switched on the light, and read for a while, a hardcover edition of John Keegan's latest military history. I read a couple of chapters and then switched off the light, even though I wasn't particularly tired. It had been a long, long day.

In the darkness I listened to the rain and the wind slapping its way around my century-old house. There was something special and satisfying about being in a warm and dry bed in the dark and listening to the wind and rain, knowing that I would be comfortable and safe for the next several hours. I thought of my guest downstairs, hoping that she felt a bit safer and happier in a dry foldout couch instead of a damp sleeping bag and wet tent. And my Annie? Not much sleep for her, I was sure, in whatever strange hotel or motel room she was residing in, down there in Virginia.

Then there was Paula. A scared, traumatized Paula Quinn, alone in a hospital room, no doubt shuddering and dreaming through the night of nearly being killed, of being splattered with the bloody bits of what had been a living, breathing, and thinking man.

It took a while for me to fall asleep.

CHAPTER SIX

In the morning, the couch was a couch again, the sheets and blankets neatly folded, as well as the nightgown. A note had been left on top of the nightgown:

Lewis—

Thanks for saving me, thanks for the hospitality. It was a wonderful night, and no more apologies for either of us, all right?

Now, back to Falconer, and the battle . . . not yours, I know, but the one I have chosen and must see to the end.

—Haleigh

The rain had stopped, but heavy gray clouds were still threatening, their color the same as the relentless ocean out there, and after a quick breakfast of tea and toast, I drove out to Exonia and its hospital.

At the hospital, there were a lot more empty parking spaces than the previous night. Only one satellite news truck from Boston had set up shop and, along a concrete planter near the entrance to the emergency room, the remnants of lit candles stood stuck there in the gray cold, the colors of the melted wax muted and dull. I strolled in, and after a minute or two at the reception desk, I took an elevator up to the third floor, carrying Paula Quinn's purse in one hand, and I think it's a tribute to my confident sexuality that I didn't mind holding on to it.

On the third floor I went past a busy nurse's station and then found myself at Room 301, and in this double room was Paula Quinn, on her side, staring blankly out a large window.

Her hair was a mess, pulled over to one side. I dragged a chair over and sat down and put her purse on the floor. Her eyes blinked at me; her head was resting on folded hands. An IV tube was still running into one wrist.

"Hey," she said, her voice faint.

"Hey," I said, reaching out, taking her warm and dry hand.

She blinked twice and said, "Oh, Lewis."

"Shhh," I said. "Take it easy."

Tears welled up, and she said, "They're busy here, I understand, and they promised they'd get to me in a while . . . but Lewis, I think . . . I think some of Bronson Toles's blood . . . it's still in my hair, Lewis . . ." and she stopped talking and her chin trembled and she started crying in silent, gasping heaves. I went over, kissed the top of her head, and looked to the nightstand, where I found a plastic washbasin and some shampoo. I ducked into the room's bathroom, ignoring the sign that read FOR PA-TIENT USE ONLY, and filled the basin halfway with warm water. There was a sharp moan, and I looked back and noticed Paula's roommate, a woman probably in her late seventies, steel gray hair, asleep against a pillow, mouth open.

I went back and spread out a towel underneath Paula's head and raised the bed some—after a fumbling few moments of trying to figure out the controls—and she started talking, and I said, "Shhh, just be still for a while, okay?"

Paula nodded, and for the next several minutes, I washed, rinsed, and then rewashed her long blond hair, and when I was done and had dumped the water, I dried off her hair as much as I could with a couple of towels, and when I sat down again, she offered me a tired smile.

"That . . . that felt so good."

"Glad I could help," I said. "How are you doing?"

She took a deep breath. "I . . . I didn't sleep well. The doctor came in, a nice Pakistani woman, and I didn't have much to say to her . . . seems like . . . oddly enough . . . I suffered a trauma yesterday, seeing what happened to Bronson, feeling what happened . . ."

Her eyes teared up, and I handed over a tissue box, and she dabbed at her eyes. "I . . . I guess I can go later today. Which would be great—but after that, I just don't know . . . I just don't know."

I took her free hand, squeezed it. "Then worry about that when the time comes."

Her face colored. "You don't understand. You're not listening to me."

I squeezed her hand. "I'm listening now, and I'm trying to understand."

Another deep breath. "What I'm saying is that the Paula Quinn from yesterday is gone, all right? The journalist Paula Quinn. The assistant editor Paula Quinn. The tough-as-nails reporter who loved crime stories, the bloodier the better . . . I thought I could be above it all, until yesterday, when Bronson was murdered next to me."

She shifted in her hospital bed so she could look at me better. "Something just snapped, Lewis. Snapped hard—and I was scared, and I was terrified, and more than that, I was ashamed. I remembered all the stories I had done before, about arsons, murders, and rapes . . . and other violence . . . and all I cared about was getting the story first, and getting it right."

"That was your job."

"I know," Paula said, the tears coming back, "and I was damn good at it . . . and I thought about the fishing co-op, with that union guy giving a speech, and then that mini riot breaking out. Some kids trying to make a stand in the lion's den, and for their bravery and their troubles, guys twice their weight and twice their ages tried to break them into pieces . . . and all I cared about was taking a good photo."

The woman in the next bed, separated from us by just a curtain, coughed and moaned again. "The same thing yesterday . . . I saw those other kids, up on the stage, challenging Bronson, and I wanted to get up there, too, to get a good photo if and when the punches started being thrown. They weren't real. None of them were real. They were just props for my tales, that's all . . . that's all everyone has been, from my very first news story, back in college . . ." Another moan from Paula's neighbor. "Now . . . I don't know. I don't think I can do this anymore, Lewis. The old Paula . . . she's gone . . . and I don't know what the new Paula is going to be like . . . and that scares the shit out of me."

I took her hand in both of mine. "Well, you won't be alone, I guarantee that."

I felt her hand squeeze back. "I'm glad to hear that. That's about the only cheerful thing I've got going for me."

I looked around the sparse room and said, "Your Mark been by yet?"

She pursed her lips. "No."

"Oh."

Paula said, "He said he'd be along shortly . . . but that he had a court hearing he absolutely, positively couldn't miss. So I'm sure I'll see him later today."

"Oh."

"Lewis, my boy, it's permissible to say more than 'oh.' Got it?"

"Got it."

So we talked again for a while until one of the overworked nurses came in and checked her vitals, and Paula yawned and said, "You know, I just might take a nap."

"Good for you," I said, and I got up to kiss the top of her head, and she moved a bit, so that my lips touched her cheek instead.

Outside in the cold, breezy parking lot, my brand new cell phone chimed, making me start for a moment. I ignored the persistent ringing until I got into the shelter of my Ford Explorer and worked the unfamiliar buttons and said, "Hello?"

The woman's voice was brisk. "Lewis? Denise Pichette-Volk here."

"Hello, Denise."

"Where have you been?"

"I've been in a parking lot, in Exonia. Next town over from Tyler. Where have you been?"

"At work. Doing my job. Something you should think about doing. For example, I left a message for you last night. Did you get it?"

"I did."

"So why didn't you call me?"

I said, "I hadn't gotten around to it yet."

"I specifically said for you to call me."

"You certainly did," I said, "but you didn't say when. Now, Denise, you have my undivided attention. We can spend the next ten minutes or so going over my various and sundry faults, or we can get to the point. So. What's the point, Denise?"

She chuckled. "My, what a piece of work you're turning out to be, Lewis."

"So I've been told."

"And here's what I'm telling you today," she said. "I want a thousand words by noon today on what happened yesterday in Falconer."

"A thousand words? By noon?"

"That's right," she said.

"Wait, when I started working on this . . . piece for *Shoreline*, it was for an issue in the spring. The deadline was at the end of the month."

Another chuckle. "That was when you started working on this nuclear protest story, before Bronson Toles got murdered. Now things have changed. I've made an arrangement where in addition to writing for *Shoreline*, you're going to be a special correspondent for an Internet-based news service that the magazine's investors have a stake in. More bang for a little buck. Your deadline is noon today. A thousand words."

I wanted to ask her more, but there was a click, and my boss had gone on to pick fights with other people.

I suppose I should have driven back home, but instead I made a quick phone call and then headed out of Exonia and to the south part of Tyler Beach, where I had been the previous day with Paula. I drove down Route 101, which bisected a wide stretch of marshland, and off to the right, I made out the center of all this controversy: the buildings of the Falconer nuclear power plant. Along the way I passed a few small straggling groups of protesters heading up to Route 1 like lost units of a distant army, struggling to meet up with their comrades.

At Tyler Beach I made a right, going south down Route 1-A past the closed motels, the closed restaurants, and the fire station and police station, and about ten or so minutes after that, I drove up to Tyler Harbor Meadows, a collection of condo units set in a horseshoe pattern that overlooked Tyler Harbor. I parked in a visitor's spot, rubbed at my hands, and about sixty seconds later, I was knocking at the door of my best friend.

Diane Woods opened the door, looking tired. She had on a pair of blue jeans, old sneakers, and a dull blue pullover sweater. "Hey," she said.

"Thanks for the time," I said. "I appreciate it."

She turned and I followed her upstairs, where we ended up in a wide living room and nice built in kitchen. Windows overlooked the condo's parking lot and the choppy waters of Tyler Harbor and, farther out, as if it couldn't be avoided, the containment dome and buildings of Falconer Unit 1. The room was decorated with Shaker furniture, oval boxes, framed prints of Canterbury Shaker Village, and other bits of New England art. There were a couple of small bookcases, the usual television set and CD stereo, and some framed photos of a smiling Diane and smiling Kara. Another set of stairs went up to the third floor, and I could hear a shower running. I looked to Diane, and she said, "Kara's taking a shower."

"I see," I said.

"Yeah," she said, sitting down wearily on a couch. "You see, all right. She's here for a meal, a shower, a change of clothes, and then back out to the protests."

"How about you?" I asked. "When do you go back to Falconer?"

"Four P.M., my friend," she said. "You?"

"Sometime today," I said. "My new boss wants a story today, a thousand words, and maybe one tomorrow."

"Two stories that quick, for a monthly magazine?"

I sat down across from her. "She's managed to link up to some sort of Internet-based news agency, help bring in a new income stream to the magazine. Part of that means me writing more than just a monthly column."

Diane frowned. "She sounds like a pistol."

"Yeah."

The shower upstairs stopped. Diane looked up and then looked down, back at me. "What else is going on?"

"The shooting yesterday," I said. "I was there."

"Ugh," she said. "I heard it was a real horror show, some people in the audience got trampled. You get away all right?"

"I did, with some bruised ribs and an aching back," I said. "One of your brother officers from Falconer tossed me off the stage when I went up to check on Paula."

"Paula? Paula Quinn? What happened to her?"

I leaned forward and folded my hands together. "She was standing next to Bronson Toles, trying to get a photo, when he was shot. She was . . . well, she got some forensic evidence from his head splattered all over her."

"Good God," Diane said. "How's she doing?"

"Physically? Just fine. No bodily injuries . . . but emotionally, mentally . . . it really shook her up, Diane. I've never seen her like this before. It's like . . . it's like she wants to stop being a reporter altogether, after all these years."

Diane sat back on the couch. "Bloody and unexpected violence like that can shake you up. I remember the first time I responded to a violent domestic. I was the first unit there, at a trailer park up near Timberswamp Road. Husband and wife, both drunk, both screaming at each other. The wife had a fishing knife in her hand.

I kept on telling her to put the knife down, put the knife down. She finally looked at me and nodded her head and said, 'Sure, Officer, I'll put the knife down,' and then she buried it between her hubby's shoulder blades."

"What happened then?"

"I got her on the floor, handcuffed. Then I got him as comfortable as possible, on the floor, next to her . . . waiting for the other units and the firefighters to show up . . . funny thing, the woman was crying, and her hubby, with the knife sticking out from his back, kept on saying, 'Don't worry, hon, it don't hurt that much.' True love, hunh? When everybody else arrived, I took a moment to go outside, find some bushes, and puke my guts out. Then I didn't sleep for a day . . . wondering if I was up to the job . . . and then I decided the only way to find out was to get back on the job."

I said, "But Paula . . ."

"I know. Violence in her vicinity isn't her job. I hope she snaps out of it. She's busted my chops a few times, along with the department, but that is her job. I don't wish her ill."

I could hear drawers and closet doors opening and closing upstairs. I said, "What do you know about the shooting?"

"Know?" she asked. "As much as your average person on the street. Bronson Toles was giving a speech, there was a disruption on the stage, and boom. Hidden sniper in the nearby woods took off the top of his head. Sniper and rifle successfully escaped."

"Any idea of the rifle's caliber?"

She shook her head. "Not that I've heard, but my guess would probably be a .308 or something equally heavy."

"Who's handling the investigation?"

"Something like this? So damn newsworthy? You know it went right to the state police, with the attorney general's office riding shotgun . . . and the Falconer cops doing what they can. Which, unfortunately for them, won't be much in a case this big. They'll probably be running down long-shot leads and fetching coffee and doughnuts."

"Do you know if they've recovered the slug that killed Toles?"

Diane stared at me and said, "All right, didn't you hear what I said before? I know about as much as the local citizen. The staties and the AG's office have this one sewn up tight, tight, tight. Just because I'm a detective sergeant in Tyler doesn't mean I have a pipeline into what's going on."

"Yeah, you're right," I said. "Sorry to press you like that."

Diane cocked her head. "Seems like a lot of pointed questions for a thousand-word story that's due to your editor today."

"It does, doesn't it."

We sat there in silence for some long seconds. Upstairs a woman was whistling a tune I didn't recognize. Diane crossed her arms and said, "What are you up to?"

I waited, and then it just clicked, like something that had been in the back of my mind for days and was finally coming free. "I want to find out who the shooter is."

"So do a bunch of other guys and gals. Guys and gals who do this for a living and who carry firearms and nice shiny badges. What's your excuse?"

"The shooter hurt a friend of mine."

She gave me a cold smile. "Hurt? Hurt a friend of yours? Lewis, a husband and a stepdad and a hero to lots of our counter-culture citizens had his head blown off in front of hundreds of people. That sort of killing gives law enforcement an enormous incentive to crack the case and find the shooter. What in the world do you think you can do that they can't?"

I rubbed my hands together. "Probably nothing, but I've got to make the effort."

Again the slight cock of her head. "For Paula, right?"

"For Paula."

65

"Thought she had a man. The Tyler town counsel."

"She still does."

"And you and Annie are still together, right?"

"We are," I said. "In fact, she's coming back here in a couple of days, so we can get reacquainted."

"Good for you."

Just then I heard the sound of footsteps coming down from upstairs, and Kara Miles, Diane's significant other for quite a period of time, emerged. Her short dark hair was still wet, and she had on loose-fit jeans, a dark gray sweatshirt, and heavy boots; over one shoulder hung a bright red knapsack. Her face lit up, and she said, "Hey, Lewis. Good to see you."

I stood up, and so did Diane. "Good to see you, too, Kara."

Diane smiled, but it looked to be a forced expression. Her hands were in both of her jean pockets, and the air seemed to crackle a bit, as if I were near an electrical generator that wasn't working right. Kara looked at Diane and Diane looked at Kara, and Kara said, "Well, I'm off."

Diane said, "I'll see you out."

Kara shifted her knapsack from one shoulder to another. "You don't have to."

"I don't mind," Diane said, and Kara turned and went down the stairs, Diane following her, and I stayed behind, my arms and feet suddenly feeling like they had swollen twice their size, making me feel awkward and out of place. There was a low murmur of voices, a pause, a sharper exchange of voices, and then a door slamming. I waited. This condo had once been a happy place, with two loving women filling it up, and now it was something else, something I didn't like.

A voice from the bottom of the stairs. "Lewis?"

"Yes?"

"Go for a walk?"

I checked a clock on the wall. Nearly eleven thirty, and it was at least a fifteen-minute drive home, and my *Shoreline* deadline for my new boss was at noon.

I grabbed my jacket. "Love to."

We walked in silence across the condo parking lot until we came to a dock that stretched out into Tyler Harbor. Diane kept pace with me and walked to the end of the dock, where she stood, looking out, and then sat down, and I joined her.

"Look," she finally said. "There's my boat. See her?"

I certainly did. The boat was a twenty-foot fiberglass Holder named *Miranda*, for the not-so-popular-among-some-cops official warning that they have to give each time they make an arrest. The sails were furled, and it was resting at anchor, maybe a hundred or so yards out. Moored to the dock was a rowboat that Diane used to get out to her when it was time for a sail. I said to Diane, "Sure, I see her."

"Notice anything odd about her?"

I looked again. "Not a thing."

Diane sighed. "Look again. Then look at her neighbors."

So I did just that. I looked at *Miranda* again and then at the other boats, the moored lobster boats, stern draggers, and other fishing vessels. Then I saw what Diane was getting at.

"She's the last sailboat out there," I said.

Diane leaned back on the worn wooden planks of the pier, weight on her hands. "So true, my friend. The very last one out there. You see, Kara and I, we always had an end-of-the-summer ritual, one last long sail down to Cape Ann and back. So far, that hasn't happened this year."

"Why's that?"

"The usual. My schedule, her schedule, that sort of thing, and now the protest movement's taking up all of her time . . . crap like that."

Out over the harbor the usual seagulls were doing their usual dance in the gray sky, and out beyond, the buildings of the Falconer nuclear power plant looked so quiet and peaceful. Hard to believe that there were thousands of people out there, in the woods and marshland, preparing for another march later today.

I leaned into her a bit, my shoulder touching her shoulder. "What else is going on?"

She turned to me, her eyes moist. "You're spooky sometimes, you know that?"

"It's October. Time for Halloween. Seems appropriate."

"Hah."

Diane turned again so that she was looking out at the harbor, the moored vessels, the stretches of marshland. She took a deep breath. "Funny thing, isn't it, that from here, you can practically see Massachusetts. Just about a mile or so away, the geography is pretty much the same, but once you cross that invisible border, my, the differences."

So many things to say, but I kept my mouth shut. Diane said, "Some time ago, a number of unelected judges over there in Boston decided people like me needed to be brought into the arena of fairness and equality, and to this day, they're squabbling over it, down there in the Commonwealth. How dare a group of unelected judges upend law and custom without getting input from the people."

She turned again, her eyes still moist, a hint of a smile on her face. "Here, though, in this crazy, independent and somewhat loopy state, what happened? The legislators in Concord got together and thought the same thing that those judges did over there in Massachusetts. The legislators heard from people, the people

68

got their input, and after a while, the same thing happened. In New Hampshire and in Massachusetts, people like me can marry the ones they love. The only difference being, in New Hampshire, they did it right. Oh, some people are still making a fuss, and why not. That's what a representative democracy is all about. Even so, what happened here . . . it was legitimate. It was from the people. I think it counts more."

Diane kept quiet. Out on the harbor a fishing boat started up, black diesel exhaust belching out. I said, "Kara and you aren't on the same page, I take it."

A brief shake of her head. "Some days, Lewis, not even the same book. Or the same library. Oh, damn it, I'm getting old, my friend, and I want to settle down—make this permanent, come out of that damn stuffy closet and just get on with my life in public, proud of who I am, and who I love. Right now, I'm going in circles . . . and I'm scared that Kara either can't or won't keep up with me."

Her voice trembled with that last statement, and for whatever good it was, I put my arm around her shoulders and left it there. She took another deep breath and then laughed. "Some of the gossipers in town, if they saw us right now, they'd be damn confused, wouldn't they."

"Serves them right."

"Sure does."

"What do the gossipers in town know?" I asked.

"Oh, hell, it's an open secret in Tyler who I am and who I live with—but damn it, I don't want it to be a secret, closed or open. I just want . . . just want to be part of life, part of being normal."

I kept my arm around her for a while, and then, her voice low, she said, "Well, I guess being part of normal is being disappointed sometimes in the one you love."

"So I've heard."

She gently disengaged my arm, took my hand, and surprising both of us, I think, kissed the tips of my fingers and placed my hand down on the dock. "You and your Annie Wynn. What do the two of you want?"

"At this moment she wants to elect a certain senator from Georgia as the next president of the United States. After that . . . we'll see where we go."

"What about you?"

"Waiting it out, I suppose," I said. "She's in the proverbial driver's seat."

Then she stood up, and I stood up next to her. The wind coming off the harbor picked up some, flipping her short brown hair around. "Some driver you've got there. Seriously, as one adult to another, Lewis . . . you look deep into her, you look hard, and if she's the one, you fight to keep her. You got that? You fight to keep her . . . because neither of us is getting younger."

"Don't remind me."

"All right, then." She paused, looking into the distance as if trying to spot her Kara out there with the other protesters, and then said, "I'll see what I can do, find out how the investigation is proceeding—but only under one condition."

"Name it."

She looked straight at me. "You and Paula . . . you're friends, but there was something there, some time ago. Right?"

"Right. It was a time ago. It's over."

"Then you do this as friends. Nothing else. For if you spoil it with you and Annie over this . . . well, I won't be happy—and you don't want to see me unhappy."

I shuddered for her benefit, and mine. "You're right. I don't."

Then she gently pushed me on one shoulder. "Get going, then. You've got a deadline to meet."

"That I do."

I walked back to my Ford Explorer, leaving her alone at the end of the dock. I pulled out of the parking lot, honked the horn, got a quick wave in reply, and saw by the dashboard clock that I had missed my deadline by almost an hour.

CHAPTER SEVEN

In my upstairs office, I sat back in the chair, looking out at my narrow front yard. I had been home for nearly an hour, and in the drive from Diane's condo to my own house, I had come up with the first few paragraphs of a story contrasting how Bronson Toles's death was another in a series of violent deaths that seemed to strike men of peace, from Mahatma Gandhi to Martin Luther King Jr., and although I cringed at the thought of having those two men mentioned in a story about a restaurant and little music-hall owner, I had an idea that my editor down there in Boston might go for it. So I wrote and wrote, and spent only a few minutes in editing, rewriting, and spell-checking, and then I sent the little bugger off by e-mail to Boston and sat in my chair to await a screaming phone call from Denise Pichette-Volk.

My chair creaked a bit. I suppose I could have oiled it up some, but I liked the little creaky sound. Made everything seem that much more real. From my office, I could make out the yard and the few clumps of scraggly grass, and then the rising hillock of rocks and boulders hiding my little slice of paradise from the passing motorists on Atlantic Avenue. This had been my sanctuary for a while, a long while, but now, like Diane Woods's, this little sanctuary was being shaken up.

I put my hands behind my head and looked at a little clock on my desk next to my Apple computer. I didn't have many plans for the afternoon, save getting something to eat and then heading back down to Falconer to see the forces of clean energy and citizen democracy struggle against—

The ringing phone thankfully derailed that string of nonsense, and when I picked up the phone, I was partially right. It was my new boss.

"Lewis," she said, "you were late getting this piece to me."

"I certainly was."

I heard her breathing. "I'll give you a pass on that."

"You will?"

"Yes, I will," she said, "but I want you to do a little rewrite, get it back to me in an hour."

I took a pen from my cluttered desk and grabbed a notepad. "What do you need?"

"The paragraph about the men of peace, comparing Toles to Gandhi and King."

I felt embarrassed that this weak part had been picked up so quickly. "Right."

She said. "I liked it. Liked it a lot. I just want you to enhance it a bit."

"Enhance? Enhance it how?"

"Add another name," she said. "JFK. Add him in as another man of peace cut down before his time. Gives a New England connection to it."

I moved again in my chair, heard that comforting squeak. "JFK. President Kennedy. Man of peace. The one who expanded our involvement in Laos and South Vietnam, ran for president on a platform of a nonexistent missile gap, whose brother set up a program to assassinate Castro, and who almost got us involved in a nuclear exchange. That JFK. That man of peace."

Denise said, "Spare me the history lesson. Just add it in and send it along, all right?"

"Sure," I said. "Added and sent. No problem."

"Good," she said. "I just saw something come over the wires. The wife and stepson of Bronson Toles plan a special kind of demonstration tomorrow at five. Make sure you're there."

She hung up abruptly, and so did I, and I spent a few minutes on the computer keyboard, despising every syllable, and then I sent the little bits of data along to another computer in Boston and sat back again, listening to the creak of my chair.

In a while I dialed a local number, and a male answered. "Hello?"

"Mark? Mark Spencer?"

"Yes," he said. "Who's this?"

"Mark, this is Lewis Cole," I said. "Just calling to check in on Paula."

The barest hesitation, and I was sure he was wondering about me, Paula's former lover, checking in on her. "She's doing okay," he said.

"Really?"

Again that hesitation. A lawyer checking his opponent? "Really, Lewis. She's doing fine."

"Can I talk to her?"

"Um, not really. She's lying down. Know what I mean?"

"Yes, I do," I said. "Look, will you tell her I called?"

"Certainly," he said. "Sorry, I need to go now."

He hung up the phone, and so did I, thinking that Mark's voice, as he talked about his girlfriend, Paula Quinn, had the same blankness of tone that I had heard in Diane's talking about her Kara.

73

After sleeping in the next day and having a cup of tea for breakfast, I puttered around the house and caught up on paying some bills and reading a stack of newspapers. Soon it was time to eat and get back to work. I grabbed my pen, notebook, and jacket, went outside and got into my Ford Explorer, and made my way up the rocky driveway and off to Atlantic Avenue. A few minutes of northbound driving later, I pulled off at a small seafood restaurant called Sally's Clam Shack. It's on a tiny strip of land between Atlantic Avenue and the beach, in a weather-beaten building that looks like it had once washed ashore, and serves the best seafood in the area. Sally's been dead for years, but her two sons—Neil and Patrick—keep it going.

Inside I was greeted with the scents of fried food, which got my saliva glands into action. Most of the service is takeout, and during the height of the summer season, the line can curl outside for more than fifty feet. There are a handful of booths in the rear, and I saw that all were filled, save one. There were a couple of guys ahead of me, waiting, wearing blue jeans, hooded gray sweatshirts, and backward Red Sox baseball caps, and I was thinking maybe I'd do a takeout order when one of the co-owners, Neil Winwood, stepped out and nodded at me and said, "Right this way, Lewis."

I felt embarrassed, but my hunger pangs were outweighing any slight twinge of shame. I followed Neil, who was limping hard on each hip and knee, having come ashore to help his mom with the restaurant some years ago when his old joints and bones couldn't take lobstering anymore. He had on black-and-white-checked pants, a white T-shirt, and an apron stained with water and flour. As I went to the booth, one of the two guys back there called out, "Hey, we were next!"

Neil shrugged, handing me a menu. "He called ahead. Reservation."

The other guy pointed to a hand-printed sign underneath the cash register that read: NO RESERVATIONS ACCEPTED. "That sign says you don't take no reservations."

Neil made a point of looking around at the sign and looking surprised. "That old thing is still up? I'll be damned. I'll have to do something about that. You guys will just have to wait a bit longer."

I know I shouldn't have smiled, but I couldn't help myself. Some time ago I had written an article about some of the famed seafood places up and down the New Hampshire seacoast, and I had mentioned this place in passing. Well, one would have thought that I was a Michelin Guide reviewer and had given them three stars, for that brief mention was framed and up on the far wall, and I never had to wait long for an order, ever.

Sure enough, it took only a few minutes before my fried shrimp and onion rings arrived, and some time later, when I was done and had left money for the check, Neil came back, wiping his hands on a towel. "Everything okay?"

"It was fine, Neil, as always," I said. Around me the place was now nearly deserted, except for two glum-looking guys with hoodies who were sitting in a booth on the other side of the restaurant. "You getting much business from the protesters?"

He sat down across from me. "You kidding? Most of those kids are packing lunches and granola. Nope, we don't get any of their business . . . but still, I do wish them success." I think Neil saw the look on my face, because he said, "Did I startle you or something?"

"A little," I said. "I mean, most of the polling I've read says the bulk of the business community in this region supports the power plant because of the reliability and relatively competitive power costs."

He shook his head. "Those pollsters, they've never called me."

I gathered up my jacket. "Never thought of you as an anti-nuker, Neil."

"I'm not," he said simply.

I kept my hand still. "Sorry, you've lost me there."

"No, I'm not antinuke. I'm antistupid. Look, nuclear power is fine, it serves a purpose, it serves a need. But you know what? When it got developed, it got an evacuation plan attached to it like a goddamn ball and chain. Up the coast in Lewington, there are coal-fired and oil-fired plants, probably just as safe as Falconer and owned by the same utilities, but there ain't no evacuation plans for them, are there?"

"Not sure I'm seeing your point, Neil."

He said, "Look out there, down the road."

I swiveled in my booth, looked out the nearest window. There was a two-space parking area, a Dumpster, and then the rock and dirt berm that made up this part of the coast, bordering Atlantic Avenue. A couple of hundred feet away was a single utility pole, and on top of that pole was a large, boxy object.

I turned back to Neil. "Evacuation siren."

"Yeah, you got that. One of fifty-six around the power plant, and if that puppy sounded off right now, in October, no big deal, right? All the tourists are gone. In the summertime, though, when you got one single two-lane road running up and down the coast, with just a handful of roads leading out of the coastline and nearly a hundred thousand people jammed here on a hot August weekend, well, it wouldn't be a pretty sight if the sirens started wailing."

"The evacuation plans get tested every year, don't they? And some sirens get tested once a month."

Neil smiled. "Lewis, you're a well-read man, and I know you've got education and have traveled some. So having said that, you're home one Sunday July afternoon having a beer on your rear deck, and you hear the nearest siren to your beachfront house kick in. What are you supposed to do next?"

My jacket was still in my hand. "I guess I'd get in my Ford and drive north, up to Maine if I had to."

Neil's smile got wider. "You'd be wrong."

"Would I?"

"Yep," he said. He motioned to the kitchen. "Hanging up there is a calendar issued each year by the New Hampshire Office of Emergency Management. Everybody within a ten-mile radius gets the same calendar, year after year. That includes you, Lewis. You know what it says if you hear a siren kick off? Mmm? You're not supposed to do a damn thing except turn on the radio to one of the designated emergency broadcast stations, and on those stations would be official information about what to do. The radio might tell you to sit still and do nothing. Or it might tell you to drive out, and give you directions. Or any one of several different scenarios. So that's what's supposed to happen."

He gestured down to the south. "So if it's a hot summer weekend, and the beaches are crowded, and those sirens start to wail . . . how many of those tourists are going to sit there and say, 'Gee, I guess we should find a radio somewhere'? No, they're going to panic, they're going to bundle up their families, get into their cars, and try to get the hell out. It'll make Hurricane Katrina look like the Rose Bowl Parade in comparison."

I stood up. "So what do we do? Shut her down?"

Neil grabbed the check and my money. "Sorry, Lewis. That's above my pay grade—but that still means I don't like the place."

. . .

In my drive to the Falconer nuclear power plant, I made a detour about a mile and a half before the plant gates, at the Seaside Campground. Unlike a couple of days ago, the way toward the main campsite was fairly open, with only a few vehicles off to the side, and the little cottage that served as an office was still closed. I pulled up near the wooden stage and felt cold. I looked at the plain wood, engine running, and then switched off the engine and got outside.

In front of the stage a few young men and women stood just staring at it, as if they were some old Christian sect from the early centuries looking down at the Coliseum. Flowers had been placed on the wood, and from where I stood, I was sure that I saw stains. In addition to the flowers there were stubs of burned-out candles.

There were also signs, bumper stickers, and such, all proclaiming the same thing: the end of the Falconer nuclear power plant and the start of something else safer and cleaner.

I was ignored, which was fine.

I turned around and was going to go back to my Ford when I spotted a couple of vehicles parked on the other side of the open grove. Two state police cruisers, a Falconer police cruiser, and a large dark green vehicle that announced with bright gold letters on the side that it was a Major Crime Unit response van for the state police. From inside my jacket I pulled out my state-issued press pass, hung it around my neck, and went into the woods. About fifty yards in, following a bit of a trail, I came to the usual yellow crime scene tape and a state police trooper and a Falconer police officer. I showed them my press pass and we had a brief and not very productive conversation in which I was advised that all public statements would be coming through the agency that runs the state police, the Department of Safety, and all inquiries should be directed to their Concord office.

And by the way, have a nice day.

I persisted nevertheless, and after a while, the Falconer cop gave up and walked into the woods. A little while later, he returned, followed by a thickset man with light olive skin and wearing a dark blue jumpsuit and black boots and a seriously irritated expression. His black hair was cut short in a buzz cut, and he said, "You the reporter from Tyler bugging us?"

"I guess I am," I said. "Just looking to ask a few questions and—"

"Tyler," he said. "You know Diane Woods?"

"I do," I said. "She's a good friend of mine."

That seemed to get his attention, and he lifted up the yellow crime scene tape and said, "Come into my temporary office, such as it is."

I followed him a few yards, and he turned, yawned, and leaned against an oak tree. "The name's Renzi, Pete Renzi. Detective with the state police Major Crime Unit, and you can ask a couple of questions—but if I find out that Diane Woods doesn't know you, then you better make sure you don't speed on state roads. Got it?"

"All of it," I said. "Thanks for the time."

"So don't waste it," he said. "What do you want?"

"What can you tell me?"

He yawned again. "Not much. One Mr. Bronson Toles, shot and killed by a single round to his head. That round hasn't been found yet, though we're looking out beyond that stage with metal detectors."

"Any sign where the shooter had been hiding?"

He gestured to the surrounding woods. "Pick a tree. Lots of trees around here have a good view of the stage. Trick is to find the right tree, and we haven't had the luck. Though we're still looking."

"Any suspects?"

He frowned. "A friend of Diane Woods and you ask such a stupid question?"

I felt warm and moved on. "A motive, then. Why he was shot."

"Well, it sure as hell wasn't random, that's for sure. So someone took the time and trouble to set up a spot to shoot at Bronson Toles, arrange an escape route, and know when he was going to talk."

"A professional hit?"

"No comment," he said, "and sorry, Mr. Cole, that's all the time I have for you today." He pointed to the yellow crime scene tape. "I trust you know your way out?"

"I do," I said.

"Glad to hear it."

When I got to my Explorer, I saw a familiar face: Haleigh Miller, talking to some of her fellow activists. She spotted me and waved, and I waved back. She came up to me and said, "Lewis, so good to see you. How are you doing?"

"Out working. You?"

She smiled though she still looked tired. "We're getting ready for the special event this afternoon."

"The one at five o'clock, with Bronson Toles's wife?"

Haleigh nodded. "Yes. Make sure you don't miss it. It's going to be . . . it's going to be something different."

"All right, I won't."

Some of her friends hung back, as if they didn't want to be despoiled by being so close to a member of the oppressor class, one who worked for the Man. Or the Woman, as was my case. "You doing all right back here?"

Haleigh said, "Oh, I'm doing fine. Sleeping outdoors and eating cold food—not as nice as it was back at your place, but I'm doing it for a greater cause, so I don't mind. Much." She laughed and said, "I really want to thank you again for helping me out the other day. I needed . . . I needed a break, and you provided it. I owe you one."

I was ashamed to admit it, but a thought came to me, one I instantly brought up. "Look, can I ask you for a favor?"

"Sure," she said, sounding innocent, not like the jaded older man talking to her.

"If you can't do it, I understand, but I'm looking to talk to someone in the movement."

"Someone in particular?"

I looked around, made sure no one else was within earshot. "Curt Chesak. The guy heading the Nuclear Freedom Front."

She folded her arms and rubbed at her elbows for a moment. "Curt? Why do you want to talk to Curt?"

"Because I'm a magazine writer," I said, not quite allowing myself to call what I do journalism. "I want to know what's going on, what's driving people, and maybe why things are happening. Curt is sort of a bogeyman to the law enforcement folks out there. He's under suspicion for a lot of criminal activities but hasn't been caught yet."

"Yet," she said, "and that's because he's a very secretive man, Lewis. He has to be, for what he does. He runs the NFF, and he has the regular antinuclear folks against him, not to mention the cops, the utilities and the unions. That's why he always wears a mask when he speaks in public. Hell, some of us don't even think Curt Chesak is his real name."

"But could you help me? At least get word to somebody that might know somebody?"

Her happy face at seeing me earlier had been replaced by something a bit more troubled. "I . . . I guess I could try."

"That'd be great." I reached into my wallet and pulled out my *Shoreline* business card. Before passing it over I had to dig out my cell phone and look up my own number—what can I say, I know cell phones are a necessary evil, but I still don't like them that much—and scribble it down.

"My home number and cell phone number are there," I said, handing her the card. "Have somebody call me at any time. I don't mind."

She looked at the card for a moment before slipping it into her coat pocket. "Okay, I guess."

Then I thought it through one more time and said, "No, it's not okay. Give me the card back."

"Why?"

"Because I'm not being fair to you," I said. "I'm using your thanks for the other night in hoping that you'll pass this card on to somebody, and that's not fair. If I'm going to do this, I'm going to do this on my own. So give me the card back."

Haleigh put her hand back into the coat pocket, paused for a second, and shook her head. "No."

"Yes," I said. "Please."

She shook her head again. "No. I don't mind doing it. I know some people . . . and I know you, Lewis. I know I can trust you. You're not a cop, you won't reveal anything, and you'll do what you say you'll do, right? You want to interview him, nothing more."

I looked at that innocent young college-aged face, decided I could go along with that, and said, "That's right. I want to interview him. Ask him some questions. Nothing more than that."

Haleigh smiled and said, "I'll do what I can do—but no promises, okay?"

"I understand, no promises."

She made to go back to her companions, then said, "Oh. I

should have asked you earlier. How's your friend doing, the reporter who was standing next to Bronson when he got shot?"

What to say? So I decided to make it quick. "She's out of the hospital."

"Glad to hear it," she said. "You know, Lewis, it's a cliché but it's true. Violence never solved anything."

I didn't know what to say about that, either, for as a cliché, it was a stupid one. Violence might not have solved anything, but in wars and conflicts and battles all across history, and continuing into the future—unless some dramatic changes occurred—violence often settled things. Permanently.

So instead of discussing philosophy with the young lady, I waved at her and got back into my Ford.

CHAPTER EIGHT

It sounds funny that at a time when there were thousands of protesters trying to break into the Falconer nuclear power plant, I had no problems gaining access, but that's where a bit of ingenuity and modern technology came into play. Off Route 1 there were two main entrances to the power plant, and these entrances were named—in a bit of utility imagination—the North Gate and the South Gate. Both gates were closed to visitors and most everyone else, but still, the protesters and media types milled about, talking to one another and passing the time.

There were also a handful of smaller service entrances, though, like the one Paula and I had used the other day, and all I had to do was call the plant spokesman, Ron Shelton, and explain that I wanted to come into the plant site, and he'd give me a time.

Which is what I did, and I drove down Stony Creek Road as before and got to the gate, where two security officers from the power plant allowed me in. By the fence were six or seven protesters, and when they saw the gate open up, they started chanting, "No nukes, no nukes." After a minute or two of driving, I didn't hear them anymore.

I followed the security pickup truck back to the plant site proper, and when we stopped at an intersection, one of the officers came back to me. I lowered the window, and he said, "Sorry, sir, but Mr. Shelton contacted us. He'd like to meet you at his office, if that's all right with you."

"That'd be fine," I said, and I kept on following the pickup truck. We drove down the main access road within the plant— past a huge billboard on one corner that read: SAFETY PAYS OFF, EVERY DAY. After about a quarter mile of driving, we made a left at a wooden sign that read: FALCONER VISITORS' CENTER. We went down a pleasant little paved lane, which opened up to a large parking lot that was filled with police cruisers from a variety of departments in the area and a half dozen or so National Guard Humvees.

I parked in an open spot as the security pickup truck drove away, then went up a sidewalk flanked by hedge work that led to an odd triangular-shaped wooden building that announced it was the plant's visitors' center. Inside there was a curved counter packed with phones, and also packed with New Hampshire State Police officers and other cops in a variety of uniforms using the phones, talking, and eating from a buffet-style table set up on the other side of the lobby.

A tired-looking Ron Shelton came from around the counter, shook my hand, and said, "Lewis Cole, from *Shoreline*, right? Thanks for coming over."

I followed him past the counter, down a hallway, to an office at the end. There was a desk and bookcases and comfortable chairs, and a large window that overlooked the rear of the visitors' center and something called the Nature Trail. Ron had on Top-Siders khaki slacks, a button-down blue shirt, and a red necktie, and though he was smiling, his eyes were red-rimmed and there were worry lines up there.

"I know you're friends with Paula Quinn, from the *Chronicle*," he said, leaning back a bit in his chair. "I just wanted to know how she's doing."

"She got out of the hospital yesterday, I know that," I said, "and I know that being next to Bronson Toles when he got shot . . . that was one hell of a shock."

"Were you there, too?"

"I was."

"Holy crap," Ron said, shaking his head. "Paula and I have butted heads a few times over news coverage, but in the end she's always been fair. I hope she gets better. If you see her, let her know I was asking about her, okay?"

"Sure," I said. His phone started ringing, but he ignored it, then rubbed at his eyes. "You heard about the special demonstration later today."

"I did."

"Laura Toles and her son, Vic, are going to be leading a march blaming us for her husband's death."

"Really?"

Ron looked at me and said, "Look, can . . . can we just have a normal conversation here for a couple of minutes, just a couple of guys? Not a plant spokesman or a magazine writer."

"You mean, off the record."

"If that's all right with you."

I paused, then said, "All right. If you say something particularly juicy, how about I ask you about it, and if it's okay, I attribute it to an unnamed utility official?"

He smiled. "You know, a week or so ago, when I was getting you signed up for access, I talked to Paula and said I didn't recognize your name, and she said you were just a columnist and were fairly new with this breaking news business—but you seem to know your way around."

I took out my notebook and pen. "I've learned from the best."

Another smile. "I'm sure she'd love to hear that. Sure. You hear anything earth-shattering that you want to use, I'll see what I can do. Other than that, we're off the record. Deal?"

"Deal," I said.

He let out a breath. "Not that I'm promising anything earth-shattering, but sometimes it's just nice to talk like a normal human being. Like the protest this afternoon. Guaranteed that Mrs. Toles and her son are going to blame us for the murder of her husband. If it wasn't for this evil power plant and all the emotions it brings out in people, Bronson Toles would still be alive, working on a new eggplant Parmesan recipe and signing up the next great breakout folk band for the Stone Chapel. Guaranteed."

"Why do you say that?"

He put his hands behind his head. "Why not? We're blamed for most everything else. Birth defects among the local population, the death of migratory birds, the lack of fish because of our cooling tunnel intakes . . . hell, when they started building this place more than thirty years ago, they recovered the skeletons of some Native Americans. The utility went to great efforts to rebury the remains with the assistance of local Native American groups, and to this day, we're still blamed for building this place on an Indian burial ground."

"You sound like one frustrated spokesman, Ron," I said.

"Oh, some days," he said, still leaning back in his chair. "You know, if we'd stop shouting at each other and stop the protests, most people would be surprised to find out how much the people who work here and the people out there demonstrating have in common."

"Like what?"

"Like we both believe in conservation, for example. Better fuel efficiency for engines and vehicles. Research into alternative energy. Reduction of our dependence on foreign oil. We both believe in that—but we're also too busy fitting into our assigned roles. The ignorant unwashed versus the corporate evildoers. Here," he said, letting his chair come forward and spinning a framed photo around on his desk, among a couple of other framed photographs. "Does that look like a corporate evildoer who clubs baby seals on his vacation?"

I took the frame in hand. It was a color photo of Ron wearing hiking boots, khaki shorts, and a T-shirt, holding a shovel, on a wooded trail, with two attractive young women dressed similarly and also holding shovels. "Nice pic," I said. "Where was it taken?"

"Up in the White Mountains, volunteering with the Appalachian Mountain Club, doing trail maintenance. Spent a glorious week up there . . . working hard, sleeping great, and appreciating the sights."

"Including the female ones?"

He grinned. "Especially the female ones. I've always spent a lot of time outdoors, hiking, hunting, fishing, and when I was in college, getting my environmental sciences degree, I spent weeks up there in the White Mountains, doing research on acid rain. You know where the acid rain comes from, that kills some of our mountain lakes and ponds?"

"Coal-fired plants out in the Midwest."

"Yeah," he said sourly, "but are the protest groups out in Ohio or Illinois trying to shut them down? Nope. They're here. Trying to shut down a power plant source that doesn't add one molecule to the problems of acid rain or global warming."

He rotated slightly in his chair and said, "Not to mention adding the Russians to the mix. Christ. Decades after Chernobyl, you'd think they'd know how to run those obsolete graphite reactors. Hell, they should be shut down, but they need power so bad over there—and here? Still stuck in the 1970s. You know, most of the people out there holding the banners and flags probably think that Japan and France are the height of civilized life, with wonderful health care and employment security, but you know what?"

"They don't mind nuclear power," I said.

"You better believe it. In France, nearly eighty percent of their electricity comes from nuclear, and in Japan—which has a reason to fear the splitting of the atom—more than thirty percent comes from nuclear. And here? The so-called leader of the so-called Free World? Less than twenty percent—and we were about to kick that number up a notch when the Kursk disaster happened." He paused, shook his head. "Fucking Russians."

I looked at him and said, "Still off the record?"

"Hunh?"

"What you just said there, about the fucking Russians," I said. "That'd make a great quote, don't you think?"

Ron laughed. "What, you want me to get fired?"

"Not particularly," I said.

He rocked in the chair again for a moment and said, "Tell you what. If you can keep a secret, you can attribute that quote to an unnamed New England utility official: 'The American nuclear industry is now being crippled not because of any problem that it caused, but because of those fucking Russians.' That way, I can get a quote out in the media that all of us here believe in, and I also get to keep my job."

I scribbled the words in my open notebook. "Sounds good to me."

"Fine." He moved the photo around on his desk, and I noted one photograph of Ron wearing a coat and tie, standing next to an attractive woman wearing a black cocktail dress. I gestured to the photo and said, "One of your trailmates from your AMC volunteering?"

That got me a laugh. "Clara? Only in some rural areas of the country. No, that's my younger sister."

"She into the outdoors and science?"

"Not hardly," Ron said. "Clara's been into music and singing since she turned twelve. Did a lot of gigs at local clubs and music halls. Came close a couple of times to breaking out and making a career out of it, but it never happened. Poor sweetie."

"I see," I said, and Ron got up from his chair and said, "Look, you don't want to be late for the next act of this circus, do you? I'll contact security, get you an escort to the south fence."

I shook his hand and went out back to the lobby, where I waited for a security officer to show up. While I waited, I looked through a number of brochures in a rack by the glass doors. I picked up one brochure titled "Radiation: Our Most Misunderstood Friend" and glanced at it for a few moments until I saw the security pickup truck roll up to the entrance.

Back at the same outcropping of rock and dirt, there were the same lines of police officers and National Guardsmen, and I spent a few fruitless minutes looking to see if Diane Woods was on my part of the plant property, but I didn't see her. Wearing my bright oversized press pass, I wandered over to the collection of newspaper reporters, television correspondents, and radio reporters, and I was surprised to see Paula Quinn standing by herself, staring out at the approaching crowds of protesters on the marsh.

I went up to her, and she turned and gave me a wan smile. "Lewis."

"Paula," I said.

She said, "Let me just talk for a moment, all right? I'm doing okay. I slept a bit better last night, had some long talks with Mark, and we both decided that like the cowboy who falls off a horse, the best thing would be to get back on the horse and get at it again. So that's why I'm here. Actually, I'm here for two reasons. One, to get out of my funk, and two, to get back to work. I've got to work, Lewis, just have to . . . or at my age, I have to think about starting over in something completely new, and frankly speaking, that scares the shit out of me."

I watched her determined face, wanting to believe every word that she was saying, but I saw only the haunted look in her eyes. "Fine," I said. "Glad to hear it, glad to see you here."

She turned and looked back out at the approaching people, and I put my arm out and gave her shoulders a quick squeeze, and she leaned into me for a moment, sighed, and said, "All I know is that we're promised something different this afternoon. You have any idea?"

I thought about Ron Shelton's conversation and said, "I have no doubt that they'll blame Bronson Toles's death on the Falconer nuclear power plant."

She said, "Oh, that's not very original, Lewis. I want to see—oh, looks like it's starting."

Unlike the other day, there was only one group of protesters coming to the fence. The Nuclear Freedom Front group was absent, and I had no idea what that meant. Another thing was oddly disturbing: The hundreds upon hundreds of people marching across the marsh grasses and mud were keeping silent. I didn't hear one word. Even the banners and the balloons and papier-mâché heads were missing. All that was there was the people, coming closer and closer to the fence line.

A shouted order from somewhere in the police line, and the police started marching down to the fence. I took a breath. I didn't like where this was going. The other day I had thought the NFF was doing a pretty good job of being ordered and disciplined, but their opponents on the other side were putting them to shame with their own sense of power and strength.

Paula said, her voice low, "I'm not sure what the hell is going on, but it's creeping me out. How about you?"

"The same," I said, noticing that Paula was standing closer to me. Around us camera crews were focusing, zooming in on the approaching marchers. A wind came up, scattering a few dead leaves. The police marched down a slight incline to the fence. A couple of reporters tried to follow them down, but I saw Ron Shelton, in hard hat and short tan jacket, corral them and bring them back to the group. That didn't seem to make them happy, but those were the ground rules for getting on-plant access, that one had to follow the directions of the PR folks.

Out on the marshes, a whistle blew. The marchers halted about twenty feet away from the fence line. A few of the demon-strators, holding up orange sticks, walked up and down the front ranks of the demonstrators, dressing the line, making it more straight.

I said to Paula, "None of the NFF demonstrators are there, see that? And the supposedly loosey-goosey unorganized group, they certainly as hell look more organized today."

Her voice was uneasy. "It's like . . . it's like the shooting has radicalized them. You know? The shooting . . . it's changed them."

Sure, I thought. *Changes.* A lot of things had changed with the killing of Bronson Toles.

Another blast of a whistle, and in the middle of the crowd, some of the people stepped aside, and I heard some mutters of astonishment from my fellow members of the Fourth Estate. A woman and a young man emerged from the crowd, holding hands, and Paula said, "That's Mrs. Toles—Laura Glynn Toles— and her son, Vic."

Then, behind them, marching slowly and as best as they could across the uneven terrain, were six demonstrators bearing a plain wooden casket on their shoulders. Four men and two women, faces set and somber.

"Holy Christ," one of the newsmen with us said. "Will you look at that? They dragged that poor bastard's body down here, just like that."

A woman from one of the Boston television stations replied, "I can believe that. Think of all the good coverage they're getting for the six o'clock news."

Laura Toles and her son marched out about five feet in front of the line of demonstrators, and then the casket bearing her husband's body came out and was next to them. As it had been the other day, a portable sound system was set up, a microphone placed in Laura's hand.

The murmuring from the press people dribbled away. I had my notebook out and saw that Paula did, too, though the hand holding a pen was trembling slightly.

"I . . . I want to speak to you, to all of you, today." Laura's voice came out strong but quivering a bit. "I . . . I know that Bronson would want us to continue . . . that the ones . . . the ones who cut him down . . . for whatever reason . . . won't be stopped . . . that the righteousness of our cause will strengthen us to continue . . ."

She stopped and sobbed for a moment, and her son put an arm

around her. Nearby a Boston television cameraman, looking through his camera, whispered, "Man, this shit is golden."

Laura took a breath, audible through the microphone, and pointed with her free hand to the casket. "There . . . in there are the mortal remains of my beloved, the one who saw things and dared to change them. My love is gone . . . what is left are just the bones, tissues, and remnants of what was once here, which once talked, breathed and loved and fought. His body is at peace . . . a body sacrificed."

She paused again, and it was amazing how quiet the hundreds and hundreds of people were, the ones gathered behind her, though it was easy to see that quite a few of them were weeping. "Yes . . . sacrificed . . . for I blame the powers that allowed this evil plant to be built, allowed it to operate, and still allow it to operate . . . though all of us know the threat it poses to us and every single living thing within miles about us. We charge everyone on the other side of that fence . . . charge them with complicity in the murder of my husband!"

I thought of what Ron Shelton had told me earlier and wished I were nearer to him; I would have loved to see the expression on his face. Now the people behind her were cheering, clapping, and even booing, and Laura raised a hand and said, "Yes! Complicity in the murder of my husband, a fine man who only wanted to feed the hungry, bring music and a message to the community, and to change this place of death into a place of life!"

More cheers, more yells, and this time, Laura allowed the noise to drift away. Her son—who looked to be in his early twenties—still had his arm around her. Laura looked back at the crowd and then to the fence line and the cops and said, "Tomorrow . . . tomorrow there will be a final memorial for my husband, at the Stone Chapel. Today . . . today we will march around the perimeter of Falconer Station, with my husband before us, to show that you may kill the messenger, you may shatter the mind that did so much for us, but you will never, ever kill the message. The messenger dies . . . but the message lives on! Forever!"

The cheers rose up, louder and louder, and then the casket started moving, and the sound system was taken away, and behind the casket and Laura and Vic Toles, the people flowed along, following them, and a chant began, soft at first, but then louder and louder:

"The people . . . united . . . will never be defeated! The people . . . united . . . will never be defeated! The people . . . united . . . will never be defeated!"

I turned to say something amusing and pithy to Paula, but she wasn't there.

I looked around at the collection of reporters and cameramen. She was gone.

CHAPTER NINE

I stayed for a while longer at the plant site, and when boredom set in, I left to go home. When I got there, I went to my upstairs office and wrote up the day's events for my mistress at *Shoreline* magazine. I wrote about the silent crowd of demonstrators marching across the marshland, the way they opened up to display the casket of Bronson Toles, the emphatic tone of his widow's words, and when I had wrapped up the story, I decided to throw in the not-so-gracious but entirely understandable quote from Ron Shelton about the Russians and their nuclear power program.

About ten minutes after I had filed the story, the phone rang, with Denise on the other end.

"Nice piece of work," she said.

"Glad to hear it."

"And I love that quote about the fucking Russians. That's beautiful. Who said it?"

"An unnamed New England utility official," I said. "Just like the story said."

"I know, but who is it?"

"Sorry, Denise. I gave my word. No identification."

I waited, hearing nothing save a light hiss of static, and she laughed. "I thought you said you weren't any good at this."

"What's this?"

"Being a reporter."

I said, "Just because you think I'm good at it doesn't mean I like doing it."

Later that night I sat outside on the rear deck of my beach house, watching the ocean move its way back and forth on the coast, in its never-ending motion of play. When I had finished with my *Shoreline* story I tidied up the joint, including wrestling with a vacuum cleaner that seemed to roll over each time I tugged on the hose. With my Martha Stewart imitation complete, I then made a quick meal of a fried ham steak and defrosted Boston baked beans, which I had earlier made from an old family recipe that belonged to Diane Woods.

I had a light down comforter on my legs, binoculars in my laps, and a glass of Australian pinot noir in my hand. Before me was the night sky in all its splendid glory, obscured a bit by a glow to the southern and northern horizons that marked cities—but looking out to the east, the only cities were thousands of miles away. I sat and watched the slow rise of the constellations, and occasionally, when I spotted the fast-moving, unblinking dot of light that marked a satellite, I brought the binoculars up and watched the passage overhead.

It was a little game I played with myself, to watch those speedy dots slide across my night sky. Sometimes when I observed the hard points of light, I was sure I was seeing a satellite. Anyway, I always got a kick out of seeing bits of light that grew lighter and darker as they flung themselves across the night sky, for usually that meant they represented a spent rocket booster, or some other space debris, tumbling along at thousands of miles per hour. I recalled with a smile a little story that had come out a few years ago, from a retired Soviet space scientist, who said that the millions of people who thought they had seen the first earth satellite—*Sputnik*—back in 1957, had in fact seen no such thing. That little point of light had been the rocket booster that had propelled the little guy into space.

So there I was, and usually these moments of peace and repose calmed me down and made me ready for a good night's sleep, but not on this October evening. I was thinking more of yesterday, seeing Bronson Toles getting murdered, and seeing my friend Paula fall to the ground. I also thought of Paula in the hospital, how much she had changed overnight, and how she had sprinted away from the demonstration earlier today. Then there was Diane Woods, doing her job, living her life in a closet, and wanting so much to break out. And, of course, my dear Annie Wynn, no doubt in some anonymous hotel room, working hard to elect a man she believed in president.

All these women in my life, I thought, looking up at the stars, all trying to live, trying to survive, trying to make a difference.

What was I up to?

I put the binoculars down, took a sip of wine, and watched the stars some more.

. . .

The next day I stopped at the offices of the Tyler *Chronicle*, stuck on the first floor of an old office building in the center of Tyler proper, which is a few miles west of its famous beach. I wandered in through the back entrance, past piles of newspapers and walking on stained industrial-strength carpet that was worn in plenty of areas. Cables and power cords snaked out through the suspended ceiling, and up ahead was a tiny warren of desks with computer terminals on top. The place was empty, save for the *Chronicle*'s editor, Rollie Grandmaison, who was sitting before his own terminal, peering at the screen over half-frame glasses, and typing with as much effort as if the keyboard had been printed in Japanese.

Rollie could have been sixty, seventy, or eighty, and if anyone knew, they weren't saying, and he had on his usual uniform of black trousers, white shirt, and black necktie, and what little hair remained was plastered over a freckled scalp. He didn't look up as I approached his cluttered desk, but he grunted and said, "She's not here."

"I can see that."

"I don't know where she is, either. I just know she's out working. Probably be at the Stone Chapel in a couple of hours, for that memorial service."

"Yeah, you're probably right," I said, "but I'm not here to see her."

That caused Rollie to look away from the screen, and before he could say anything else, he had a fit of coughing that turned his face the color of a stop sign. Another secret was the status of his health, which was why Paula had gotten a promotion some months ago to assistant editor, to help out Rollie.

If Rollie was grateful for that, though, he kept that emotion as secret as his age and state of health. When he stopped coughing I said, "I'm actually here for a favor, Rollie. I was hoping to look through your clip file."

"What for?"

"Want to see what kind of stories you've got on Bronson Toles and the Stone Chapel."

He took off his black-rimmed half-glasses, rubbed at his eyes, and said, "Anyone else I'd tell 'em to go screw, that I had better things to do, but Paula . . . well, consider it done. Go on down to the cellar and I'll send along my college intern for the fall."

I looked around the empty office. "You're still getting interns? And paying them?"

Rollie said, "Oh yeah, we're still getting them, but we're not paying them. Those days are gone. Most of the time, we use 'em where we need 'em. Filing, answering the phone, filling out classified ad forms."

"Don't think they'd learn much by doing that," I said.

Rollie grinned. "They're learning a lot, I promise you. About real life, and buddy, for most of 'em, that'll be the most important thing they ever learn."

In the basement of the Tyler *Chronicle* it was damp and musty, with a sump pump in one corner that Paula told me often fought a losing battle over rainwater seeping in. On wooden stands there were filing cabinets and bound back issues of the *Chronicle,* and in one corner an abandoned darkroom from the days when photos came about from a mixture of film, chemicals, photo paper, and odd men and women who often seemed to have sniffed too many of the chemicals over the years.

Before me was a scarred wooden table, and deposited on the

table by a quiet college-aged boy who had a phone headset attached to one ear was a thick green file folder, and with open notebook in hand, I started going through the clip file for Bronson Toles and the Stone Chapel.

The old smell of the glue and tape tickled at my nose. The first clippings were stories about a mansion that had once belonged to Bonus Norton—a wealthy Tyler businessman from the early 1900s—that had burned to the ground in 1977, with the only surviving structure being an adjacent stone chapel that was used by Mr. Norton so he didn't have to travel far away from his beloved home on Sundays to attend services. Further articles went on about the ruins being bulldozed, a small-scale housing development going on the property, and the stone chapel and its land being bought by a collective led by a graduate student from Harvard named Bronson Toles. From there, the clippings told stories about different rock bands and folk groups that played at the Stone Chapel—now fully owned by Bronson Toles—and how the Stone Chapel was known as a place where groups made their debut before "breaking out."

Which was true, for there was a clipping from *Time* magazine in 1983 listing the number of famous bands that got their start at the Stone Chapel. More clippings followed, with more photos of Bronson Toles—one showing him at an event, recording the music with one of those old-fashioned reel-to-reel recorders—and then, in the late 1980s, Bronson branched out into protests, social justice causes, and the like. Nuclear freeze, organic food, free-range chickens, sustainable coffee, renewable energy, and the usual other issues. A number of presidential candidates also showed up at the Stone Chapel to get Bronson Toles's blessing, and twice over the years, the Stone Chapel was threatened with closure because of increased utility bills and property taxes. Somehow Bronson rallied, and along the way, a few years back, he married one Laura Glynn, who became Laura Glynn Toles, and there was a happy wedding photo of the groom and bride and best man—a very young Victor Glynn Toles—standing inside a flower-strewed Stone Chapel.

So there it was. A man's life and career in one thick folder, with space for the next clipping, his murder and subsequent funeral.

I checked the time. The memorial service for Bronson was set to begin in less than a half hour.

The Stone Chapel was located next to a housing development called Norton Meadows, at the upper end of Tyler, just a few hundred yards away from North Tyler. The beach was nearby but not visible; what was visible was the hordes of people lining up to try to get inside. I parked and grabbed my reporter's notebook and my ever-useful press pass, and I lucked out, for the press pass did have value this morning. Off to the left, by the full parking lot, was a yellow rope line with a handmade sign dangling in the breeze that read: MEDIA THIS WAY.

The Stone Chapel was made in a sort of faux Romanesque style, with tall stained-glass windows, and double wooden doors that led inside. To the rear was a small attached two-story cottage that was probably the living quarters for the Toleses. The media entrance was a side entrance off to the left of the chapel, and a somber-looking young man with a handlebar mustache, patched jeans, and a tie-dyed T-shirt looked at my press pass and gestured me in. Inside, the place was packed, standing room only, with a raised stage at the near end. Light came from the stained-glass windows and lamps hanging down from black chains. The area roped off for the media was near a stone wall that held framed photos of musical groups that had played at the Stone Chapel, each photo with a grinning Bronson Toles standing nearby, and a couple of him sitting behind some recording gear.

There was also a wide cork bulletin board with photos of the workers here at the chapel, and among the dozen or so photos, I noted one of Haleigh Miller, my UNH contact, smiling and standing with a group of young people, including Vic Toles, Bronson's stepson. Other photos of young ladies were there as well, most of them with Bronson Toles standing with his arm around them.

Banners were hanging from rafters up in the ceiling, promoting either the usual leftist causes or musicians, and even with the people inside, it was fairly cool. Up on the center of the stage was Bronson's casket, a green and white flag draped over the plain wood. Also up on the stage were speakers and microphones and stools for musicians, and there were a few people up there, talking to each other. Vic Toles was standing by himself, arms crossed, staring at the casket of his stepfather, while his mom was a few feet away, talking to someone in an animated way, lots of hand movements, facial expressions changing like the flipping pages of a book from humor to anger to sadness. The someone she was talking to was wearing pressed jeans, a black T-shirt, and a black suit coat, and he had sunglasses perched above his carefully coiffed blond hair. He stood there with arms folded as well, nodding here and there.

Somebody nudged me. I turned and smiled. It was Paula Quinn, looking tired, wearing khaki slacks and a black turtleneck sweater.

"Hey, good to see you," I said. "I was worried yesterday. I didn't see you leave."

"Well . . . I chickened out. Something about the marchers and seeing the cops and National Guardsmen in all their paramilitary gear . . . it seemed like something violent was about to break out . . . and I didn't want to be there."

"It stayed pretty quiet, all things considered."

"I know, I know. I just . . . panicked. It's hard to explain."

"Try me," I said.

"Lewis—"

"Look, we've got time, and I really want to know what happened."

Then it looked like Paula shrank into herself, as if I had just had a visual premonition of what she would look like fifty or sixty years down the road. She started to speak, stopped, then caught herself and said, "I felt . . . exposed. Standing on that bare patch of ground, with all those people around . . . and the woods out in the distance, beyond the marshes. It sounds crazy, but I was thinking about the sniper who killed Bronson. I'm sure he had a telescopic sight. Am I right, Lewis? A shooter like that, he'd have to have a telescopic sight to make that kind of shot."

"You're probably right," I said.

"Then the bastard saw me," Paula said, voice quivering. "He saw me when he was aiming at Bronson. He had to . . . and I've been thinking about that. That he saw me, then moved his rifle just a bit, and pulled the trigger—but what if I had moved instead? What would have happened? It would have been me dead up on the stage, not Bronson."

"The killer was aiming at him, not you," I said, "and you're here."

She took in a deep, shuddering breath. "I know that. I know I'm here. I also know there's a killer out there who saw me, who took note of me . . . and suppose he liked what he did to Bronson and decided to go after somebody female next? What then?"

"Paula, the chances that—"

"So when I was up there, at the plant site, with all those people, I started getting nervous. Scared. I imagined that the shooter was still out there, in the woods, watching us all . . . and maybe he was going to kill Bronson's wife the next time . . . or his stepson . . . or maybe he saw me out there, standing there, and he knows what I look like, and . . . I had to get out of there, Lewis. I had to get out of that plant and Falconer and go home and lock the doors and have a good cry."

"I see," I said. "So how are you doing today?"

Paula stayed quiet and motionless, and then she shook herself, and some sort of transformation occurred, for now she seemed to be her own age. "Oh, I'm hanging in there—and I'm glad to be here . . . honest, I am."

"Really?"

She shook her head, smiling. "No, not really. I have to be here, I have to keep working—though to tell the truth, I'd rather be curled up in bed, reading Jane Austen, with the computer, cell phone, and landline phone off."

"Come on, you've told me that you've read and reread all of her books at least a half dozen times."

"True, but you know what? It's comforting, you know? No surprises, nothing bloody, everything genteel and soft, the good ones get their rewards in the end. After last week—it's pretty seductive."

"I see."

She gave me a rueful laugh. "Jane Austen . . . it's all fantasy. As well written and special as it is, those books show a slice of upper-class, privileged life. When sweet Jane was living and writing her books, a starving ten-year-old girl could be hanged in London for stealing a loaf of bread."

Then came the hum of a sound system being turned on, and as I had the day before, I gave her shoulder a squeeze, and as she had the day before, she turned away.

CHAPTER TEN

The memorial service started, and then went on, and then went on. No offense to the memory of Bronson Toles, I was bored to tears after the first half hour or so. Speaker after speaker went up and rambled or ranted about the man, about oppression, about imperialism, and oh yeah, about a certain nuclear power plant. I took notes the best I could, wondering how regular news reporters could do this, day after day, without turning to heavy drinking. At least when I was a lowly columnist, I could choose my own topic, something that interested me. I really had no interest in being here, save for keeping my fairly well-paid job. It wasn't just me, I either; could see some of my fellow scribblers yawning, with some of the more sneaky ones texting on their cell phones or PDAs. Even some in the audience seemed restless, with the applause and cheers declining for each subsequent speaker.

After time dragged on for another hour or six, Laura Glynn Toles came to the microphone, and the crowd came alive, cheering and applauding and whistling. Her eyes were red-rimmed, and she looked as if she had gotten maybe a handful of hours of sleep over the past couple of days. She had on a long multicolored peasant skirt, heavy boots, and a gray cable sweater. She came across the stage and touched the bare wood of her husband's casket. More cheers. Laura walked up to a microphone and held up both of her hands. To her side was Vic, applauding, biting his lower lip, tears rolling down his cheeks.

When the applause and cheers finally died away, Laura bent her head to the microphone and said, in a hoarse whisper, "I'm . . .

I'm so sorry that I cannot speak for very long . . . for my voice is slipping away . . . though my spirit is still fighting."

The cheers came up again, and again she raised her arms to silence the crowd. She coughed a couple of times and then lowered her head. "I . . . I have nothing more to add . . . to add what my wonderful friends have said before about my husband, my soul mate, my fellow traveler on the journey to make this a safer and more sustainable world."

A few more cheers, but others in the crowd tried to silence their friends, to let her continue talking. She took a few moments to wipe at her eyes and said, "What . . . what I have to say next is important . . . but sad . . . I have to say . . . that with my dear husband's death . . . it has . . . the time has come to close the Stone Chapel."

The place erupted with shouts, cries of "No!" and more yells. By me the reporters had stopped yawning and texting and were busily writing up their notes, taking photos of the slim form of Laura, up there onstage. She shook her head and turned away, then came back to the microphone. The crowd eventually became quiet, and she coughed again and said, her voice even more hoarse, "We have done so much here . . . but it is time to move on. This place . . . this place was kept alive by Bronson . . . and with his death . . . I cannot run it by myself."

"We'll help you, Laura!" came a woman's shout, and more cheers. She smiled and said, "No . . . this was Bronson's place . . . his and his only . . . and I know someone will eventually reopen the Chapel . . . maybe someone here in the audience . . . but there is something more important . . . for all of us. That is . . . the day after tomorrow . . . the day after tomorrow . . . all of us will be there in Falconer, there in Falconer to march across the marshes, march over the fence line, and march onto Falconer to shut her down!"

With that last phrase, she had raised her fist, and now she said again, louder, "Shut her down! Shut her down!"

The audience quickly took up the cheer, echoing her, making it louder and louder, and it seemed like the banners overhead were fluttering from the impact of the hundreds of voices.

There was a brief media availability in the Stone Chapel's green-room, where performers would wait until being called on-stage. Laura Toles was stuck in a corner, surrounded by camera crews and radio reporters with extended microphones, and she looked like a female quarterback in a huddle with her team-mates, though she certainly didn't look like she had any control over them. Lots of questions were being tossed her way, and she was doing her best to answer in a voice that was raspy and hoarse.

I edged up the best I could and then stepped away. The frenzy here was for the electronic media, and although I guess with my new marching orders from Denise Pichette-Volk I was somewhat electronic, I felt out of place with my pen and note-book.

In another corner of the room, where chairs had been piled up, Vic Toles stood by himself, watching his mother do her best with the loud questions being directed her way. I went up to him, and he looked at me and gave me a nod, and I nodded back. He had on worn dungarees and one of those blue and white sweaters that were supposedly popular with preppies a decade or a cen-tury ago.

"Lewis Cole," I said. "*Shoreline* magazine. Sorry about your loss."

He nodded. "Yeah. Thanks."

"Mind if I ask you a couple of questions?"

"Knock yourself out."

"Is your mother serious about wanting to close the Stone Chapel?"

He was in his midtwenties, lean, with short brown hair and a puffy look about his face, as if he had been up for twenty-four hours straight, which was a reasonable guess considering what he and his mom had been up to.

He said, "Even with Bronson running the joint, with all his energy and connections, it was a month-to-month challenge. You know? Signing up the acts, trying to get good talent, working in the kitchen . . . only one day off a week, on Monday . . . yeah, most times, it was a hell of a grind. So with Bronson gone . . . why put up with it, you know?"

"I see," I said, writing carefully in my notebook. "You know, I went through some newspaper archives about Bronson Toles and the Stone Chapel, and I never got a handle on how he and your mom met."

Vic smiled a little, like it was an old memory that was amusing. "Our rescuer—that's what my mom called him. You know, she turned out to be right."

"In what way?"

"Didn't know my real dad at all," Vic recalled, looking away from me just for a moment, as if looking at something far away. "My mom dropped out of real life before I was born, moved into a commune in the upper part of Vermont. Called the Northeast Kingdom—one of the most remote places in God's New England you'll ever see. My dad was a part-time logger, full-time hash smoker, and got in a fight with a runaway chain saw and lost. So my mom raised me up there with the others, homeschooled me. We lived off the land, fished, hunted, starved and froze in the winter, and used a two-hole outhouse. Me, I was young, it was an adventure—but I think Mom got tired of it. Then Bronson came by, on some sort of safe-energy tour, and the two of them clicked and . . . there you go . . ."

"Sounds like a good story," I said.

"A good real-life story," Vic said. "I grew to really know him as a dad, even went along with him adopting me. You know . . . first time I used a flush toilet was when I moved to Tyler. Funny, hunh?" Then he wiped at his eyes a couple of times and turned away and said, "Enough, okay?"

"Sure," I said, putting my pen and notebook away. "Enough."

Outside I met up with Paula, and she said, "Off to my office and file, Lewis, if I can get the energy up. A hell of a story, hunh? The Stone Chapel, closing. See you later."

"You, too, Paula—and good to see you."

She smiled. "Good to be seen, but . . . only by you. You know? I'll be one happy girl when they catch that damn shooter."

When she left I moved through the moving crowd of journalists and cameramen, something caught my eye. It was the guy that had been up on the stage, talking to Laura. He was speaking into his cell phone and getting into a black BMW with Massachusetts license plates. A Realtor, getting ready to sell the joint on Laura's behalf? I was too far away to talk to him, but close enough to write down his license plate number. Maybe I could wheedle a trace from Diane Woods, though that was proving more and more difficult lately with more stringent rules from the new police chief.

"Lewis! Lewis!" I turned and saw a slight woman pushing her way through the journalists. It was Haleigh Miller coming up to me. I could tell from her puffy and red face that she had been crying during the memorial service. I went over to her, and she said, "The meeting with Curt Chesak. It's set up for tonight."

I couldn't help it. I stared at her in amazement. "How the hell did you do that?"

She said, "I told you I had friends . . . and some connections. So are you still interested?"

"Absolutely."

"Tonight, six o'clock. At the parking lot of the Laughing Bee doughnut shop, in Falconer." She wiped at her runny nose. "I've . . . I've got to get going. The occupation the day after tomorrow is going to keep us all busy. Oh, what a sad, sad day . . . to lose Bronson, to lose that voice, and now"—her voice broke— "I'm out of a job. I mean, it was just a job while I'm in school, but God, it meant so much to me . . ."

Seeing her like that made me feel like I had two left feet and two left hands. "You heard what Laura said. Maybe somebody will take it over."

Haleigh managed a smile. "Maybe, but even then . . . it will never be the same, will it. Never be the same."

For a moment I remembered being her age, when it seemed possible that you could outline your life's course for the next twenty years, and I said, "You're right. It'll never be the same."

At home I scrounged lunch from whatever was still within the stale date that was existing in my refrigerator, and when I was finished writing my piece for *Shoreline* on the memorial service, my phone rang, and it was Paula Quinn.

"How are you doing over there by the ocean?" she asked.

"Doing fine," I said. "How are you doing at the *Chronicle*?"

"Lousy," she said, sighing. "I just . . . I just don't have the energy for this, Lewis."

There was a *click-click* on the phone line, meaning an incoming call was heading my way, but I ignored it. "Go on," I said.

Another sigh. "Deadline is in a half hour, and Rollie keeps on staring and staring at me, and when I look at the computer screen . . . nothing's coming out. Nothing at all."

Another *click-click* on the phone line.

I closed my eyes, recalling all the times I had seen Paula at the scene of multiple-car accidents, arsons, and the occasional untimely death. Each time this young blond woman with the slight body would go in and come out with the story, and get it done with hours to spare. Whoever was on the other end of this phone line was not Paula Quinn.

"What do you need?"

"Excuse me?" she asked.

"What do you need? How many words?"

No answer, and I thought for a moment that she had hung up the phone in anger. Then she spoke, her voice lowered to a slight whisper, like a little girl asking a storefront Santa Claus for a gift and not sure if she was going to get it.

"About eight hundred words. That's it."

"Your e-mail address the same?"

"Lewis, you can't be serious, this is—"

"You'll get your eight hundred words, but only if you let me get off the phone. You can take those words and rearrange them anyway you like, but I won't let you miss deadline."

She tried to speak, failed, and I said, "I'm hanging up now. Check your e-mail in-box in a while."

After hanging up the phone I went back to my notes and the story I had filed for *Shoreline,* and took a breath and went to work. I'm sure Denise Pichette-Volk wouldn't have been thrilled at what I had been doing, but I didn't care. Paula needed help, and if it meant breaking what few rules journalism had left, I was okay with that.

Boy, was I under a deadline. I wrote and wrote, and the phone rang once and I could hear the answering machine downstairs pick up, but I kept on typing. When I was done and had sent the story as an e-mail attachment to Paula, I looked up at the clock and saw I had done it with ten minutes to spare. Nice job. I got up and stretched some and went downstairs and checked my answering machine, where I had missed a message from my dear Annie Wynn.

Damn.

I picked up the downstairs phone and started dialing frantically, and I sat back on the couch in relief when she picked up.

"My dear boy, where the hell have you been?" she asked. "You must have been on the phone when I called. Why didn't you pick up?"

"I was . . . I was helping someone out, and I was on the upstairs phone. No caller ID screen on that one."

There was a din in the background of her phone, and I said, "At the airport?"

"I am," she said. "About to get on a plane, go for a 6:00 P.M. meeting in Arlington, and then I'm catching an early flight tomorrow to Manchester. Will be there at 9:00 A.M. Or have you forgotten our date?"

"Not for a moment," I said, hoping she believed me, "and I'm glad it's tomorrow. Looks like my day is wide open."

"Glad to hear that. Who was so important on the phone that you couldn't talk to me?"

Ouch.

"Paula Quinn, from the *Chronicle*," I said. "We were both at a news event this morning, and she needed some help on a story."

Annie said, "Oh, that sounds nice. Is that all the help she needed?"

"Absolutely."

"Good," she said. "Because I don't want to come up there and have to kick her ass, and then yours."

I smiled. "No ass kicking required. You just get up here."

"Fine," she said. "Southwest Airlines, arriving in. Manchester at 9:00 A.M. You be there, friend, or I'll think you're sniffing around your old girlfriend."

I was going to say that what Paula and I had was more complicated than the old boyfriend/girlfriend routine, but I let it be.

"Deal," I said. "Are you packing anything special in your luggage?"

A low laugh that warmed me. "Just you see." There was an echo of an announcement in the background, and she said, "Flight just got called. See you tomorrow."

"Oh yes," I said, and I hung up the phone.

Just before 6:00 P.M. I was parked in a gas station lot across the street from the Laughing Bee doughnut shop in Falconer. In this part of town, Route 1—or Lafayette Road—was three lanes, with a turning lane in the center. At one time there had been rows of old colonial houses lining this road, but they had all been bulldozed, burned, or converted into office space. Now this stretch of Falconer had grocery stores, box stores, fast food restaurants, muffler shops, a store that sold pornography, jewelry stores, and lots and lots of firework stores. Not to pick on the fine people of New Jersey, but for those thinking New England was all white church steeples and fine green lawns, this stretch of New Hampshire looked like it belonged at an exit off the Garden State Parkway.

My destination this early evening was the small parking lot of the Laughing Bee doughnut shop, and as I sat in my Ford Explorer, I had a bit of doubt about why I was there. There was that drive, of course, of finding out who had traumatized my friend Paula, and as an afterthought—as cold as it sounds—the killer of Bronson Toles. But to what purpose? The state police and the Falconer police had better resources than I did. What I did have was that stubborn drive to make it all right, and that's what prompted me to start up my Explorer and drive across the street. If I had a hand in getting the shooter, then Paula wouldn't have to worry anymore about a nameless, faceless killer out there, staring at her through a rifle's telescopic site. Maybe that would help her get back to the old Paula.

Besides, whatever I learned tonight could be used for *Shoreline*, and to keep Denise Pichette-Volk . . . well, if not happy, at least satisfied.

The logo of the Laughing Bee doughnut shop was pretty self-explanatory, with a grinning bumblebee in flight, holding a variety of doughnuts in its legs. The store was closed, and there were two other vehicles parked in the lot: a hybrid Prius and an old Chevy pickup truck. Both vehicles were empty.

I looked at the dashboard clock: 6:05 P.M.

I guess fighting against the Man meant not worrying too much about appointments and such. Then again, maybe my escorts were hiding in one of the vehicles. I turned around and the parking lot was still empty.

The dashboard clock said 6:10 P.M. I rapped my fingers against the steering wheel. Five more minutes and then I'd be out of here,

Curt Chesak or no Curt Chesak. I waited some more. Three National Guard Humvees motored by, and a straggling line of protesters across the street jeered at them.

It was now 6:17 P.M. I started up the engine and—

Somebody rapped a hand against the driver's window.

I lowered the window, and whoever was there stepped back.

"Don't look back at me, all right?" came a male voice. "You look back at me, and the meet is off."

"All right," I said. "I won't look back."

"The rear doors open?"

I made sure by toggling a side switch. There was a *click,* and then the door opened, and my visitor got in. "Don't look back," he warned again. "Look back and—"

"Yeah, I got it," I said. "If I look back, the meet is off."

"Nice to see you got it. Now drive. Go out and take a left."

I pulled out into traffic and turned left and followed my unseen visitor's directions. We drove south for a few moments and went through an intersection that marked the closed South Gate of Falconer Station, where there was a crowd of about fifty or so demonstrators waving signs, chanting, and posing for a couple of television crews that had illuminated the area with a harsh light. A billboard inside the gate announced that Falconer was producing safe energy for one million New England homes, and that sign had been defaced by what looked to be paintball guns.

My escort in the rear seat snorted something as we drove by, and I said, "You say something?"

"Yeah, I did. Sheep."

"What sheep?"

"Those sheep," he said. "Sheep posing for other sheep, everyone doing their roles—but, buddy, me and my friends, and Curt Chesak, we sure the fuck aren't sheep."

We drove south for a couple more minutes and, following my

unseen escort's directions, I took a left and a right and another left, and I was in a residential area of Falconer, with trailer parks and tired-looking Cape Cod homes. At one point there was a dirt road off to the left in a thick grove of pine trees, and I was tapped on the shoulder.

"There. Take that left."

I drove down that dirt road a few more yards, and he said, "Stop."

I stopped and put the Ford in park, and he said, "All right, shut the engine off. Here's a few rules before we proceed."

I switched the engine off and said, "Where did you learn this? At some professional protester class at school?"

"Very funny," he said. "No, my dad, he worked for the big bad CIA. Didn't tell me about anything he did for real for the agency, but did teach me some tradecraft. Has proven very useful. So here's the rules. When you step out, you're going to leave everything electronic behind. Got it? Cell phone, pager, PDA. Everything like that stays behind."

So I worked some and did as I was told. I didn't like it one bit, but this young man behind me was in the driver's seat, no matter where I was sitting. When I was finished he said, "One more thing. And if you don't agree, then—"

"Let me guess. The meet's off."

"Yeah. The meet's off."

"What's the one more thing?"

He said, "I'm sorry, but it has to be done. Curt Chesak is one of the most wanted men in New England, and his security is paramount. So we're going to step out of your gas guzzler here, and there's going to be a hood placed over your head. Just for a while. You'll be taken to see him, have your interview, and then be brought back here."

I didn't like any of it, not one bit, but I also didn't like the thought of Paula Quinn, home by herself, shivering with fear over the thought of being in a killer's sights again.

"All right, but I have something to share with you."

"Go ahead."

I said, "This goes well, I get to see Curt Chesak, or friend, I'm going to make you very, very unhappy."

"Some threat," he said, voice just a bit sneering.

"No," I said. "Some promise—and I'm ready."

CHAPTER ELEVEN

So I stepped out into the cool October air, and my companion stepped out as well, and in a practiced move, he slipped a cloth bag over my head. It felt like one of those cloth shopping bags that stores encourage you to use to save the earth, which I thought was fairly humorous. My escort took my arm and said, "Just a few feet down the road, all right? Then we're going to go for a short ride. In the meantime, if you give me your keys, we'll move your Ford back to the doughnut shop parking lot, put your key on one of the rear tires."

"Why can't it stay here?"

"Because it can't. If you think we're low enough to steal your vehicle, don't worry about it. Curt gave specific orders that neither you or your ride was going to get messed up."

Happy that my auto insurance was up to date, I reluctantly passed over my keys. I then let him lead me on down the road, and I made out the sound of a car engine. As he held my arm I said, "Since we're getting pretty familiar with each other, mind telling me your name?"

He laughed. "Why should I?"

"Why not? Or are you wanted by the police as well?"

"Not yet," he said. "Not yet. You can call me . . . Todd. How does that sound?"

"If it works for you, that's fine."

The sound of the car engine grew louder, and then we stopped. I heard a car door being opened, and Todd said, "I'll help you in. Put your hands out some, that should help."

I managed to get into the rear seat without falling on my butt, and Todd came in next to me. My hands on the seat revealed it to be some sort of soft leather, and I said, "I'm disappointed in you folks. These are leather seats. Not very environmentally correct, are they?"

Todd said, "Not too soon to cancel everything, if that's what you want."

"You're boring me with those threats, Todd. So put them away for somebody else."

The car was put into gear, and for fifteen or twenty minutes we drove around, with sharp turns, brakings, and a few backups. I guess Todd and his driver thought I had some sort of super-human power so I could count the turns and keep track of the time by tapping my feet or something, but I was just finding it stuffy and clammy inside the shopping bag. The car went down another bumpy dirt road for a distance and then stopped.

"All right," Todd said. "A bit more walking and we're there."

The door came open, and I stepped out, helped up by Todd. He said, "Lift your feet up. There's a trail here, it's kinda rough."

So for a long series of minutes I was led along some sort of trail, and twice I tripped over exposed tree roots, but Todd kept me up. Another time a branch whipped my face, and he muttered, "Sorry about that," and then there was an "Almost there, and we're going across a footbridge, so be really careful."

There was the smell of mud and saltwater, and my feet echoed some, walking across rough wood. Then I smelled a fire burning and heard a few voices, and then we stopped.

Todd said, "We're here. Okay? When you're done with Curt Chesak, then I'll take you back—and when he says the interview is over, then the interview is over. All right?"

"Oh yeah," I said. "Sounds swell."

With that, the hood came off my head, and I took a deep breath and then opened my eyes, took out a handkerchief, and wiped at my sweaty face. I was in a small clearing in a pine forest. Out beyond some of the trees there were small campfires. Before me sat a man on a camp stool. He had on work boots, blue jeans, and a gray sweatshirt. His hands were folded in his lap, and he was wearing a black watch cap and a red bandanna across his lower face. He had large ears, prominent, and it seemed his eyes were brown. Between us was a small campfire. I looked behind me, saw a camp chair, and sat down. There were other activists there as well, in the shadows and firelight, and most wore ski masks or some kind of face mask.

"Mr. Cole," he said.

"Mr. Chesak," I replied. "Is the bandanna really necessary?"

"I'm wanted by a number of people and a number of police agencies. I don't want to take chances."

"Is Curt Chesak your real name?"

I could sense his smile behind the bandanna. "A question that's not going to be answered tonight. So try something else."

"Your fellow protesters over there," I said. "Are they wearing masks for my benefit, or because they don't trust one another?"

"Everyone you see is here because they are trustworthy," Chesak said. "Some feel comfortable keeping their faces covered, on the off chance we're under some sort of surveillance, or if there's a police raid."

I took out my notebook and pen. There was enough light for me to take notes, if I wrote large enough. "Thanks for the interview."

"You're welcome. You should also thank the young lady who pled your case—otherwise, you wouldn't be here. Larger and wealthier media organizations have tried to be in your position, and none have succeeded."

"Maybe they didn't like the thought of being shuttled around half the county with a grocery bag over their head."

A slight shrug of his wide shoulders. "The price that must be paid to keep me where I belong."

"Where is that exactly?"

"Leading the members of the NFF, the Nuclear Freedom Front."

I scribbled something in my notebook. "I see. How did you come to lead the Nuclear Freedom Front?"

"By direct action, how else. I started with local actions, and when the NFF came together, I was chosen."

"Why the NFF?" I asked. "Out there are thousands of protesters with the Coalition for a Livable Future, and maybe a few hundred of you folks, the NFF. So why the NFF?"

He said, "Have you spent any time with the Coalition?"

"Not that much."

"You know what they're good at doing?"

"Protesting."

"Sure," he said, as the campfire between us crackled and burned. "Protesting. Discussing. Talking. Oh Lord, can they ever talk. That's what they're very good at. Talking. And that's why we have the NFF. We're more interested in direct action, Mr. Cole. That's our strength. Maybe not our numbers, but our dedication."

"I've seen your dedication," I said.

"Thank you."

"I saw the dedication of a couple of your followers, too, the other day, when Bronson Toles made his last speech. Two of your NFF members were up on the stage, disrupting Bronson's speech."

"They were making a point," Chesak said, "that it was no longer a time for talking but a time for taking. Look, Bronson Toles was good at raising money, getting publicity—but doing what has to be done, that was lacking in his department."

"What's your department, then?"

"What do you mean by that?"

I flipped a page in my notebook. "The coalition is having their big demonstration the day after tomorrow. Let's say you were in charge, and you had . . . oh, some magic power that allowed you to succeed, do exactly what you hope to do. So what would that be?"

My question seemed to catch him off guard for a moment, and then he said, "Wow. That's some question. That's some dream. All right, bottom line, we plan to go over those fences, go past the cops and National Guardsmen, and occupy the site."

"What about the nuclear reactor?"

"We plant to shut her down."

"How?"

Again I had the sense he was smiling at me behind his red bandanna. "It may be hard to believe, Mr. Cole, but among our ranks are disillusioned members of the nuclear power industry, as well as veterans of the nuclear navy. We know that power plant's vulnerabilities, its weaknesses. Even without getting past the heavy security to the plant's control room, we can shut her down. Once that happens, Mr. Cole, that death plant is not going to reopen ever again. That place is not only a ticking time bomb, ready to go off at any second, but its mere presence here is polluting the environment and the people living in its shadow."

It was a challenge, keeping up with his fast talking, but I did my best. "All right. The plant is shut down. That means New England loses about eleven hundred megawatts of power. What does the region do without that power supply?"

"It makes adjustments," he said. "Alternative power. Conservation. Better refrigerators, better lightbulbs, better appliances. Hell, this region did fine without air conditioners for a couple of hundred years. Giving those up sounds like a small price to pay for safe energy."

"That kind of adjustment can take a while," I said.

"That's what we hear, all the time. Be patient. It'll take a while. Things can't happen overnight. Well, when we occupy and shut down Falconer, that'll be a shock to the system, something sudden and unexpected. Change will have to occur. There will be no other choice."

Another flip of my notebook. "Some might ask, who or what gives you the right to do something so drastic?"

"It's called self-defense, Mr. Cole. In the New Hampshire state constitution, it even says that the citizens have the right to act on their behalf if there's a greater danger involved. That danger is just over there, less than a mile away—and we citizens are doing to do what it takes, and we're going to shock the system, to make it take notice."

Well, I thought, *time to go really nuclear and see what happens.* "What about the murder of Bronson Toles?"

"What about it?"

"Was that a shock to the system, something that had to be done?" I asked.

He stared at me for a bit, the light from the campfire casting dark shadows over the part of his face that was visible. "I'm not sure what you're driving at, Mr. Cole."

I said, "It's no secret that the coalition and the NFF don't get along that well. Or that you and Bronson Toles didn't have the best of relationships, either professionally or personally. Or that—"

Chesak interrupted me and said, "If you're saying that either me or a member of the NFF were responsible for Bronson Toles's murder, you can stop right there."

"How can you be sure?" I pressed him. "Wouldn't it be to your advantage to have Bronson Toles removed from the scene, leaving just one visible leader for the antinuclear movement? Maybe even get some coalition members to join you?"

"I wouldn't want most of them," he said sharply.

"Why? Aren't they dedicated enough to the cause?"

"You know what they're dedicated to? I'll tell you what they're dedicated to—they're dedicated to talking, talking, and reaching a consensus. That coalition . . . they're made up of scores of groups, some of them primarily anti nuclear, others pro women, pro Native American rights, anti corporation . . . hell, there are a couple of groups over there that are pro hemp, for reforming the marijuana laws. Each group is called an affinity group, where decisions are made collectively. Can you believe that, trying to get twenty or thirty people to agree on anything? Hell, a group that big couldn't decide on what to have for breakfast!"

"Yet these groups—"

Chesak was on a roll and wouldn't let me talk, and he said, "Each affinity group has a facilitator. Not a leader, no, a leader is too fascist a term. So each group has a facilitator, and each facilitator meets with the others in a grand council, where they hammer out how they're going to protest, which part of the fence line they'll march to, and even what time they march—but that's not the end of it. Each facilitator has to go back and convince his or her affinity group that they've made the correct decision. And if not, well, the affinity group hammers out their position, like, no, we don't want to march at 9:00 A.M., we'd rather march at 10:00 A.M., and then the whole grand circus starts up again . . ."

When he took a breath, I said, "Sounds like the NFF is better organized."

"You got that right, and you have to be better organized. The stakes are too high to allow all this time wasted on talking and consensus. Which is why I'm certain no NFF member had anything to do with the murder of Bronson Toles."

"Sorry," I said. "I don't see the correlation."

He leaned forward a bit. "Because I know the NFF, I know how they operate, how they think—and I know no one would do anything even remotely like that shooting without my knowledge or say-so."

"So you knew about the plans for those NFF members to disrupt Bronson Toles's speech."

"Eh?"

I made a point of going back over my notes. "You just said that you know how the NFF membership operates, thinks, acts, and that they wouldn't act without your knowledge or say-so. Therefore, you had to know about that disruption."

Chesak's eyes narrowed. "I have nothing to say about that. I will say, as the leader of the NFF, I know the members. I know we had nothing to do with Bronson's murder. I also know that most of the stories about Bronson and his saintly life are so much bullshit. Nobody has the balls to report on what kind of guy Bronson really was."

"What do you mean?" I asked.

"You ever go to the Stone Chapel for a performance?" he asked.

"No, I never have."

Chesak said, "Well, if you had, then this won't come as a big fucking surprise to you. About ninety-nine percent of his employees—servers, dishwashers, ticket takers—were all young women. Young good-looking women, and you can bet he was getting a lot on the side. Part of being a business owner, eh?"

"Maybe," I said.

"Let me guess, what I just said isn't going to make it into print, is it."

I didn't like where this was going and said, "Not sure of that."

"Yeah. Right. That's the kind of response I was expecting. With that, Mr. Cole, this interview is done."

With each passing minute with Curt Chesak, I found I was liking him less and less. I said, "Just one more follow-up, if you don't mind."

"Go ahead," he said. "Make it quick."

Another flip through my notebook. "A couple of days ago, out there on the marshland, you called yourself the coordinator of the NFF. Now you've been telling me that you're its leader. Which is it, then?"

Again his eyes narrowed. "I run the NFF because the members know me, trust me, and have confidence in my decisions. I'm sure you've heard of that kind of leadership, Mr. Cole."

"I have, but it's been a while." I closed my notebook. "About seventy or so years ago. Political guy in Germany who gave great speeches and would allow no dissent from his decisions. I think the term used was something called *Führerprinzip*. Leadership principle. I'm sure you've heard of that, haven't you?"

He stood up. "This interview is really over." He walked into the darkness, and I heard one more word: "Asshole."

So be it. I tucked the notebook away in my back pocket. I had been called worse.

· · ·

The man I knew as Todd called out to me. "Turn around, Mr. Cole."

I followed his instructions, and he came up to me, and the same shopping bag was placed over my head. He said, "It looks like that interview didn't go so well."

"How could you tell?"

"Curt had some choice words to say about you when he went into camp. Said it was a waste of time. Said if he could, he'd give that UNH bitch a slap upside the head for getting you in here."

I said, "Can I give you a message to give back to Curt?"

"Sure," he said, taking my elbow. "What is it?"

"If he has an urge to slap somebody upside the head, he's got my business card, with my cell phone number. Anyplace, anytime, and leave college-aged girls out of it."

Todd sighed. "Fine. Let's go."

We moved along the path, and I was processing in my mind what I had learned, what I had done—which wasn't particularly much—but I felt good that I was out and about, doing things, and the worst that could happen was that in the end, I'd have another story to file that Denise Pichette-Volk would be pleased to see, since it was a scoop.

Yeah, the worst that could happen.

I guess my imagination had failed me right about then.

About ten minutes into our walk, a muffled voice called out, "Todd! Curt wants you back at the camp."

We stopped. "What for?"

"How the hell should I know? He just sent me along, told me to finish this job and to send you back."

"But Henry . . ."

"Hey, no names! Jesus, do I have to remind you of everything? I'll take this clown back to the car, get him on his way."

Todd moved back down the trail, and the man called Henry grasped my arm. "Let's get moving," he said, his voice still muffled, as if he were wearing a bandanna as well. "I want to get back 'fore dinner is served."

Unlike Todd, Henry didn't seem to care very much about the speed at which we were moving. I stumbled twice and said, "Hey, would you mind slowing it down?"

He laughed. "Sorry. Like I said, I want to get back soon."

We kept moving, and then I stumbled again, and one right after another, a series of branches started whipping at my face. I stopped and said, "This isn't the way back."

"No kidding."

"Yeah," I said. "No kidding—and the masks and the games are over."

I moved my hands to take the cloth bag off my head, but my escort was faster.

He grabbed my wrists, pushing them together, and I felt something hard and plastic wrap around them, snug. A tie-wrap, similar to what cops use when they need to secure someone fast and quick.

"No, buddy," he said, lowering his voice. "The games are just ready to begin."

Henry got behind me, twisted my arms, and then propelled me through the woods, pushing me, going faster, as more branches struck my face and shoulders.

"What the hell—" I started, and he twisted my arms again, and he said, "You know, in movies, this is where the bad guy, and

I admit, that's me, explains everything to the victim, and that's you, why what's about to happen is going to happen, and you know what?"

He jerked me to a halt, the bag still on my head, my hands fastened before me, and he added, "That's never made sense to me, so why start now?"

He shoved me, hard, in the small of the back, and I stepped out into nothing.

CHAPTER TWELVE

I fell and heard a gunshot, and then there was a sharp, cold splash of water, and I raised my legs, hoping to get some depth into the saltwater, and there was another gunshot, and then another. With my bound hands in front of me, I got the grocery bag off my head, saw darkness and shapes, and I willed myself to keep still, to keep my arms and legs from flailing, from making a noise, making a sign of my presence.

I floated up, cold, shivering, and my head broke through the water. A nearly full moon was rising, illuminating the surroundings in a cold white light. I had been tossed into one of the wide tidal streams cutting through the salt marsh, and I could make out my assailant up on the grassy bank, looking down at me, pistol in hand. Every fiber and ounce of my being was convinced to move away, to dive in the water away from this man, and with a great struggle, I did exactly the opposite.

I slogged toward him, as fast as I could, and he raised his arm, and then I couldn't see him anymore. The embankment where he was standing four or five feet above me had been cut away by generations of incoming and outgoing tides, scooping out some of the soil, leaving the place he was standing on as an overhang.

I caught my breath, waited. I could hear cursing up there.

Waited some more. I gingerly moved away, making sure I was under the muddy and grassy overhang. Now I could make out the stench of the mud that came from the saltwater tides bringing in and out fish, trash, and seaweed. I was in sloppy mud that rose to midshins, and I kept still, knowing moving around would cause slurping and gurgling noises that would draw my shooter to me like an insect to an open flame.

Waited.

No sound from above.

I started shivering, closed my arms around myself. Waited some more. I could make out the sound of feet rustling in the marsh grass as my shooter stood a few feet above my head.

Waited some more.

Kept on shivering.

At some point I knew I'd have to figure out what the hell had just happened, who the shooter was, and why I was targeted, but that point was a long way off. Right now I had to stay still, stay warm, and then get the hell out of this marshland before I got hypothermia, got shot, or got caught in an outgoing tide trying to swim with bound hands.

Waited some more.

I couldn't tell if my assailant—the man called Henry—had moved, but I also knew I couldn't stay here much longer. It was getting colder, and the water seemed deeper around my legs. I had to move. Just had to, and I had a yearning to be home, where there were strong locks and several weapons, any one of which I wished I had with me.

Waited. A cold breeze came through, making me shiver, and I decided it was time to move, now was better than doing nothing, and—

I flinched at the sound of another gunshot.

Realized this one was a distance away.

Chances of two shooters operating at this time of night in these salt marshes?

Not a good chance, but I'd take it. My shooter had moved and hopefully had shot at a shadow or a night creature moving suddenly away.

Took a breath, started slogging.

Time dragged on, strength draining away, as I fumbled my way through the muddy streambeds, the stench strong in my nostrils. Eventually I realized I was traveling in a winding route that was just wasting time and distance, for I was deep enough in the streambed that I couldn't see a damn thing. So I hoisted myself up by grabbing on to an overhang, pulled myself over the lip, and rolled over on the salt marsh, my hands cut and bleeding from the sharp grasses.

I tried to catch my breath, staring up at the few stars that were shining defiantly through the powerful blaze of the moonlight. I rolled over on my belly—my shooter Henry out there, if he was the man that had killed Bronson Toles, had access to a scoped rifle and maybe a night-vision scope as well, so I kept a low profile. Out in the distance were the blinking lights of the Falconer nuclear power plant. That was to the north. I didn't want to go east and keep stumbling through the marshes and streambeds and end up at Route 1-A. So south it was, where I thought I could make out lights from some homes.

I slithered across the salt marsh, grass, and mud, then flopped over in a depressed area of an embankment. I sat up and tried tugging at the plastic ties about my wrist. I moved one wrist and then the other, wincing at the pain cutting through the skin. I even tried gnawing on them with my teeth. Nope. The plastic ties were staying for a while.

After a couple of minutes of futility, I got up, shivering again, and looked to the distant lights over there marking Route 286, which led down to the Massachusetts side of the seacoast and a few restaurants and homes. If I kept on moving, I could be out of this nightmare in less than an hour.

I started slogging, sinking into the mud through the marsh grass, holding my arms out in front of me, trying not to think of what had just happened, just trying to think of the problem at hand, and trying to—

I suddenly came to a drop-off, my feet slipped, and, off balance because of my bound wrists, I tumbled over and struck my head in the darkness.

Dreams. I was dreaming that I was eating saltwater taffy, and that the taffy was melting in my mouth, dripping down my chin, choking me, making me cough, making me—

Woke up with a start, coughing out a spew of saltwater. I coughed again and looked around. I was in the bottom of a saltwater streambed, legs splayed out, head throbbing like hell. Water was around my chest and had been in my face. The tide was coming in. If I had stayed here unconscious, I just might have drowned. I moved, got up, swayed, and vomited in one sharp spasm, bent over, my wrists still bound and aching.

I looked around. I had fallen down into this streambed, and there, a rock was exposed. Must have hit my head there, and hit it hard.

I scrambled and moved and got up on the other side of the embankment. I was really shivering hard, and I took a look around, and there, off to the east, was a pink glow.

Dawn was coming.

I started moving, coughing, shivering, head and wrists hurting like hell.

Eventually, after some long minutes, I came to a place where the salt marsh came up against some worn pastureland, with a distressed fence consisting of leaning bits of timber and some strands of rusting barbed wire. The sun had risen far enough to lighten everything, and I pushed my way over the barbed wire. Up ahead the land rose, and there was a chicken coop and some tired-looking chickens poking and prodding at the dirt. Next to the chicken coop was a double-wide trailer sagging at one side. There were two flagpoles off to the right, one flying the American flag, the other the black-and-white POW/MIA flag.

I stopped for a second on the rear lawn, then started walking up to the house. I was sure that from here the dirt driveway—which boasted an old VW Beetle and a Chevy pickup truck—would lead off to a road, and from there . . . well, I'd figure something out.

Then a door burst open from the side of the house, and a burly man with a thick black beard, wearing black Wellington boots, gray sweatpants, and nothing else, stepped out, glaring at me, pointing a shotgun in my direction.

It looked like the time for figuring was over.

He stepped closer to me, his chest covered with a mat of gray and black hair, except for a couple of areas where I saw pink scar tissue.

"You're trespassin'," he called out.

"I certainly am," I said, "and I apologize for that."

He came closer, the shotgun still pointing at me. He said, "You one of them protesters?"

"No."

"A reporter?"

"Not really," I said. "I live up on Tyler Beach. The name's Lewis Cole."

He lowered his shotgun a bit. "What the hell happened to you?"

"I . . . I got into trouble. Some of the people out there in the woods, they didn't like me being there. So they tied up my arms and tossed me into the salt marsh."

"Why'd they get pissed at you?"

"They didn't like where I've been, what I've said."

"Were they antinukers?"

"There was just one of them," I said, "and we didn't have a chance to discuss energy options."

The shotgun was now pointing at the ground. "You a vet by any chance?"

"No," I said, "but I did work for the Department of Defense for a number of years."

He grinned, his teeth firm and white. "The name's Bert Lang. Served twenty years, New Hampshire National Guard. Now I live on disability and whatever else I can scrape up, like a bit of plumbing and electrical work, maybe some drywall if my back ain't aching. Friend, you look and smell like shit."

"Can't help that," I said, "but I did trespass on your property. I'm sorry about that, Bert."

"Hell," he said, stepping closer. "That's no problem. Real problem is those hippies and protesters out there, and those damn news media, they think they can troop across my land for better pictures, or a place to shit or piss, or whatever. Think they own the joint. But you . . . here, hold on."

He lowered the shotgun to the ground, came back up, and with his thick hand reached into a back pocket and took out a Filipino-style butterfly knife, folded the knife into place with an expert flip of his wrist, and came over to me. I held out my wrists, and he gently, almost tenderly sliced through the plastic tie-wraps.

I couldn't help it, I gasped in pleasure and rubbed at my free wrists.

"Bet that feels damn good, now, don't it, Lewis."

"It sure does."

He flipped the knife back and returned it to his pocket and then picked up his shotgun. I said, "Look, can I bother you—"

Bert grinned. "Nothing's gonna be a problem. You wanna call the cops about what happened to you?"

"No."

"You wanna get cleaned up some, and me give you a ride?"

I kept on rubbing my wrists. "That'd be great, thanks."

I came up to the double-wide, and from inside I heard some dogs barking, and Bert yelled out, "You boys in there shut your yap, you got that?" He turned and said, "I'd let you in and all, but those dogs would be all over you the sec you got inside."

"Oh, they bite, then?" I asked.

He laughed. "The hell they do. They'd lick you to death, that's what they'd do. Hold on . . ."

Bert slipped inside the double-wide, and after a couple of minutes, he came back out with a couple of dark blue towels, a sponge, and a white bucket filled with soapy water. He had also thrown on a T-shirt—FREEDOM ISN'T FREE, depicting a screaming eagle holding an American flag in its talons—and I washed up the best I could.

"That ride offer still stand?"

"Where do you need to go?"

"I'm hoping my Ford's parked over at the Laughing Bee."

Bert said, "Shit, I don't see why not. I usually head over 'bout this time for coffee, doughnuts, and some of the best lies ever told. You 'bout done over there?"

"Yes," I said, holding back one dry towel, "but I'd like to use this later, if that's all right with you. My pants are sopping wet. I don't want to mess up your truck seat."

A big laugh from that. "Bud, if you saw what my dogs did to the inside of my truck—that's mighty nice of you, but I won't mind. Come along, let's get going."

He took the bucket, sponge, and wet towels and walked me up to a Chevy pickup truck that was three colors: green, rust, and primer. I got in, and despite Bert's prediction of what I would see— and there were stains and dog hair galore on the upholstery—I spread out the towel and sat down. He got in on the other side and said, "Cripes, Lewis, looks like you dinged your head there somethin' awful."

I put my hand up to the rear of my head and winced in pain as I felt the egg-shaped bump back there. I took my hand down, and it was smeared with blood. Bert said, "Would have made more sense to use the towel for your head."

"I'm sure," I said.

"You wanna go to the hospital in Newburyport?"

"Thanks, but no," I said. "I just want to get home."

"Fair enough," he said, starting up the truck, which took only three tries and an amazing backfire that shuddered through the truck's frame.

In the fifteen-minute drive to the Laughing Bee, my new best friend talked about growing up in Falconer, his service with the New Hampshire National Guard, and his various pains and disabilities. Along the way, some early-morning protesters were straggling along the side of the road, and Bert said, "You notice anything strange about those antinukers?"

Now that I was in a warm truck cab and not thrashing around the marsh, various aches and pains started announcing themselves, including the thumping big ache at the back of my head, where I had earlier struck that exposed rock. I said to Bert, "A number of things, but what have you noticed?"

We stopped at a traffic light intersecting Route 1, and I was happy to know that I was just a few minutes away from getting to my own vehicle, if Todd back there had told me the truth about moving it to the doughnut shop's parking lot. Bert looked both ways and then pulled out. "They're either young or old, you know? Oh, there's a dusting of other ages, but mostly it's the old folks and young'uns. Meaning, it's those who are retired, or who can afford to skip school for a week or two."

Bert slowed the truck down as a number of protesters straggled across the road, heading to a gas station parking lot where a coffee truck had parked. He watched them line up for coffee and doughnuts and said, "You know . . . if I was lucky enough to be their age and in school, I sure as hell wouldn't be down here in the mud, muck, and marsh grass. I'd be hitting the books, hitting a few brews, and trying my hand at some rich chicks."

He laughed and moved ahead, and there, in a lonely spot all by itself, was my Ford Explorer, as promised, at the Laughing Bee doughnut shop. Bert pulled in and said, "There you go, Lewis. Hope today's a better day than last night for ya."

I shook his strong and rough hand. "Thanks, Bert. Really appreciate it."

"Buy you coffee and a fat pill?"

I opened the door. "Thanks for the offer, but I really want to take a shower and get into some clean clothes."

Bert joined me in the parking lot and slapped me on the back. "Can't rightly blame you. Take care, now."

"You, too."

I walked to my Ford and as promised, found my key sitting on one of the rear tires. Then I stopped, went through my pockets.

No notebook.

It had to have fallen out somewhere out in the marshes, or the water, or anyplace else.

Damn.

I got into the Ford, started up the engine, and turned the heat up full, and I suddenly had this nagging feeling that I was forgetting something.

I opened up the glove compartment, took out some paper napkins from my infrequent visits to drive-through burger places, and gently placed a couple on the back of my head. The ache intensified.

Took the paper towel away. Bloody as hell.

Still . . . what was going on? What was I forgetting?

I looked at the dashboard, at the light blue-green numerals that told me what time it was. It was 8:45 in the morning.

The little voice in my mind kept on nagging me.

What was going on?

I saw the numerals flick over from 8:45 to 8:46.

Still I sat.

Come on, I thought. *Are you going to sit here all day, watch the clock change until it reaches 9:00 A.M.?*

9:00 A.M.

Today.

Oh, crap.

In about fourteen minutes, if they were on schedule, Southwest Airlines would be depositing my Annie Wynn at the Manchester Airport, where she would expect to be picked up by a healthy, happy, and well-dressed and well-groomed Lewis Cole, if not bearing gifts, well, at least bearing a welcoming smile.

From Falconer to Manchester was a drive of about forty-five minutes.

I pulled down the shift lever, got the Ford into drive, and got the hell out of Falconer.

CHAPTER THIRTEEN

One bit of good fortune was that the drive was mostly highway, and as I quickly exceeded the speed limit, I fumbled a bit with my free hand on the passenger seat, where I retrieved my cell phone. If Annie was on the ground, I could at least tell her I was on my way.

Good plan, except my cell phone's battery had drained away overnight. No juice. I suppose I could have gotten off at a highway exit and wasted valuable time looking for a store or gas station that had one of those old relics called a pay phone, but I didn't like the odds. So I goosed my excess speeding along New Hampshire's Route 101 by another ten miles an hour, hoping that any state troopers on duty this morning would be down in Falconer.

The Manchester airport had grown a lot since I moved back to New Hampshire, but it still had a small-state airport feel to it. Some time ago, in a burst of lunacy, the people running the joint decided to stick it to their southern neighbors and call the place the Manchester-Boston Regional Airport, which no one ever uses in talking or writing about it. The name change was done to drag in business from weary Massachusetts travelers, but still, it took some derangement to share the name of your airport with a city more than fifty miles away. I always thought the place should be named for the first American to fly in space—a New Hampshire native—but no one ever asked me, and so the nutty name remains.

Nutty name or not, I was able to park in a short-term lot that, after a spirited run across a lane of traffic in front of the terminals, got me inside in just under sixty seconds.

I looked around the small terminal, at the large metal moose that greets our visitors, and then scrambled upstairs to the waiting area. There, sitting at a table outside of Dunkin' Donuts, was a very cross-looking Annie Wynn, who had a pile of luggage at her feet and who was putting her cell phone away.

I quickly strolled over to her and said, "Annie—"

She interrupted me and said, "Do you have any idea how long I've been trying to call you? I've been here since . . . holy crap, Lewis, what happened to you?"

All the way over to Manchester, I'd been working through what to tell her, and I said, "Had an accident."

She stood up, now concerned. "Car accident? Are you all right?"

I stepped up to her. "Not a car accident . . . but I'll tell you on the way back to Tyler. All right?"

Annie wrinkled her nose and said, "No offense, handsome, but you're not getting a kiss from me until you take a shower. Maybe two of them."

I bent down, picked up her two bags.

"Deal," I said. "Let's go."

We walked quickly out of the terminal, back to my Ford, and in a minute or two, we were leaving the short-term parking lot, where we paid the magnificent sum of two dollars.

Days like these, I do love my little state and its quirky airport.

It was a pleasure to drive to Tyler Beach without worrying a state trooper would pick me up, and it was a pleasure to see and hear Annie right next to me, without a phone line in between, but what wasn't pleasurable was trying to explain to her what had happened to me the night before.

"All right," she repeated for the third time. "You were taken to a hiding place for these fanatical antinukers, and then were nearly killed when some character named Henry took you out and took a shot at you?"

"That's right."

"And even after stumbling around the marsh for about half the night, nearly drowning, getting lost and whatever, you still don't want to go to the cops?"

"I don't."

"Why the hell not?"

"A number of reasons," I said.

"Lewis . . ."

So I told her the number of reasons, she countered a few times, and this charming discussion lasted until I drove down the

139

collection of bumpy ruts that led to my house, with a steady rain starting to fall.

Instead of going into the shed that serves as a garage, I made a sloppy turn in front of my house and faced my Ford back up the incline of my driveway, leading back to the parking lot of the Lafayette House. I put the Ford in park and said, "I'm going to pop inside. If I'm not out in two minutes, drive away and call the Tyler cops. Ask for Detective Sergeant Woods. Tell her what I just did."

Annie said, "If you're trying to scare me, you're doing a hell of a job."

"Not scaring," I said. "Being cautious."

I touched her hand and stepped out, then strolled up to the front door. I unlocked it and quickly checked the living room, upstairs, and then, back downstairs, the small dirt-floored basement area that holds my oil furnace and not much else. Clear. I went out and gave her a cheery wave, climbed back into the Ford, and drove it into the garage, and a minute or two later, we were in the living room of my home, her baggage on the floor.

Annie said, "Look, I appreciate what you've said, but I really think you need to go to the cops."

"No, I'm sorry," I said, hanging up her coat in the downstairs closet. "If I do that, then it's official. When it becomes official, it becomes news. When it becomes news that one Lewis Cole of Tyler Beach was the victim of a kidnapping and perhaps an attempted murder, then a lot of old stories from last winter are going to be dug up. About me and Senator Jackson Hale."

"We can handle—"

"Annie, please," I said. "You're a few weeks away from the November election, your guy is in the fight of his life, and I'm not going to provide ammo for his opponent."

Annie said, "But it's . . . hold on."

"What?"

She came up to me, put a hand to my head, gingerly touched the bump there and the clotted mass of blood about my hair. "Christ on a crutch, Lewis, you're hurt."

"You should see the other guy," I said.

"I thought the other guy was a rock," she said.

"True."

"Lewis . . ."

"Not a good comparison, I admit."

She took my hand. "Upstairs. Now. We're going to take a look at that before anything else."

"Just a sec," I said, and I went to make sure the front door was locked and the dead bolt slid into place, and then I followed Annie, walking up the short set of stairs to the second floor. With her coat off I noted her black hose, short tan skirt, and a couple of other things. As she reached the second floor, I said, "Since when are garter belts and stockings back in fashion?"

She turned and flashed me that impish redheaded smile that had intrigued me the first day I met her, and she said, "I don't follow fashion trends, sweetie. I set them."

I went with her into the bathroom, and she left and came back with a straight-backed chair that I keep in my office for those few visitors actually curious enough to spend time in that little book-lined cubby. I sat down and noted that the bedroom door was open, and I could see the nightstand next to the bed. In the top drawer of the nightstand was my 9 mm Beretta semiautomatic pistol, and underneath the bed, on a foam cushion, was a 12-gauge Remington pump-action shotgun with an extended magazine. Even in my current state, I knew I could get to both weapons in seconds if somebody tried to break in through the front door.

"Off with your shirt," she said, wrinkling her nose at my odor, no doubt, and after that sodden bit of clothing hit the tile floor, she went "tsk tsk tsk" and got to work. I sat and took it fairly well, with only one or two winces, as Annie cleaned up my hair and gently touched my bump, then put on a bit of gauze with surgical tape.

She stepped back and said, "Not a bad job, if I do say so. If your head had been any softer, or that rock any harder, you would have needed some stitches."

"Thanks," I said. "Anything else you've got for me?"

"No, but you've got to take a shower, and either wash or burn those clothes, Lewis. I mean . . . I've stuck with you for the past hour, but there's a limit to what a girl can put up with."

I stood up, kissed her for a moment, and started taking off my clothes.

"No offense, m'dear," I said, "but it looks like after a long flight, you could use a shower yourself."

She leaned back against the bathroom counter. "Flight was under two hours. Not long at all."

"Now you're being technical?"

"You forget I'm a lawyer, young man," she said.

"Details, details," I said, moving over to turn on the shower, and when I turned back, she had taken her blouse off and was reaching behind to unsnap her black lace bra. I gave her a look, and she shrugged.

"No time to get caught up in details," she explained.

Some sweet time later we were resting in bed, her head on my shoulder, her fingers idly running across my chest. She blew a bit of air across my shoulder and said, "Remind me again why you thought it was a good idea to talk to this rabid antinuker guy."

"Part of my research."

"Unh-hunh," she replied. "Research for a story for your magazine, or for Lewis Cole, defender of the faith and lady folk?"

"A bit of both," I admitted.

"What did you hope would happen when you talked to the antinuke guy? That he'd throw up his hands and confess?"

"Nope. I just wanted to ask questions and to poke around and stir things up. You stir things up, interesting items can pop to the surface."

She pinched me in a delicate spot, and I yelped. "Or interesting items like a magazine writer can be tossed in a swamp."

"Wasn't a swamp," I said. "It was a salt marsh."

"Okay. So stirring things around is your strategy. What is your endgame, what do you hope happens?"

"With me stirring things around, showing up at odd places, asking inconvenient questions, I hope somebody gets nervous. I hope somebody makes a mistake. I hope somebody steps out of the shadows . . . and I find out who the shooter was."

"Then what? Tell the cops?"

"Eventually."

"Mmm . . . eventually. What does that mean?"

I shifted in the big warm comfortable bed. "Eventually means that once I'm convinced I got the right guy, then he ends up with the cops interested in him. That's what. Then I let the law enforcement professionals take care of it."

"You don't think they're already doing that now?"

"I have a personal interest," I said. "Sometimes that lets me do things and go places they can't."

"Strange way to get the killer of that Toles character under arrest."

I said, "This is going to sound cold, but I don't care that much that Mr. Toles got himself killed. What I do care about is that this shooter has practically destroyed an old friend of mine, a friend who is hiding out scared, afraid that she's the next target."

"She could go to the cops for protection," Annie said.

"True, but there's a limit to what they can do. Always a limit. You know the towns around here. They're stretched thin as it is. There's no witness protection program, no way for her to get twenty-four/seven protection from a small-town police force."

She gently stroked my hair around where the gauze and tape were still in place. "So it's your job, then."

"Not a job."

"What is it, then?"

"Friendship," I said. "Friendship and loyalty."

With that Annie moved around so that she was now lying on top of me. She kissed my nose, her red hair hanging about her face, her warm smooth flesh melding into me.

"All right, friendship," she said, "but if you decide to go back to days of yore, when you were wooing Miss Quinn, then I'm going to give you a bump that will make the one you have back there look like a mosquito bite."

I leaned up some and kissed her back. "One wild woman at a time is my limit."

She sighed in apparent contentment and said, "Your wild woman is getting a bit hungry. You think she could get some late breakfast in this joint?"

"I don't see why not," I said. "Care to join me downstairs?"

"Ack," she said, pulling the sheet and comforter up to her shoulders. "I've been flying from one state to another in this great land these past several months, and this is the most comfy bed I've been in since. No, sir. I'm not leaving. My big boy is going to give me a kiss and go downstairs and make us some breakfast and bring it back up. Is that all right?"

I kissed her freckled nose. "Since when can I ever say no to a redheaded wild woman?"

So I went downstairs and puttered around in the kitchen, and in a while came back upstairs with orange juice, instant coffee, scrambled eggs, toast, and sausage links, and while we ate, Annie said, "I promise to keep things on a nonpolitical keel here during my day off, but my God, I'm enjoying every second of this. It's like parachuting back into the world of reality after spending months in cloud-cuckoo-land."

"Cloud-cuckoo-land?"

She nudged me with her shoulder. "It is what it is. It's day after day, one miserable long slog after another . . . it's not a race, Lewis. It's a goddamn long marathon—and just a couple of weeks more. Just a couple of more weeks."

"Then what?"

"Like most marathoners who finish a long race, I plan to throw up, drink a lot, and sleep for a day or two."

"Sounds like fun."

"Only if you're around to join me."

"In a heartbeat."

We finished up our breakfast and, being the gallant man that I am—or so I was told—I gathered up the dishes and brought them downstairs. I was tempted to toss them in the sink, but the latent Boy Scout in me kept me in the kitchen to wash and dry and put everything away.

When I got back upstairs, Annie was doing something fancy with a scrap of black lace and said, "I'm in the mood to play some more. Are you up for it?"

"Not sure," I said. "My head still hurts a bit."

She gave me a naughty look. "Which one?"

"Don't you lawyers have a process called discovery?" I asked.

"We do."

After tossing off my robe and joining her in bed, I said, "Then get discovering, woman."

Much later, after another mutual shower and mutual drying off, we went downstairs, where I built a fire in my stone fireplace, and Annie curled up on the couch in an old UNH sweatshirt of mine and not much else, with a down comforter wrapped around her legs. Outside a cold rain was falling, splattering against the sliding glass doors that led out to the rear deck overlooking the Atlantic Ocean.

"Two things, my boy," she announced. "One, you're going to take that television remote and turn on something that is nowhere near a cable news channel. Turner Classic Movies or something similar would work well. Then you're going to take the remote and hide it."

"Hide it?" I asked, feeling refreshed and comfortable, wearing an old dark blue terrycloth robe.

"Hide it," she repeated. "This day is my day off with you, and I'll be damned if I'm going to be sucked into watching the latest campaign news, of who's up, who's down, and what else makes the world go round. However, knowing the political junkie I am, I can't trust myself. So hide it."

"Deal," I said, getting the remote, flipping it on, and finding TCM, just as she had requested. They were in the middle of coming attractions, but I was hoping something good would show up. Annie burrowed into the comforter and said, "Second thing, my boy, your wench is starving again and requires a fine meal. That means no cheeseburgers, no pizza, no hot dogs, no pastries, nothing I would get in a conference room, an airport lounge, or a 7-Eleven. Deal?"

"Deal," I said. "And for dessert?"

She winked at me. "Depends on how your head is feeling."

I went into the kitchen, hid the remote in the silverware drawer—some hiding, I'm sure that Annie saw what I did—and then made a phone call to the Lafayette House across the street from my home. I got hold of Ramon—and I'm embarrassed to say I didn't know his last name—who was the chef for the Lafayette House, and I explained to him what I needed.

"Jeez, Lewis, I don't know," Ramon said from the hotel's kitchen, and in the background I could hear shouts and dishes being tossed around. "Most times it's okay, but a takeout today . . . . we're getting slammed."

"I'm going to make it worse," I said. "I can't leave the house, so you'll have to have someone deliver it here."

"You can't leave the house? What's that? You under arrest or something?"

Or something, I thought, looking over at Annie curled up on my couch, a nice fire roaring along, the sound of the rain and wind striking my old home. Even though it would take only ten minutes for me to go up to the hotel and get my takeout order, I wasn't going to leave her behind. Not with my Henry out there, the guy who tried to drown me and shoot me in the space of a few minutes.

"Yeah, house arrest with a woman friend."

He chuckled. "All right, m'man, maybe I can squeeze something in, but I can't send somebody over, it's a hell of a—"

"Fifty bucks."

"What?"

"Fifty bucks to get it delivered."

"Oh, come on, that's—"

"One hundred dollars, Ramon. One hundred dollars."

There was a pause on the other end of the line, and then his voice whispered, "That's some house arrest. Okay. A hundred it is. You'll get your food in a half hour."

I hung up the phone. Annie was watching me, her face gently smiling, but I sensed something else behind those eyes.

CHAPTER FOURTEEN

Thanks to whichever god rules cable channels, when I joined Annie on the couch, TCM started showing *The Lion in Winter*, with Katharine Hepburn and Peter O'Toole. Annie graciously shared the down comforter with me as we watched the film, and she said, "God, yes, the Dark Ages, when cutthroat politics really mean cutthroat politics."

So I joyfully settled down with my woman, aching but feeling loose-limbed and refreshed, and looking at the nearby clock to see how much longer dinner was going to be. Another twenty minutes or so, if things went well. The rain was really coming down harder, and wind was splattering some of it on my rear deck windows, and Annie cuddled in closer to me and said, "My God, I'd forgotten places and times like this still exist."

I said, "It's here for you, whenever you want it."

She laughed. "My life the past few months has been living out of suitcases, finding a place that does dry cleaning in an hour, and trying not to eat pizza four days in a row. I haven't been home to Boston in weeks, my mail is probably two feet high, and after the election, I swear, I'm going to collapse."

"Then collapse here," I said.

"Mmm," she said, "you know, I was thinking about after the election and—"

The ringing phone cut right into her, and I pulled myself free to answer it. "Lewis?"

It was Paula. "Hey," I said. "How's it going?"

She laughed, but her voice sounded brittle. "Better . . . last night I managed to get a good two hours' sleep, and I didn't have a nightmare. So I've got that going for me . . . . and did you see today's *Chronicle*?"

Annie's face was impassive. I said, "No, I haven't."

"Well, my story . . . hell, your story was in it. I just wanted to thank you again."

"No problem, Paula," I said, and with that, Annie's left eyebrow rose. "Glad I could help."

"The big demo is set for tomorrow," she said. "I'll see you at the usual place?"

"I'll try," I said.

"Want me to pack a lunch for us?"

"If you'd like, that'd be fine," I said.

She was quiet, and Paula said, "You're not alone, are you."

I said, "That's absolutely right. And you?"

She sighed. "The honorable Mark Spencer has a meeting later on with some financial types looking to support him for his state senate run. He may or may not join me for dinner. In the meantime . . . thanks again. And you take care."

"You, too," I said, and hung up the phone. I went back deep into the couch and Annie reassembled herself against me. On the television screen, Peter O'Toole, playing Henry II, was chewing up the scenery as only he could. Annie asked, "Paula?"

"Yep."

"What's up with her?"

"She wanted to thank me for helping her out with a story the other day. We'll probably see each other at tomorrow's demonstration."

"She still has her boyfriend?"

"For the moment," I said.

"What do you mean by that?"

"Her boyfriend is the town counsel for Tyler. He's considering running for state senate. That seems to be taking up his attention more than Paula."

Annie said, "Sounds like a dick."

"No argument from me."

"Still," she said, squeezing me under the comforter, "if she dumps him and is back on the market, I have first and last dibs on you."

I kissed the top of her head. "And all the dibs in between."

On the screen, Katharine Hepburn, playing Queen Eleanor, was being as commanding and elegant as only she could be when the phone rang once more. I muttered something inconsiderate and answered, and it was another woman in my life, Denise Pichette-Volk.

"Lewis?"

I said, "The same."

"The last piece you did caused quite the stir. Especially that 'fucking Russians' quote. What do you have for me next?"

What I had next was my reporter's notebook, lost somewhere in the mud and grass of the Falconer salt marsh. Annie stirred, and I kept my arm firm around her. I said, "How does an exclusive interview with the head of the Nuclear Freedom Front sound?"

"Really?" she asked.

"Really," I said. Okay, the notebook was gone, but I was certain I could re-create most of my conversation with Mr. Chesak with a fair degree of accuracy. If not, well, what was he going to do? Take off his cheesy disguise and show up at the *Shoreline* offices to complain?

"When can I have it?"

"Sometime tomorrow," I said.

"Why can't I have it today?"

"Because I'm taking today as a sick day, that's why," I said.

"Oh," she said. "How sick are you?"

"Sick enough," I said, and hung up the phone. Annie giggled and said, "My God, the women just won't leave you alone, will they."

"The burden of being popular," I said.

"Your boss?"

"As much as I hate to admit it, yes, my editor at *Shoreline*."

"She sounds like a real pistol," Annie said.

"More like a howitzer," I said.

That earned me another intimate snuggle, and I checked the time. Less than ten minutes to go, and Annie saw me look at the clock and said, "God, my stomach is about ready to declare war on the rest of me. This had better be good."

"It will," I said. "Promise."

As if the ghost of Alexander Graham Bell were cursing me for some long-forgotten Scottish joke on my part, the phone chimed again, and as I reached for it, Annie pushed me aside and said, "Unh-unh, this time, it's my turn." She grabbed the phone and smiled at me and said, "Mr. Cole's personal assistant speaking. How may I assist you?"

It was a funny bit, but then her face paled and she passed the receiver over to me without a word. I took the phone and heard a familiar muffled male voice on the other end.

"So you made it, asshole," the voice said.

"Apparently so."

"Guarantee, you won't be so lucky next time," he went on. "I missed you, but pal, I rarely miss—and never on the second try. Got that?"

"Bold talk for a loser who likes to take shots at a guy who's got cuffed arms and is knee-deep in mud," I said, and I hung up the phone.

Annie's eyes were very wide. "That him?"

"Yeah. What did he say to you?"

"He said, 'If that fucker Lewis Cole is next to you, let me talk to him.'"

I said, "Sorry. I wish I had taken the call instead."

"I don't care about the language," she said. "I hear worse in the span of ten seconds in my job. Cops?"

"Not worth it," I said.

"The call could be traced and—"

"He sounds sharp," I said. "Which means a disposable cell phone. Which means no tracing. Beside, a call to the cops . . . in a matter of days, I'd be back in the news, and so would your candidate. Not going to happen."

"So what's going to happen, then?"

I got up from the couch, rearranged the comforter around her, and then traced the phone line to the jack in the nearby wall. I pulled the phone line free, held it up so she could see it.

"No more phone calls. No more interruptions. Just you and me."

Then there was a pounding on the door.

I dropped the phone line and looked at my heavy door with the dead bolt, and tried to keep my voice cheery. "Looks like our meal's here. Stay on the couch and I'll take care of it."

I raced upstairs, the bottom of my robe fluttering, and went into the bedroom, which smelled of soap, exertion, and the pleasing scent that Annie wears. I got to my wallet on the nightstand, pulled out five twenties, paused, and then pulled something else out. From the nightstand drawer, I took out my loaded 9 mm Beretta. I didn't check to see if it was loaded. It was. I know I'm breaking a half dozen rules and commonsense approaches, but all of my weapons are loaded. When somebody is breaking in at 2:00 A.M. is no time to fumble around looking for ammunition. There are no inquisitive children in the house, and none visiting anytime soon, so I was comfortable with my arrangement.

I switched off the safety, dropped the pistol in the large right pocket of my robe, and went back downstairs.

On the television screen, a sword fight was ensuing, and I went to the front door and hesitated for just a second before using the peephole. No, I didn't like being exposed like that, so I moved over and looked out the near window. I saw a young man dressed in jeans, windbreaker, and a Red Sox baseball cap worn backward, looking miserable in the rain, holding two large white plastic bags in his hands.

"You Mr. Cole?" he asked, his face splotchy with a red and white complexion.

"Yep," I said, and he sighed and passed over the packages to me.

"Here ya go," he said, and I passed over the five twenties, which brought a smile. "Christ," he said, deftly pulling one twenty out and shoving it into his jeans. "I thought Ramon was dicking with me, that somebody would actually pay for a home delivery. Thanks, bud."

"No problem," I said, ducking back into the house, locking the door, and heading off to the kitchen. As I spread out our feast— and told Annie to stay still—I slipped the Beretta out of my robe and put it in the silverware drawer, next to the remote. It was getting crowded in there, but I would put up with it.

Some time later, after a dinner of grilled lobster tails over rice, with a side of salad and grilled veggies, and a bottle of a French Bordeaux that I had been saving for a special occasion, Annie put another chunk of firewood in the fireplace, retired back to the couch, and stretched out. I cleaned up and restored everything to the kitchen, and Annie called out, "Mr. Cole?"

"Yes, ma'am?"

"You know what my mama said about rainy fall days like this?"

I folded up a dish towel. "Nope. What did your mama say?"

"She said, 'Days like these, you'd want to spend in bed with a good book, or someone who's read one.'"

I went back out to the living room. "Feel like exploring my library?"

She said, "I feel like something. Let's go upstairs and find out."

I awoke with a start, dreaming that I was mucking around in the salt marsh while bullets zipped over my head. I shifted in the warm bed and looked at the bright red numerals of the nearby clock radio. It was 2:10 in the morning. I moved a hand across to the other side of the bed.

It was empty.

I lay still for a few moments, then heard the furtive noise of someone working at a keyboard. I sat up and looked out the bedroom door. A small glow of light was coming from my office. I threw on my robe and went out to my office and saw Annie sitting at my desk, working on my Apple computer.

"Hey," I said.

"Hey yourself," she said, still looking at the computer screen.

I leaned against the doorjamb. "Thought you were taking a day off."

Her gaze didn't move away. "I did, sweetie. If you check the time, you'll see it's a new day—and in a few hours, I'm going to ask you to take me to the airport. I was having a bout of insomnia, and thought I'd get up and check my in-box. It's a creepy feeling to have been away for a day and to have one hundred and nine unread e-mail messages waiting for me. Ugh."

"I can imagine," I said.

Her hands hesitated for a moment, and then she turned to me, her face wan in the light from my computer. "Can you?"

"I think I can," I said.

"Then you have a better grasp of things than I do, Lewis," she said. "Because I can't imagine being in your shoes. I can't imagine being assaulted, getting a threatening phone call, and then going to answer the door with a loaded pistol in your robe pocket. All without contacting the police."

"Like I said," I pointed out. "Going to the cops means some publicity, and I don't think publicity is what you or your campaign needs right now."

A brief nod. "Sounds good. Sometimes, though . . . I get the feeling you don't mind being on the outside, doing your own thing, maybe making your own rules."

"True enough," I said.

"Well, that's outside my world, my friend," she said. "My world is of rules, broken and bent, but still, rules—and of the law. Being a member of the Massachusetts Bar, I have a respect for the law. Not a healthy respect, but still, respect. Your world . . . I'm afraid our worlds will collide in one hell of a bang one of these days."

I made a point of looking at the digital clock in my office. "Not this day, I hope."

She shook her head, smiled. "No, not today. Also not today is something else we're eventually going to discuss."

"Which is what?"

"What I wanted to talk about yesterday, for a bit. About when the election is over. About when you and I recover here. Lewis . . ."

I said, "Things in politics aren't going to end because of the election, are they."

"No."

"Even if Senator Hale loses?"

"Even if he loses. Win or lose, I've been promised—in writing—either a position in the new administration, or in Senator Hale's office in Washington."

"You've done a hell of a job for him."

"You're damn right I have," she said, "and I deserve it."

"Going back to Boston and working on wills and probate . . . doesn't seem as attractive, does it."

"God, no."

"So what, then?"

She turned back to the keyboard. "This was something I wanted to think about on my day off. Buddy, I am no longer on my day off, and I've got scores of e-mails to get through."

I went in, kissed the top of her head, and put my hands on her soft shoulders. "Then we'll talk about it later."

"Only if I get through these e-mails. You're a dear man, but having you here is a distraction. Lovely as you might be."

Another kiss to the top of her head. "Message received and understood."

I went back to bed and eventually fell asleep to the sound of Annie's fingers tapping on my keyboard.

. . .

A few hours later I took Annie back to the Manchester airport, and in the hour or so drive to the west, she used her BlackBerry to make phone call after phone call and to text the scores of people she owed messages to. She had taken a shower, begged off breakfast, and was dressed in a sharp black outfit that said *serious woman on a serious mission*.

When we got to the airport and I pulled up to the single large building that served as the terminal, the serious woman left for a moment and the tender woman appeared. She touched my cheek and said, "Thanks for the day and night of sanity, Lewis."

"My pleasure," I said. "At least three times."

She giggled and we kissed, and I got out and retrieved her luggage, and she said, "I hope I didn't scare you earlier this morning."

"By taking over my computer without asking permission and looking for my hidden porn collection?"

She gently kicked me in the shin. "Cad. No. About what happens after the election. About me. About you."

"No," I said. "Not scared. I know we'll do well, whatever happens. That's for later. You've got a man to elect president."

Annie hugged me, and I felt her hand run up my side, where I was wearing a Bianchi shoulder holster and my Beretta, and she whispered, "Armed, are you?"

"Yes."

"And you've got a man to catch."

"I do."

"Then do it," she whispered, "and don't get yourself killed. Because I'll be so pissed you'll run scared, even if you're dead."

I rubbed her back. "Deal."

We broke apart, and she grabbed her luggage and started

walking into the terminal, talking again to her BlackBerry, towing her wheeled bag behind her. I waited and waited as she approached the sliding glass doors.

Waited some more.

The doors slid open.

Annie walked through.

Stopped.

Turned. Smiled and threw me a kiss.

I threw one back.

It had been worth the wait.

CHAPTER FIFTEEN

After spending an hour in my office writing a story for *Shoreline* about my oddball interview with Mr. Chesak of the Nuclear Freedom Front—and doing a fairly good job, if I do say so myself, with my reporter's notebook turning into sludge somewhere in the Falconer salt marsh—I got into my Ford and started driving south to Falconer for the big demonstration due for later that morning.

I took out my cell phone and made a call to Ron Shelton of the Falconer nuclear power plant, and got my first big surprise of the day.

"Say that again?" I asked, sitting still at a traffic light on Route 1 in Tyler.

"Sorry, Lewis," he said. "I've been told not to allow you on the plant property, and before you ask me why, you know the answer."

"No, I don't. Do tell."

He sighed. "That story the other day. About the unnamed utility executive who said, quote, 'those fucking Russians.' Well, that came back and bit me in the ass, big-time."

"I didn't identify you by name, Ron," I pointed out, "and you cleared the quote. So what's the problem?"

"The problem is that a real executive at the plant saw a reporter depart the visitors' center, and then read a story you filed, about twelve hours later, with that pungent quote. Two and two were put together, and I was called into the executive's office for a grilling. So when I was put on the spot about what reporter was in a power plant's offices . . . sorry, I had to give you up, Lewis."

"And you? What happened to you?"

"Some sort of half-assed investigation is going on, and I'm in the center of it. To calm things down, I had to ban you. Sorry again."

The light ahead of me changed. There was the honk of a horn behind me. I started driving.

"Gee, thanks a lot, Ron," I said. "So how long am I banned from the plant site?"

Another sigh. "Don't know. I'll see what I can do."

"The big demo is taking place in about an hour," I said. "Don't do me any more favors."

I clicked off and resumed driving.

The U.S. Marine Corps—an organization I've long admired and had dealings with in a previous life—has a saying that marines improvise, adapt, and overcome when faced with challenges. This challenge was one that I was certain any marine could handle before his or her first cup of coffee in the morning, but it was one I still had to address. So I kept on moving south along Route 1 until traffic started backing up and slowing down, and I luckily found a space at the Laughing Bee doughnut shop and, despite my history of parking there, dropped off my Ford. I had a small knapsack that I slung over my shoulder—to go along with my 9 mm Beretta in my shoulder holster—and I made a quick stop at a nearby 7-Eleven, where I picked up a couple of bottles of water and a ham and cheese sandwich of uncertain provenance. Then I went back outside and started walking.

Getting to the demonstration proved to be fairly easy. I followed some stragglers, and then more protesters joined us, and then we started moving through the woods. Trails had been cleared, with splotches of white paint on tree trunks marking the way, and soon enough, more and more people were joining us. I had my press pass outside my coat, and for the most part, I was ignored. The protesters formed into clusters, marking affinity groups that worked among themselves, and each carried flags or banners naming the particular group. I saw one that was from the University of New Hampshire, but I didn't see Haleigh Miller among its members. When we emerged onto the salt marsh, cheers went up, getting louder as more and more people streamed out.

I stood for a moment on a hummock of grass and dirt, watching the marchers. Once they came out of the woods, they fanned out across the marsh, some banging drums or cymbals, others waving banners and flags. I saw two protesters—in their late twenties, both male—pose for a photograph, holding up a large pair of wire cutters in their arms, gas masks poised on top of their heads. Cheers erupted from the nearby demonstrators as they did that.

Next to me was a news photographer, and identification marking him as being from the Associated Press hung around his neck. He was tall and wore khaki slacks, a black turtleneck, and a mesh, camera equipment vest, and around his neck a number of cameras and lenses hung like odd Christmas decorations. He nodded in my direction and said, "Lots more people than I thought."

"Impressive," I said.

He raised a camera and said, "Makes you wonder if they can actually do it."

I looked out at the hundreds and hundreds of protesters moving like a multicolored river across the flat salt marsh. "If they have any organization, they'll go over that fence like Sherman through Atlanta."

The photographer laughed. "Now that'd be some pix. See you around."

I stood there for a bit longer and then joined the masses. More chanting, more drumbeats, and a few papier-mâché puppets bounding along. Helicopters were buzzing overhead, and I recognized one as being from the New Hampshire State Police, and two from Boston television stations.

The going was tricky, with flat areas of marshland cut open here and there by streambeds. The first demonstrators across the marsh had prebuilt wooden spans that they dropped across the deep streambeds, and I was impressed. Maybe they would do it, after all.

The lines of people moved along, and then they spread out. I stood a little apart and scribbled notes, noting the number of people, the colors of their clothes, their signs protesting nuclear power plants and supporting green power, and there were more cheers as round weather balloons went up in the air, each trailing a thin rope holding flickering bits of ribbon. The helicopters seemed to note the new arrivals, and they moved away, and again I was impressed. This was more of an organization than I'd thought.

I looked to a small rise of dirt, brush, and crushed rocks, the foundation of the chain-link fence and barbed wire marking the southern boundary of the Falconer nuclear plant. On the other side of the fence was a long line of police officers in dark jumpsuits, with batons and helmets. They looked pretty organized, as well.

There was a crackle to the air, a nervous energy of forces in motion that were about to collide, and the sensible part of me warned me to walk away.

Instead, I got closer.

Up near the fence line I went, along with a few other members of the news media, as the lines of protesters dressed themselves, going down the marshland in front of the fence line for a few hundred yards. I scribbled some more notes, shifted the small knapsack on my back, and looked around.

More chanting, more shouting, more fist waving, signs moving up and down.

I waited some more.

The morning dragged by.

I shifted my feet in the salt marsh, yawned, and walked around some.

A couple of reporters were huddled together, talking to their news desks on their cell phones.

The chanting, the shouting, and the fist waving had died away. Some of the protesters were actually sitting on the mud and grass.

What the hell was happening?

A couple of demonstrators went by me, arguing between themselves, and I got in their way and held up my press pass and said, "Guys, what's going on?"

The one on the right, wearing one of those colorful wool hats from the Andes with droopy sides, looked at me with flashing eyes and said, "None of your fucking business, you corporate shill."

His companion was more cooperative. He had on a long denim

jacket covered with buttons, including a black-and-white one stating: ANARCHY RULES! He coughed and said, "Going on? I'll tell you what's going on. A goat fuck, that's what's going on. All these people out there . . . and no one knows what to do next. Hell, we know what to do next—get a move on and go over the fence! But they'd rather sit and talk and reach a consensus, debate how many representatives should get together to reach a decision, how many of those reps should be men, women, gay, transgender, handicapped, Native American . . . fuck that shit, man."

I scribbled as fast as I could, and then the first one said, "Yeah, look over there. Those asshats know what to do."

I looked up to the fence line, where a gate had opened up, and the black-clad cops were marching out to face their opponents.

When I looked back, the two dissidents had moved away, heading to the nearest tree line.

The shouts and the chanting dribbled away as the cops came out, and behind them, beyond the fence line, the National Guard troops moved down the hill to take their place. They marched out in fairly good order, across the grass and uneven ground, stretching out in a line. The hundreds of protesters moved away a bit, and then they stopped.

There was about fifty yards separating the two groups, and the sudden appearance of the police seemed to surprise the antinuclear forces. I went over to the mass of protesters with a few other reporters—including the tall AP photographer—and I gave up taking notes before long. It was just too confusing, with lots of rumors, loud voices, and plaintive talk along the lines of "What are we going to do now?"

The Associated Press photographer caught my eye and said, "What do you think?"

"Tactics," I said. "For an unorganized mob like these folks"—and I could hear some murmurs behind me from those who disagreed with my observation—"it's one thing to go up and attack an object, like a fence, but now you're facing cops. It's more serious. You have to be face-to-face, person against person. Whatever existing plans there were have just been tossed into the trash bin, and it'll probably take them a while to figure out what to do next."

The photographer brought a camera up to his face. "Tactics. Yeah, I can see that."

Then somebody punched me hard in the side.

I turned. A slight woman with short dark hair stood there, fist balled, and she laughed. "I should have known it was you, Lewis. Speaking about tactics and disorganization. How do you like being out here with the unwashed masses?"

Kara Miles, Diane Woods's significant other, stood next to me, bringing a smile to my face. She had on jeans, Timberland boots, and layers of clothing up top, and her ears were festooned with the usual studs and earrings.

"How goes it, Kara?"

She paused, as if she didn't like the question, and I noticed she was wearing a blue scarf, and so were a number of other protesters behind her. Two of them—young women with long blond hair in braids—held up a hand-painted banner that read: TRUE BLUE!

"We're doing all right," she said. "Trying to figure out what's going to happen next. Some of the affinity groups want to engage the police, appeal to their better nature. Others want to sit down and just squat for a while. Some just want to go charging over. I mean, there's not even a hundred cops and National Guardsmen over there, and we've got thousands."

Some of her friends nodded in agreement with what she was

saying, and I said, "Hate to be a history geek again, but remember what Napoleon said."

"An army marches on its stomach?" she asked coyly.

"Nicely done," I said. "I was thinking of something else he said. That God's on the side of the heaviest artillery."

One of the women holding the banner called out, "But we have truth on our side! We'll win! Just you wait and see!"

Kara rolled her eyes and said, "Do me a favor?"

"Sure."

She gestured to the line of police officers. "Diane's over there. If you get a chance, could you get a message to her?"

"Of course. What's the message?"

Kara stepped closer to me. "Tell her I'm going to be a good girl today. I won't get arrested. Got it?"

"Gotten—but I'm not sure I understand it."

She stared out at the line of black-clad and helmeted police officials, one of who was her lover and companion. "It's a kind of peace offering. Not much, but . . . I want to tune down some of the static. We've been having . . . challenges lately."

I thought about Annie, about our day together, about what a postelection life might mean to both of us.

"Aren't we all," I said.

A burst of cheers erupted when a small group of people came out from the tree line, and like puppies running to a bowl of kibble, most of the reporters went over to this group, which consisted of Laura Glynn Toles and her son, Vic, and a couple of other demonstrators. Laura and Vic were walking arm in arm, and they had black armbands on their right arms, and they did their best to ignore the reporters coming at them, thrusting microphones and cameras in their faces. Laura had on a long jean skirt, thick boots, and a heavy yellow barn jacket, and her face had the screwed-up intensity of someone desperately trying not to cry. Vic, wearing green cargo pants and a thick red down coat, looked grim as well.

They stopped at a slight rise of land that was the highest point for yards all around, and I decided to acknowledge whatever journalistic duty I had and moved in as well, pushing some against the huddle of journalists. I caught bits and pieces of what Laura was saying.

". . . we're here to show our commitment to the cause, even in the face of grave danger . . ."

". . . no matter what happens today, our fight will continue . . ."

". . . yes, my decision is final. The Stone Chapel will be sold. I just hope some progressive gathering will step forward to purchase it . . ."

Then one of the male activists who had accompanied the Toleses stepped out in front of Laura and held up both hands. "Folks, please, that's enough, please. Give them some privacy now, all right? Please?"

Some of my fellow reporters called out a few more questions, but Laura and her son turned away and walked a few steps, and kept their backs turned. I turned as well and walked away, and shortly thereafter, so did the other reporters.

For nearly a half hour not much was going on, so I decided to cross the open field and talk to the cops—well, one cop in particular. I walked away from the milling group of demonstrators and news reporters and started across the marshland to the line of cops. A couple of other people had gone ahead of me, and as I got closer, I had the oddest feeling I had done this before. I'm not much for believing in hunches or past lives, but there was something very familiar about the scene, about two camps of people with an open strip of land between them . . .

I stopped and looked back at the protesters, the flags, the banners, the balloons rising up above them, the papier-mâché heads, and then I got it. A documentary I had seen on the History Channel a few months ago about the war in the Western European trenches in 1914 and the unofficial Christmas truce, when German and British soldiers emerged from their trenches to meet in no-man's-land, to exchange tobacco, candy, and even uniform badges.

A brief glimpse of humanity during a four-year slaughter.

I kept on walking to the police officers, conscious of the weight of the pistol under my jacket, hoping none of the law enforcement folks would notice.

Those that had gone ahead of me included a couple of reporters doing their best to interview the stolid and unresponsive cops, and a couple of protesters, trying to get . . . well, I'm not sure what they were trying to do. They were an older man and woman, both with white hair, both wearing sweatshirts covered with buttons embracing a number of political positions, and they were speaking earnestly to the line of police officers.

The man said in a loud voice, "In your heart of hearts, you know what you're doing here is wrong. Please. Come join us. Come over to our side. Refuse to fight for the corporations, the polluters, the ones who spoil our environment. Make this a special moment, a moment of history, showing people power at its best. Like the fight against the Berlin Wall, the fight against Marcos, the fight against nuclear war. Join us—surprise the corporations. Drop your weapons and walk this way."

His female companion said, whenever he paused, "He speaks the truth . . . he speaks the truth . . ."

I got closer to the cops and started looking at the stern faces, and at one particular stern face I stepped over and said, "Detective Sergeant Woods. You're looking fetching today."

That earned me a quick smile, and she said, "Lewis . . . don't have much time to talk."

"How about a little time?"

"I don't see why not. Come this way."

She stepped back out of the line, and her fellow officers shuffled a bit to let me go through, and I felt that odd sensation of being in a foreign territory, under some marque or protection offered by my friend Diane. There was something else as well; the cops looked strong and menacing in their riot gear, helmets and gas masks strapped to their legs, batons in their hands, but from where I was standing, they looked woefully outnumbered.

I'm sure they would deny it to a man—or a woman—but I think they were terrified by the numbers opposing them.

Diane stopped after a few paces and took off her riot helmet. Her hair was matted down from wearing the gear, and she wiped a hand across her forehead.

"Well?" she asked. "What's going on?"

"Got a message for you."

"Really? Who? The secret master of the antinukers?"

"Nope," I said. "Kara."

That stopped her. She eyed me. "You kidding?"

"Not for a second."

"How did this happen?"

I said, "I met her a few minutes ago, with the rest of her affinity group."

"Yeah," she said with a tinge of tiredness in her voice. "The True Blues. So what's the message?"

The talking from the older man grew louder, more insistent. His face was now scarlet. I said to Diane, "The message is that she plans to be a good girl today. She won't be arrested."

Diane's face brightened up, a good thing to see. "Really? She said that?"

"Yes. What does it mean?"

She was smiling. "Means . . . means a lot. She's going to do what she feels is right, without the possibility of embarrassing me. Look . . . if she was going to be arrested . . . it could get sticky if some reporters with too much time on their hands decided to poke around about my relationship with her."

Sure, I thought, knowing why I hadn't gone to the cops over the previous day's attack. I didn't want to drag Annie and her job into whatever nonsense was going on with me. So, something Kara and I had in common, besides our obvious good taste in women.

"That sounds like good news," I said.

"It is," she said. "Best news I've had in ages. Hey, look up there, beyond the fence line. See anybody you know?"

Even at this distance, I recognized the slim figure of the assistant editor and reporter for the Tyler *Chronicle.* "Paula," I said.

"Yep. She's up there . . . and why in hell are you down here?"

Listening still to the harangues of the older man and his friend, I said, "The evil corporate masters that run the show around here officially disinvited me."

She laughed. "Sorry about that, pal."

I kept looking up at the figure of Paula, and just for the hell of it, I waved at her. I was pleasantly surprised when she waved back. Diane said, "She's looking better. At least from my vantage point."

"Really?"

"True," she said. "Before we marched out here, I saw her chatting with some of her fellow news types. She was laughing and joking with them—not much, I know, but it is better, considering what she's been through. Right?"

"Right," I said.

She looked at me, her face still alight, and she said, "I owe you."

"For what?"

"For bringing me news that made my day."

"Diane—"

"No," she said, putting her helmet back on, reaching to grab the chin strap. "Two bits of news for you, my friend. The first is that that the shooting of Bronson Toles—it's a dead end, from what I hear. No real forensics evidence. The slug that nailed him wasn't found, even after hours out there with metal detectors. So the thought is, as crazy as it sounds, that it was a professional hit. A sniper in the woods waiting for his moment, then taking it and slipping out."

"A pro? Are you sure?"

She tightened the strap. "Sure as I'm going to be. Though that's not for public consumption, Lewis. So in your travels, you might think of who would benefit from Bronson Toles getting whacked, and who would have the sources and means to do so in a professional manner."

She didn't have to say any more. I recalled a visit the other day to a crowded union hall, where I'd been escorted in by a man with lots of sources and means.

"Thanks for the update. What else do you have?"

Diane started going back to her fellow cops. "In a while, I think things are going to go to shit, and rather quickly. Lot of angry and upset people who've rallied and marched—they're not going to turn around and go home after spending all this time and energy. They're going to try to occupy the plant site, and to do that, they're going to have to go through us."

"Can they do it?" I asked.

Her voice was bleak. "We have our orders, Lewis. Nobody's getting near the fence line. Nobody's getting near, over, or through."

"Those are some heavy orders."

"Oh yeah," she said, her eyes looking pale. "A few decades ago, back when this place was being constructed, there was another big-time demonstration. The governor was a real law-and-order type, wanted to send a message, so all the protesters were arrested. Nearly fifteen hundred. They were put up in National Guard armories, cost the state a bundle of money, and made lots of headlines for the antinukers' cause for weeks. Current governor ain't that dense. No arrests unless absolutely necessary. Just keep them away from the plant site, make sure there are no arrested martyrs, and that's what we're going to do. So watch yourself. Be careful. All right?"

"I will," I said.

Then I walked back across no-man's-land.

CHAPTER SIXTEEN

It happened a couple of hours later. Some cheers rose up from the mass of protesters, and a couple of hundred of them started marching across the open salt marsh, heading to the row of cops. They went in staggered lines, arm in arm, and about a dozen reporters and I trotted alongside, trying to keep up. It was worse for the television crews, who tried to maneuver across the slippery mud and grass and gullies while carrying their gear. As the line of protesters got closer and closer to the cops, in one seemingly practiced move, the cops removed their helmets, tugged on their gas masks, and put the helmets back on.

One of the reporters called out, "Oh, Christ, watch out!" and from the line of cops, two metal canisters flew out beyond them, landing on the grass, where they blew open in white clouds.

Tear gas.

Like an immediate flashback, my Department of Defense training from years ago sprang up from long-dormant memory cells. Tear gas. Also known as CS gas. The prevailing wind blew it right at the center mass of the protesters. There were screams, shouts, and I moved off to the left, getting away from the wind-driven clouds that drifted over the lines of demonstrators.

The clouds rolled over, they blew away, and the lines of demonstrators had collapsed. Some had run away, a few were still standing, but most were on their hands and knees, or collapsed on their sides. Then the police started to move, holding their batons lengthwise in both hands. They marched in formation, in tempo, and in a matter of seconds they were upon the protesters.

It was short, it was brutal, and it was hard to look at, especially since I knew my friend Diane Woods was there, in the middle of it. Some of the protesters tried to stand up, and the black-clad cops pushed them back. More shouts. More pushing. The people broke and staggered back to their original line as the cops moved as one, pushing, poking, and prodding. Even those who couldn't get up, who were disabled by the tear gas, were grabbed by their wrists and arms by the cops and dragged until they started moving, crawling. . . . The press people near me were taking photos, taking notes, and broadcasting what was going on. I caught the sharp tang of the tear gas, the smell of fear, and the stench of the salt marsh and mud and grass.

"Holy God," one of the reporters near me said. "Holy God."

My notebook was in my hand, along with a pen, but I didn't have to take any notes. I knew I would never forget what I was seeing, would never forget the shouts and screams and the police officers doing their jobs, as disagreeable as it was.

I shrugged off my knapsack, opened it up and pulled out a water bottle, and took a long swallow. Until I had drunk the water, I didn't realize how thirsty I had been. I finished off half the bottle and was still thirsty. I looked to the cops. In good order they had marched back to their previous position. Over at the mass of protesters, some had given up, had started straggling back to the woods line, and then—

I couldn't believe it. Another group had come out of the mass of antinuclear activists, arms linked, marching, and they were going slow, and they were singing. The wind shifted and I recognized the song.

"We shall overcome . . . we shall overcome . . ."

Something thudded deep in my chest. This had gone someplace different now, was something more than just an antinuclear demonstration in front of a New Hampshire nuclear power plant. No, this was something else. This was the power of the state opposing a group of its citizens. I didn't have that joking cynical feeling anymore about being here out on the salt marsh. Right now, I didn't know what to think.

More tear gas, more clashes, and the demonstrators fell back again, some sobbing, others falling down while some of their companions, wearing T-shirts over their coats marked with red crosses, poured water over their faces.

I drank some more water and watched what was going on before me, hoping this day would come to an end.

. . .

Tired from standing all morning long, and with the sun high up, warming my skin, I found a dry spot of marsh grass and sat down. I was close to the demonstrators, who were milling about, some singing, others talking, some huddling together in groups, hugging. From one affinity group I saw a young blond woman emerge and go over to a water dump of about a dozen half-gallon jugs of water, where she used one to wash her face. I got up quickly and approached her and said, "Haleigh."

She lifted her face. Her blond hair was soaked, and her eyes were red-rimmed and swollen. Her jeans and UNH sweatshirt were splattered with mud, and she had a pink ribbon fluttering from her right arm.

"Lewis," she said, her voice hoarse. "One hell of a day, isn't it?"

"That it is. How are you doing?"

She wiped at her eyes and face with the sleeve of her sweatshirt. "Okay . . . I guess. I mean, none of us thought we'd walk right in . . . but we thought we could get over the fence, in large enough numbers . . . oh, it's a hell of a mess. The cops . . . they're good at what they do."

"What's next?"

She coughed. "We try again."

"You think the third time's going to be the charm?"

Haleigh attempted a smile. "That's what we're here for."

I said, "Look, the cops aren't going to let you pass on through, singing gospel hymns, no matter how dedicated you might be. Don't you think you've done enough, Haleigh?"

She wiped at her face again. "No. Not enough. Never enough. We've marched, we've rallied, and we've come here together, Lewis. We're not going to give up—not today, not ever."

I said, "Haleigh, you're—"

"Please," she said. "Don't try to convince me otherwise. I know you've been places, seen things, done things. I know you probably think this is all silly and immature." She looked back at the mass of people, some of them lining up, ready to go at the police again. "We're doing what we think is right. No matter what the police or the government or anybody else thinks. We're doing what we think is right. Do you understand?"

I had a faint memory of being that age, of being so righteous, so self-assured. "I do."

A better smile this time. "Good." She reached into her jeans pocket and pulled out a length of pink ribbon. "I'd like to give this to you, if you don't mind."

"What does it mean?"

"It's the symbol of my affinity group," she said. "The Pink Panther Patrol. Since nuclear power isn't good for birds, people, or animals. Including pink panthers."

I took the ribbon, thought for a moment, and then slipped it through a knapsack strap. Maybe I was violating whatever journalistic boundary I was supposed to maintain by being a cool and neutral observer. But I saw she appreciated what I had done, and that was fine enough for me.

I said, "Your fellow antinukers might think I'm a professor or something."

"Or something," she said, "since everybody in the Pink Panther Patrol is female."

Then, a surprise. A quick peck on my cheek and she said, "Do your job, but be close to us this time. I think we're going to do it. Just you watch."

"All right," I said. "I'll be watching."

. . .

After all the planning and talking and discussion, it was the approaching tide that forced this last and hardest confrontation. Water was starting to ooze and trickle into the open cuts and gullies in the marshland, and from the intensity of the meetings going on among the diminished ranks of protesters, I got the feeling this was going to be their last stand. Or their last march. A tall bearded man stood apart from one group of activists and said, "We've got to stop debating! We've got to stop talking! There's no more time!"

A couple of people yelled back at him, and he pointed to the ocean and shouted, "That tide's coming in, no matter how you feel, how you decide! In a couple of hours, we're going to be knee-deep in water! The time is now!"

That last call seemed to galvanize the remaining demonstrators, and even though it was their third try, more people were lining up, linking their arms together. Some of them cast foul looks our way, to the members of the news media, and I had an idea of what they were thinking: They were putting everything on the line for what they believed in, and all we were doing was recording their pain and sacrifice, and for what?

For something called the news.

At the end of one line, I saw a group of college-aged women linked arm to arm, all of them wearing fluttering pink ribbons on their arms, and this bit of news was no longer just news to me. Someone I knew was up there on the front line, ready to face a long line of cops, and maybe at a different time and place, Haleigh and Diane could be friends of a sort, friendly neighbors and such, but now time and circumstance had made them opponents.

Now the protesters started marching, slower but more steadily, and the lines of people quickly widened as they marched, as if they were trying to outflank the formation of police officers, and it seemed like they might actually do it. With the rows of marchers expanding quickly to the left and the right, the ragged crowds of demonstrators engulfed us reporters. I tried to keep up, breathing hard, chest thumping along, the knapsack bouncing on my back. Off to the left a cameraman from one of the Boston television stations fell onto the mud and grass, and his correspondent—a young man in a fine-looking suit and wearing knee-length rubber boots—struggled to get him up off the ground. Ahead and ahead the long lines moved, and a woman nearby started singing a Christmas carol, of all things: "Joy to the World." Her voice was strong and sharp, and when she finished the first verse, she yelled out, "Sing! Come on, sing!"

She broke into "Hark, the Herald Angels," and other voices joined her, and through the moving mass of people, the dark line of police officers stretched out as well, and more canisters flew overhead, landing before us, bursting into tight white clouds. By now, though, most of the approaching activists had handkerchiefs over their faces, dipped in water or something else, and a few even had their own gas masks.

The line faltered, some fell, and the wind cast away more of the gas, and they kept on moving, moving ahead. A flash of a movie memory came to me, of seeing the epic *Gettysburg*, of the long line of Confederate troops moving up, marching, Pickett's doomed charge against the fortified Union lines, and then there were shouts and screams as the activists drove into the line of cops.

Chaos. Shouts. The cops no longer looked like American police officers but like uniformed and armed oppressors, a Third World aura about them, and they pushed back, pushed back, using their batons, pushing and swinging, and there were screams and yells. Some of the activists actually broke through the open line of cops, making their way to the fence line of the Falconer nuclear power plant. They ran, but they didn't get far, as a gate opened and reinforcements trotted out, and these had small canisters in their hands, and they sprayed in wide motions, spraying Mace into the faces and eyes of the demonstrators. Those few who had gotten beyond the police line fell or stumbled back.

In the melee I was in, the singing had stopped, and a couple of stronger ones started chanting: *"The whole world is watching! The whole world is watching! The whole world is watching!"*

I moved to the left, away from a knot of protesters who were pushing and pushing up against the cops, and I slipped on some mud, and that slip is what saved me.

Something hard punched against my back, and there was a sharp pain near my spine, like a bee sting. I fell to the ground and the hammer blow struck me again. I fell on my face and belly, rolled over, tried to see what cop was going after me with a baton.

I looked up, eyes tearing.

It was no cop.

The man was in jeans and a dirty gray windbreaker, and his face was hidden by a red bandanna. In his hands he held a thick pole of wood, and at the end of wood, hammered in, was a long metal spike. Though his face was hidden, there was merriment in his eyes, and I knew I had been with this man once before.

Henry, the man who had seized me after my visit with Curt Chesak, ready to finish the job.

He raised the pole with the metal spike at the end, and I kicked out, catching him in the shins, and he backed away with a yelp just as there was a soft *pop!* and we were engulfed in a cloud of tear gas.

· · ·

My eyes burned shut as I rolled and crawled. I willed myself not to breathe, but I couldn't help myself, and my lungs seized up, burning as well. The odor was bitter, pungent, and mucus started roaring through my sinuses and into my mouth. I coughed and coughed and spat and spat, and my chest burned. About me there were cries and coughs and the sounds of choking. I tried to crawl some more and buried my face into the mud and grass, the stench of the mud friendly and warm after the sharpness of the gas.

In a while there was a hand on my shoulder, and I pushed it away, and a woman's voice said, "It's all right, it's all right. Roll over, sir. We'll take care of you."

My eyes were still shut, and I rolled over, wincing at the pain between my shoulder blades and the pressure of my knapsack back there. Warm water was splashed across my face and a cloth moved it around, and more water came down and I blinked and sat up, coughed some more.

Kneeling before me was an older heavyset woman with a soft smile, her thick gray hair pulled back in a ponytail. She was in jeans and rubber boots, and over a dark blue sweatshirt she had on a very large white T-shirt that had a homemade red cross painted on it.

She offered me a paper cup of water, which I drank eagerly. "Thanks," I said. "Thank you . . . thank you very much."

"Glad to help," she said. She took the empty paper cup from my hand and folded it gently, then placed it in a large cloth sack. In front of her were some water jugs and an open satchel, with cloths and bandages and other medical supplies. Around us other people dressed in the same white T-shirt were keeping vigil with other people on the ground. At some distance away, the police officers had lined up again, at the ready.

"Are . . . are you a nurse? Or a doctor?"

She grinned, revealing a dimple on one side of her face. "No, just a volunteer. Part of the Quaker congregation from Porter. Here to observe . . . and to help. Are you feeling better?"

"Yes, yes I am," I said, and then I noticed that my butt was sopping wet. The tide was marching in. "Thank you again."

She started gathering her belongings and said quietly, "I saw you earlier, didn't I?"

"I don't know. Did you?"

She zippered shut her satchel, got up, and grabbed a water jug. "Yes, I'm sure of it. You were talking to a photographer about us, and what we were going to do. I'm pretty sure you made a smart-aleck comment about these people being an unorganized mob. Am I right?"

"I'm afraid you are," I said, my face still burning. "I'm sorry I said that about you."

She said, "No, that wasn't me you were talking to. I have nothing against nuclear power. Not at all. My uncle actually works over there at the power plant. I *am* against the power of the state using force against people. That's why my fellow Quakers and I are here. To help out. To bear witness. To protect the people where we can."

"Thanks again," I said. I wiped at my face with both hands and saw I was standing in about three inches of water.

As she started walking away, she pointed to the cops and the power plant and said, "If that's the opposite of being an unorganized mob, then you can have it. I want no part of it."

She walked to a couple of young women sitting in the mud and water, arms around each other, crying. She knelt down and went to work. I looked around, saw little groups here and there, but no longer was there a mass of people. It had all broken up. They were slowly slogging their way back to the woods, back to their encampments. The only sign of organization was the long line of police officers patiently standing, gas masks on and batons in their hands.

Diane was over there, Diane, my oldest and dearest friend.

I bent down to pick up my knapsack, saw the pink ribbon—torn and muddied—and started walking away as well, the knapsack in my hands.

I stopped after a moment, though. I looked down at my green canvas knapsack, at the two long tears in the back. My back started stinging as well. I ran my fingers through the rips, thought back to where I had stumbled. That length of wood with the spike at the end—if it had been driven into the base of my neck, it would have severed my spinal cord and I would have been a dead man, in there among the crowds of people and the police officers and the tear gas clouds.

Underneath my jacket was my 9 mm Beretta. Fat lot of good it had done me.

I resumed walking and looked around me. The protesters had scattered into small groups or lines of people slogging through the rising tide, heading to the higher ground marked by the tree line. I couldn't see Laura Toles or her son, Vic. I walked some more and heard loud voices. There. Off to the south. Kara Miles was arguing with three of her fellow activists. Hands were raised, fingers were pointed, and even this far away, I could see how scarlet Kara's face was.

I wondered if Diane was having a similar fight with her fellow police officers.

CHAPTER SEVENTEEN

Some long time later, I got back to my Ford Explorer, but the movement of people and slow traffic meant the usual fifteen-minute drive to Tyler stretched almost to an hour. The protesters that had been at the salt marsh had come back to Route 1 in Falconer and were now gathering at the main gate of the power plant for some sort of vigil, and I didn't care anymore. I just wanted to get home, which is what I did, by circling around on some back roads and getting to Tyler Beach, where there were some tourists and beachgoers, and no one carrying a sign, or a baton, or anything else.

As I was driving down High Street, about ten minutes away from home, my cell phone rang. On the other end was a woman, and after a brief conversation, I made a U-turn and headed back into the center of town.

I parked at the rear of the Tyler *Chronicle* building and walked in past the circulation department—usually one overworked man assisted by young men or women hired on a temporary basis—and went up past the piles of newspapers to the newsroom, which is just a collection of battleship gray desks clustered in the center of an open office area. It was late afternoon, and Paula Quinn was at her desk, rapidly typing away on a computer terminal.

She glanced up at me as I approached and gave me a quick smile. Her skin was pale, and it looked like she had lost some weight, but I was encouraged by the smile. "Have a seat, if you'd like," she said. "Thanks for stopping by to check in, and—Christ, what the hell happened to you?"

I sat down in the chair, stretching out my muddy feet. "Was in the middle of the demonstration, out in the salt marsh. Not high up with dry feet and free coffee like some journalists I know."

Paula resumed her typing. She had on a dark green turtleneck shirt and a gray sweater over it, and her fingers looked cracked and dry. "Yeah, lucky me and the others. Hold on—I just want to finish the story and find out what the hell happened to you."

"Deal," I said.

I took in the newsroom while Paula typed. There had been a time when the newspaper had several full-time reporters and photographers, but that time had gone away some time ago. Besides Paula, there were two other full-time reporters now, plus a number of stringers, usually bored housewives or recent college grads, all trying their hand at journalism, and usually failing.

"There," Paula said, slapping one more key. "Done and sent. How were things from your side of the fence?"

"Muddy. Rough. Lots of tear gas, lots of pushing around. Number of hurt people. You?"

"Some quiet. Like those northern congressmen and families gathering to watch the Battle of Bull Run from a distance. Looked pretty messy."

"It was."

She said, "I thought you were going to be on the plant property for today's demo."

"Me, too, but I got exiled by Ron Shelton. Seems like his corporate masters didn't like my last filing."

Paula started going through some papers on her desk. "Dropping the F-bomb about our Russian friends and blaming them for the protests from local residents—not really a good plan for developing community relations."

I looked at her working diligently to pile the papers into some sense of order, and I said, "How are you doing?"

"Better," she said, her voice flat.

"Really?"

"No, not really," she said, "but I want to stop feeling this way, I want to stop whining about it, and I want just to move on. You know? If I peed standing up, I'd say that I wanted to man up and get on with it. Womaning it up doesn't have the same ring to it. Whatever it is, I want to do it. I don't want to be afraid anymore."

"Paula—"

She held up a hand. "Enough about me. Please. What happened to you?"

"Police line was standing there, holding still, when the anti-nukers marched up to meet them. I was in the middle when both sides collided. Tear gas, batons, lots of pushing around—a real mess."

She said, "One of our better stringers was there, filed a report. I did the main story—and it looks like it's over, on their part at least. Word I hear is that the bulk of the regular demonstrators are heading home, but there's still a hard core out there, ready to take the stage."

"The Nuclear Freedom Front, right?"

Another pile of papers was set to rights. "You are correct, sir. The Front says it's their turn, either tomorrow or the day after—and that they don't intend to stop."

"Oh, that's wonderful," I said.

"Yeah," she said. "Hold on, I want to drop something off on Rollie's desk."

Paula got up and walked away, and I looked at my muddy boots. As she came back from the front of the newsroom she said, "Christ, Lewis, what happened to your back?"

"What do you mean?" I asked, turning my head.

She reached out and touched the rear of my jacket. "It's all torn up back here . . . and . . . Lewis, there's blood. What happened?"

What to say? The truth, I guess. "Somebody among the demonstrators took offense at your humble correspondent and took a swing at me."

Her fingers were still playing with the rear of my coat. "With what?"

"A length of wood. With a spike at the end."

Paula's hands were on the collar of my coat. "Off. Right now."

"Paula—"

"I see blood back there, bud, and you're not leaving here until I take a look. Now. Up and off."

I stood up and shrugged off my coat, wincing some, and then undid my Bianchi shoulder holster with my Beretta automatic pistol, and Paula's eyes widened at seeing my weapon, but she didn't say a word. I took off a pullover sweater and a long-sleeve sport shirt, and Paula said, "All right. Walk this way."

She went off to the side of the room, where there was a unisex bathroom, and she said, "Come on. Let me give you a bit of a wash."

"What's it look like back there?"

"Heavy scratch," she said. "Could be worse."

I stood still and looked at myself in the mirror, saw the tired eyes, the damp short hair, and I winced again as Paula wet a paper towel with some warm water. She gently washed at my back and did it again and again. "There," she said softly. "Looks better. Let me put some antibacterial cream on it."

Underneath the mirror was a plastic first aid kit, and she opened it up and took out a tube and then spread the cool cream on my back. "All right," she said. "One big Band-Aid later and you're all set."

"Thanks, Paula. You've got great hands."

She laughed. "So I've been told."

Paula closed up the first aid kit and replaced it on the wall. Then, in the small confines of the brightly lit room, I looked at her and she looked at me. We stared at each other, and there I was, standing shirtless before a woman I had once been intimate with, a woman who had now performed first aid on me.

She stepped closer, put a hand on my shoulder. "Good to see you."

"Always good to see you."

Paula came closer and I let her, and then the phone rang. And rang. And rang. She smiled, lowered her eyes, and brushed past me back out to the main office. I followed her and got dressed, looking at the rear of my jacket, knowing it was going in the trash when I got home.

On the phone, Paula said, "Okay. Okay. When was it found? Really? Okay . . . thanks, you're doing a good job. What else can you tell me? Unh-hunh, unh-hunh, okay . . . I'll meet you at the police station as soon as I can. Depending on what's left of the demonstrators. Thanks."

She hung up the phone and gathered her purse, reporter's notebook, and coat. I said, "What's up?"

"As if we don't have enough going on—there's been a murder in Falconer. Lucky for me, my stringer was at the police station when the news broke."

"What happened?"

She put on her coat, got her keys. "Body found floating in one of the streams in the salt marsh. Bullet wound to the back of the head. A couple of antinukers got lost trying to get out of the salt marsh and found the body. Looks like it's been out there for a couple of days."

"Male or female?"

"Male, guy in his early twenties—and he was wearing some pins for the NFF."

Even though I was dressed, I now felt colder than I had in a long time. I recalled my time the other night in the marsh, when I had escaped from the shooter, the man called Henry. After he tried to nail me, and after I escaped, I'd heard one more gunshot, at a distance.

Yeah. Made sense. The man called Henry had shot the man called Todd, to eliminate a witness and—

"Lewis?"

"Yes?"

"I really need to go—and . . . will you walk me to my car?"

"Absolutely," I said.

Outside I walked Paula to her red Toyota Camry and watched as she got in and started the engine. As she backed out, she blew me a kiss, which I cheerfully returned. I kept watching as she merged into Route 1 traffic, and then I got in my own vehicle and headed home.

At home, it was time for a clothes dump and a shower and turning up the thermostat for the furnace, and I heated up a can of corned beef hash in a big black iron skillet, sprinkled some grated cheese and some ketchup on the top, and ate the hot and greasy food and enjoyed every bit of it. Then I made a call to Annie Wynn and got her voice mail, and then called somebody else and left a message on his voice mail, and then I went upstairs to my office and wrote my daily contribution to *Shoreline* magazine.

With this all squared away, I went downstairs and switched on the television and surfed through the news channels, looking at the coverage of the protests, and I had a little shock of recognition when I saw myself standing with the demonstrators. How about that. I had a quirky moment of humor, too, thinking that if Denise Pichette-Volk had been watching this particular newscast, she would have seen me at work.

Then I watched a bit more, and saw the coverage from the station over in Manchester, which had a breaking news segment from Falconer about the discovery of the murdered young man in the marshland. Not much to report—Paula had more information than they did back in her office—and I lay still on the couch, thinking. I had a good idea that the man who had shot Bronson Toles was either the same man who had tried to do me harm or someone connected to him. Either way, there was a dead young man that I was connected to.

So I was thinking, *Contact the Falconer cops or not?*

I got cold, drew the comforter around me, and remembered my talk with Annie. Too much going on with her and her senator for me to stir things up.

So no, no police contact. Not now.

Snug in the comforter, the low drone of the oil furnace heating up my cold beachfront house, I fell asleep.

During the night the sharp ring of the phone woke me up, and I stumbled around in the dark until I retrieved the receiver. A male voice was on the other end, the same that had called when Annie was visiting. He started up with a threat, and I wearily said, "I've been threatened by better, jerk," and hung up the phone, unplugged it, and then went upstairs and to bed.

Next to me, underneath a pillow that still had the scent of Annie, I placed my loaded pistol.

In the morning I went to Blythe's Breakfast Nook, up on Atlantic Avenue in the town of North Tyler. It was situated on an outcropping of granite that had good views of the Isles of Shoals out on the ocean and the nearby waves coming into a part of North Tyler that didn't have any beaches at all, though on some warm days, fortunate viewers could see harbor seals sunning themselves on the rocks. This day, however, most of what we saw was the gray Atlantic Ocean rolling into some wet boulders, the sky and the distance obscured by low clouds.

I sat with a window view across from my breakfast guest for the morning, Felix Tinios, resident of said North Tyler, security consultant, former inhabitant of Boston's North End, and current employee of Joe Manzi, head of the New England Trade Union Council.

Felix had on pressed jeans, black shoes, and a black turtleneck sweater, and as usual, he looked well showered and coiffed. He looked at me oddly as he sat down and said, "Carrying, aren't you."

I had on a Harris tweed jacket over a blue oxford shirt and khaki slacks, and I said, "Yes, I am. Guess I need a new tailor."

He laughed and picked up a menu. "No, you need a new attitude, Lewis."

"What do you mean?"

Felix opened the menu and said, "You have a look about you, of being uncomfortable. Like you're at some high-society dinner, sitting next to the hostess, a beautiful Brazilian model with stunning cleavage, trying desperately not to loudly pass gas."

"Thanks for the image."

"You're welcome," he said. "Still, I wouldn't worry too much. You only have to worry about cops with sharp eyes and others with . . . a professional background."

"Lucky me."

We ordered, and it took only a few minutes for our meals to come out: eggs Benedict for Felix, pancakes with sausage links for me. When we finished eating he dabbed at his lips with a cloth napkin and said, "What's up?"

"Number of things."

"I've got some time, so go on."

I folded my hands on the white linen tablecloth. "The shooting the other day of Bronson Toles. In Falconer. You hear anything that's not been made public?"

One of his eyebrows rose. "Lewis . . . the type of way these things were settled in my circles—back in the day—was either a one-way trip out to Boston Harbor or two taps to the back of the head. A sniper shot like that . . . sorry, out of my area."

I said, "Sure. Your circles. What about the circles you're currently traveling in?"

He picked up a tall glass of orange juice and champagne, took a healthy sip. "The union boys? Please. That's a bit too direct, even for them."

"Like the other day, at the rally at the fishing co-op, when some of those fine union brothers beat the crap out of some college students?"

He shrugged. "You're a student of history. You know how unions and union members respond when they feel their livelihoods are threatened. Not condoning it, not explaining it, just telling you as a fact."

"Sure," I said. "Here's another fact. The local economy is rotten, and will remain rotten for the foreseeable future. Then a winning lottery ticket arrives in the form of the federal government and the owners of Falconer Station. Thousands of good-paying union jobs, ready to start, except for some antinukers raising a fuss. Those antinukers are led by a local charismatic leader. They're pretty much united, pretty much know what they want to do. Then the leader gets his head blown off."

Felix said, "That's the problem with being a leader. You stand apart. You become conspicuous. You become an easy target."

"Sure," I said. "So if you're a union fellow who's not too tightly wrapped, and you think one guy is standing between you and good jobs for you and your brother and sister union members . . . quite a temptation."

"I'm sure the state police have looked into that, Lewis."

"There's always more that can be done."

"What do you want me to do? Hmm? Tick off my employers by asking such . . . insensitive questions?"

"No," I said. "I'll ask the insensitive questions. All I want you to do is to get me a meeting with Joe Manzi. The sooner, the better."

"For what purpose? To ask him his opinion of local prevailing-wage laws?"

"Not hardly," I said. "I want to poke, prod, ask questions about him and his followers. See if I can shake things up."

"Shake things up so . . ."

"I think you know my techniques, Felix," I said.

He frowned slightly. "Yeah. I do. You want to stir things up so that the shooter makes his presence known."

On my back the bandage itched. "Either he or his friend has already made their presence known. What I want now is a name and an address."

"Hence you're carrying a weapon."

"Hence, yes," I said.

"Risky work."

"But necessary," I said.

"Why?"

"Why what?"

He cocked his head. "Look, did that tear gas out there screw up your head? You're asking me to set you up so you can, quote, stir things up, unquote. So I want to know why . . . why is this important for you? Simple question. Don't you think?"

In the warm and comfortable confines of Blythe's Breakfast Nook, it seemed odd, and I knew it, but I cleared my throat and said, "Paula. Paula Quinn."

That got his attention. "The reporter from the *Chronicle*? The one I saw you with at the rally in Falconer a few days back? That Paula Quinn?"

"Yes."

"Thought you were still out and about with Annie Wynn."

"I am."

"Sounds complicated."

I said, "She was on the stage with Bronson Toles when he got shot. She's . . . been different ever since then. Traumatized. Shaky. She feels like the shooter is out there and may come after her, take care of business. She feels like a target . . . and I don't like her feeling that way."

"So you want to make it right?"

"I do."

Felix grinned. "Hell of a hobby you got there, Lewis."

"One of several."

A young waitress in a short black skirt and a tight white blouse came over, dropped off the check, and offered a wide grin for Felix, nothing for me, and then walked out. Felix eyed her for a moment and then backed out of his chair.

"Give me a couple of minutes," he said. "I'll see what I can do."

He walked out of the dining room, cell phone in hand, and I looked at the check and put my American Express card down on the slip. I watched the waves rolling in, and the waitress came by, picked up the bill and my credit card. In a couple of minutes,

Felix came back, joined by the waitress, who put the check down in front of me.

Felix said, "To my surprise, it's set. Five o'clock this afternoon, at Uncle Paul's Diner in Salisbury. All right with you?"

"Perfect," I said. "How did it work out?"

A slight shrug. "He's pleased with my service so far. So I guess I caught him in a good mood. Oh, and one more thing."

"What's that?"

"I didn't tell him your real reason for seeing him. So do what you have to do."

"Not a problem," I said.

I signed the check and found a little surprise: Slipped in between the paper and the credit card receipt was a business card for the restaurant, and on the back was scrawled the name of our waitress—Amanda—and a Tyler phone number. I slid the business card across to Felix and said innocently, "I believe this is for you."

He picked up the card, smiled. "I believe you're right."

"How do you do it?"

"Do what?"

"Now it's your turn to be dense," I said. "You know what I mean."

The smile remained on his face as he made the card disappear. "Must be my rugged good looks."

"What am I," I asked, "the proverbial chopped liver?"

Felix got up from the table. "No, not rugged enough."

"So says you," I said, getting up as well.

CHAPTER EIGHTEEN

I spent a while later that day running errands, picking up my mail at the Tyler post office, and doing some grocery shopping, and once again my day was interrupted by the chiming of my cell phone. Surprised who was at the other end, I agreed to a quick meeting near my house, in the parking lot of the Lafayette House.

When I got to the parking lot, it was about half full, and there was a slim man with eyeglasses standing in front of a dark blue Saab sedan. I pulled into an empty spot and said, "Mr. Shelton."

Ron Shelton, spokesman for the Falconer nuclear power plant, seemed to blush. He had on dress shoes, gray slacks, and a thin tan down windbreaker. "Hey, Lewis. You can leave the Mr. Shelton aside."

"Oh," I said. "Does that mean all is forgiven with your evil corporate masters?"

"No, it doesn't," he said. "Although they're not really evil. Just misguided." It seemed like he was trying to make a joke, but he wasn't smiling.

"Good for them," I said. "Why the offense over what I reported?"

"Ugh," Ron said. "Please don't remind me. I almost got suspended over that little comment of yours."

"Hate to disagree, Ron, but the little comment wasn't mine. It was yours. I merely reported it."

"Yeah, all right, I'll give you that one. Thing is, I really didn't think you'd report it."

"You thought wrong," I said. "It was a newsworthy comment."

"Too newsworthy," Ron said. "My boss didn't mind that much, but his boss, and her boss, raised holy hell, and since you were at the plant site the day before that F-bomb was printed and attributed to a utility official, and I was the only person to meet with you—my boss stepped in for me, said you were left alone in the visitors' center for a while, could have talked to almost anyone."

"Nice history lesson," I said, "but why this meet? Could have told me this over the phone."

Ron rubbed one hand over the thin brown hair on the top of his head. "I could have . . . a few years ago, but now . . ."

The whole sense of him changed, seemed more cautious. "What's up?"

"Hunh?"

"What do you mean, a few years ago?" I recalled something I had read back then and said, "The utility takeover. Four years ago."

Ron nodded. "That's right. When we were locally owned, we had ties to the towns and the state capitals. Even the top guys and gals came from around here. When that Florida consortium took over, everything changed. Including the live-and-let-live attitude. There's a real cutthroat attitude among some of the higher-ups about keeping track of and destroying one's enemies—and that's why I'm here."

"Because?"

"Because you raised a stink and some folks are interested in you, and from second- and third-hand accounts, I've learned that they find you interesting because . . . you used to work for the Department of Defense, didn't you?"

"Some years ago," I said.

"That's what got their interest. That you were at the Pentagon, and that they couldn't learn any more than that. So consider this my apology for getting you banned from the plant site. Some folks with lots of money and sharp elbows are looking at you."

"Your odd apology accepted," I said. "So that's why you're here, face-to-face, instead of talking over a phone. You don't want somebody's boss's boss listening in to what's going on."

"Hate to admit it, but you're right," he said.

"Not often I get told that," I said.

He smiled. "You sound like my sister, Clara. Always sharp, always joking."

"Your sister the singer?"

"That's right."

"Last time we talked, you said your sister was an up-and-coming singer, playing local clubs and halls. She still singing?"

Ron frowned. "Sort of. She's married now, kids, and she's the cantor at the temple in Porter. She could have made it, but . . . well, let's just say some of the people you meet in the local clubs would make sharks look like guppies. The bastards. You know, I always thought the proudest moment of my life would be to buy a CD of her music, to see her on one of those national television talent shows—but it never happened." He glanced at his watch. "Sorry. Gotta get back to the plant. We've got another demo coming up soon."

"After yesterday's battles, I didn't think the protesters would be up for another round."

"They're not," Ron said. "It's the Nuclear Freedom Front's turn. They promise to do what their rivals didn't do. Enter the plant site and shut us down."

"They sound confident."

"Yeah, they sound deranged, but that didn't come from me." He glanced at his watch again. "Anything else?"

A number of anything elses were jostling for attention, but one came right to mind. "How many people have you got working at Falconer?"

"Between full-time staff and contractors, about eight hundred."

"Out of those eight hundred, how many are avid hunters? Who use high-powered rifles?"

"Not funny," he said, his face set as he walked back to his Saab.

"Wasn't meant to be," I said.

"Whatever," Ron said, opening the car door. "I'll give you this, though. I do know that detectives from the state police have been talking to security, going through personnel records—looking for suspects. That's it."

"Good enough," I said. "Thanks."

At home I put the groceries away, checked the mail, and looked over the copy of today's Tyler *Chronicle*. There was a big story with photographs of the previous day's demonstration, but since I had been there, I didn't care to reread what I'd felt, tasted, and smelled. Instead, I looked down at the bottom of the page and saw the story I had been looking for. It had been co-written by Paula and the stringer, a woman named Melanie Reisinger.

I glanced through the story. Falconer police and state police were investigating the discovery of a murder victim found in one of the stream tributaries in the southern part of the salt marsh, near where I had spent that long night flailing around.

I sighed. The victim was one John Todd Thomas, twenty-two, a graduate student in foreign relations from Colby College. His father was retired from government service, one way of hiding his work with the Central Intelligence Agency. His mother was a high school teacher in Arlington, Virginia.

John Todd Thomas. The young man who had escorted me to see Curt Chesak, and who had been gunned down by my adversary, whoever the hell he was.

Cause of death was a gunshot wound.

I folded up the paper, left it open to that page, and put it on the counter in the kitchen, where it would mock me every time I walked by.

A few hours later, I parked next to Uncle Paul's Diner in Salisbury, Massachusetts, the community right across the border from Falconer. The diner was painted dark blue, with its name inscribed in yellow Gothic letters. Salisbury is about the same size as Falconer, but without the tax burdens of its immediate neighbor to the north or the tax benefits of having a multi-billion-dollar power plant in the backyard.

I got out of my Ford and went into the diner. On the glass doors were various stickers and such, including one for the local Kiwanis Club, which met here every Thursday at noon. I was was struck by the reassuring and comforting smells of cooked food and grease.

On either side of me were booths, and in front of me was a long wooden counter with round stools; beyond that was the kitchen area. Off to the left, at the back of the diner, was Felix Tinios, sitting by himself, and he nodded at me as I went closer. Two booths beyond Felix was Joe Manzi, also sitting by himself, and in the booth behind Joe were two heavyset men wearing the nylon jackets of the New England Trade Union Council. One of the two men I recognized as being the unsuccessful gatekeeper from the other day at the fishing cooperative, the one who had tried to keep Paula and me from going inside.

Joe stood up, extending a hand, which I shook. Despite the reputation he had for being a champion of the working class who had it pretty easy, his hand was strong and rough. His face was bright red, his dark hair slicked back, and he was solidly built, with wide shoulders that seemed to take up most of the booth.

"Cole? Lewis Cole?" he asked, his voice a bit raspy.

"Yes," I said, "and thanks for seeing me on such short notice."

He looked past me for a second, in the direction of Felix. "Well, you come with a good recommendation. I've trusted Mr. Tinios with a lot these past few weeks, and if he says you're okay, then you're okay."

I pulled out my reporter's notebook and said, "That's nice to hear, but whatever happens, don't blame Felix."

The smile was still on his face, but there was a suspicious look about his eyes. "You think this isn't going to go right?"

"Not at all," I said. "Just want to be prepared."

"Hah," Joe said. "Just like the Boy Scouts."

"Sure. Like the Boy Scouts."

So I started off slow and polite, asking him all the basic questions about his upbringing, his work in the trade unions, and how he got to be head of the New England Trade Union Council. He answered them with the practiced ease of someone who was used to being questioned and had ready-made answers for everything.

Well, I thought, *most everything . . .*

"Can I ask you some questions about the violence?"

"What violence?" he asked with an innocent tone of voice.

"Ah," I said, looking down at my notes. "A few days ago I was at a rally, at the Yankee Fisherman's Cooperative. Saw you talk there for a bit before a couple of antinukers jumped up and started protesting. Last I saw, they were getting hammered by some of your fellow union members."

I could hear murmuring from behind Joe's booth, from his two companions, but Joe didn't seem to mind. "That might be your memory. I just remember that they were interrupting a meetin' that they had no right to interrupt. They were disturbing the peace, they were interfering with our peaceable right of assembly. They were the ones who started it, not us."

"Still, they were beat up, weren't they?"

More murmurs from behind Joe. "They were jostled around some, but yeah, maybe they got tuned up a bit. Why not?"

"Why not let the cops handle it?" I asked, pen still in hand.

"You were there, right? You know how crowded it was. Besides, it was our place, and our time to speak. What, we should have waited five or ten minutes for a couple of cops to work their way through the crowd to get up onstage? Let those clowns have the floor? Why in hell should we do that, then?"

"Oh, I don't know," I said. "Maybe a little waiting would show a willingness not to go to the fists right off the bat."

He leaned a bit over the booth's light orange tabletop. "Look. Unions and their brothers and sisters didn't get here, and get what was owed them, by being nice, by lettin' people step over them, talk over them. Okay? They did it by voting, by organizing and yeah, sometimes, by doing a little direct action. Maybe that was wrong. I'll admit it. But you know what? Since those creeps got tossed out in the parking lot, roughed up a little bit, maybe them and their friends will think twice about crashing a gathering like that and trying to take over the stage."

I looked at his sharp eyes and said, "You folks really don't like those activists, do you."

He snorted. "Here's a story for you, and how come this story never gets out in the paper? Hunh? Who are those protesters out there, anyway?"

"They'd say they're just concerned citizens, that's all," I said. "Petitioning their government and their neighbors."

"Hah. Citizens. I'll tell you who they are. High school students or college students. Or dropouts. Or senior citizens with their brains a bit scrambled. Or professional leftists or people who just love to join each other for a party and a good time and to tell each other how much they miss Vietnam or Woodstock."

I said, "I saw some of them yesterday. They were getting tear-gassed, shoved around, pepper-sprayed. Didn't look like a party. Or a good time."

"So you say," he said, "but on the news, it looks like a ragged band of losers. And you know what?" Now his voice was getting heated. "Let's say you're one of my union brothers, a guy trying to raise a family. You've been on welfare for six or eight months, or living off whatever savings you got. Or you're a union sister, a single mom, trying to raise a couple of kids on your own. Then you get word from your union hall. If a couple more federal agencies just sign off on a couple of permits, then, boom, the hiring is going to start up again."

I said, "I think I know where this is going."

"Maybe you do, but I'm gonna tell you anyway. They get word that hiring is gonna start, good jobs at good wages. Maybe they don't have a college degree, but they're smart where it counts, in their craft, whether it's welding or painting or carpentry. Then just as the news gets good, the Russkies act like the idiots they are, the feds get cold feet, and these pampered high school and college kids come out of the woodwork, ready to march around, smoke dope, and get laid at night in their tents. One big fucking party. And if the second unit gets canceled, they can go home and tell their trust-fund moms and dads how special they were, while thousands of workers out there across New England look to see when their food stamp eligibility runs out."

I was scribbling so fast that my hand nearly cramped. He paused, his face even more red, and I knew he was losing patience with me, so I had just one more thing to ask him, which I had the feeling would set him off like a vial of nitroglycerin dropped from the top of a building.

"You've made a good point, about how your workers don't particularly like the activists," I said. "When it comes to the shooting of Bronson Toles, did—"

Surprise of surprises, he didn't explode, or try to throttle me, or stomp out. He just held up a callused hand and said, "Sure. Easy excuse. Pin it on the nutso union guy. Look, Lewis, there's a hell of a lot of difference between roughing up a couple of college kids who jump up on your stage and try to interrupt a news conference and blowing off some character's head. What the hell would that gain us? Nothing, that's what. In fact, the state police came by and some detective, Italian guy . . ."

"Renzi," I said. "Detective Renzi."

"Yeah, that's right. He talked to me and my leadership council about the shooting, and I said, have at it. Here's a membership list. Talk to anyone you want. Anybody gives you grief, talk to us and we'll bring 'em in to talk to you. We don't have anything to hide."

"So did the state police do just that?"

He said, "Talk to the cops. I don't want to say anything to screw up their investigation. But c'mon, think about it. What kind of benefit would it be if it happened that one of our brothers whacked that antinuker? You think if one of my guys got arrested, that it would be a good thing? Hell, no. It'd just piss off the antinukers and anybody who was on their side. Plus, it'd also piss off those folks that are on our side, like the businesses lining up to get the contracts if the licensing goes through. So if that's what you're driving at, Mr. Cole, that one of our guys shot down that antinuker, forget it."

"You sound pretty confident," I said.

"Confident, sure," he said, "but hell, not one hundred percent. Maybe somebody out there with a grudge against Toles, or a score to settle, or something to do with the unions and protesters, some nutcase, okay. I'll give you that. But we're a pretty tight-knit group, Mr. Cole, and I can almost give you a one hundred percent assurance we had nothing to do with Toles getting killed."

I wrote some more in my notebook, and he said, "That's it, isn't it."

"Excuse me?"

He grinned, leaning back against the fake wood seating. "All those polite questions earlier, about me and where I grew up, and my first job, and my first union elections, that was just a setup. The real meat of what you were looking for, it was all about Bronson Toles getting murdered. Right?"

"I like to be thorough," I said.

"Yeah," Joe replied, looking at his wristwatch, "and I like being prompt for my next meeting. So if you'll pardon me, we're done here."

"I guess we are," I said, folding my notebook shut. "Thanks for your time."

"Good luck in whatever the hell it is you're doing," he said, and behind him I saw one of his two companions making a call on his cell phone. I walked out of Uncle Paul's Diner, with Felix Tinios glancing at me with a bemused look on his face, gathering up his coat, ready to do his job, as I was wrapping mine up.

I got into my Ford Explorer, started her up, and backed out onto the street. It was dusk, and my plan was to head back home to Tyler, look at my notes, and write something vaguely interesting and noncontroversial for Denise Pichette-Volk down there at *Shoreline*.

That was my plan.

Funny thing about plans. They often don't take other people and interests into consideration.

CHAPTER NINETEEN

I traveled north a bit on Route 1, the traffic sparse at this time of night, and up ahead were some flashing amber lights. I saw a pickup truck with the logo of the Salisbury Public Works Department straddling the road, with a man in a reflective orange vest directing me off to a side road with a flashlight with an orange cone at the end of its lens. I made a turn to the right, down a country road with no streetlights and not much in the way of houses. I'd driven about a hundred yards when a car pulled out and got in front of me. Right about then, glancing at my rearview mirror, I spotted a set of headlights behind me, accelerating.

Then I braked, for the car in front of me started slowing down just as the one behind me kept on speeding up, and in about fifteen seconds—and about the time I recalled Joe Manzi's buddies had been working their cell phones—I was boxed in. The car in front of me, an old Chevrolet Impala with a dented trunk, slowed down, as did the vehicle behind me, a dark blue Ford pickup truck, and then I had to hit the brakes hard as the Impala in front of me and the Ford behind me came to a stop.

Despite what was going on, I had to admire their technique. I unzipped my jacket, waited.

The Impala's door opened, and a man came out carrying a tire iron. He came up to me, and in my side view mirror, I saw another man get out and come in my direction, also carrying something.

I rolled down my window. Their second mistake of the evening. They should have flanked me, on either side of my Ford, because I wouldn't be able to keep my eye on both of them. This way, coming at me on the same side . . . they just made my task that much easier.

I decided to open the door and get out.

Yes, their first mistake of the evening was forcing me over.

I stepped out, and the man in front called, "Did we tell you to get out, asshole?"

"I guess you didn't," I said, and he said, "Damn straight," and with a sharp blow of the tire iron, he smashed my left headlight.

I turned and saw that the other guy approaching had a baseball bat in his hands, and I recognized him as the unsuccessful gatekeeper from the other day. He called out, "I knew you was going to be trouble the moment I saw you, back at the fishing co-op, you asshole."

I said, "Then you're a perceptive fellow."

I kept my head moving, one to the other, one to the other, and the guy with the tire iron decided to take one more whack at the broken headlight, like poking at a sore tooth or something. The man with the baseball bat said, "We heard the questions you were asking Joe back there at the diner, we know what kind of jerk you are. So we're here to tell you you're not gonna write any story about the unions, you got it? We've had enough with the out-of-towners raising hell, with the newspaper reporters raising hell, with the TV stations getting all soft and moist about those poor protesters. It ends here tonight, got it?" To emphasize his point, he rapped the side of my Ford.

"Ever hear of the First Amendment?" I asked, keeping my head moving, back and forth, back and forth. The guy with the tire iron was standing still by the left front fender.

Baseball bat man laughed. "Ever hear of getting your head

busted? You will, 'cause it's gonna happen, right now, and there's no wop around to save your ass like last time."

I felt like sighing. So it would have to come to this. I reached under my coat, pulled out my 9mm Beretta, and said, "Funny thing, guys, Italians sometimes do show up when you really do need them."

There was a round in the chamber, so I didn't have to work the action, but I did pull back the hammer, so it made a loud and satisfying click. I turned to the guy up front and said, "Drop the tire iron. Hands behind your head, and get over there with your friend."

Another turn, and I said, "Baseball bat, on the ground, now."

With my pistol out, the whole atmosphere changed, and so did the demeanor of my new best friends. The guy up front dropped the tire iron with a loud clang, and he shuffled over to his buddy and said to me, "Look, let's be reasonable here, okay? We were just funnin' with you, that's all, and—"

"Quiet," I said. "Just keep your mouth shut."

Now, with them standing side by side, it was easier to cover them. Baseball bat man, without the bat, looked slumped and smaller, and he said, "Pal, look, we were just—"

"Shhh," I said. "Please don't insult me. You've just threatened me, but insulting me . . . just making it worse. So do be quiet— and I'm not your pal. Got it?"

The one on the left nodded, but the one on the right stood there, legs quivering a bit.

I kept the pistol aimed at the gatekeeper. "Joe sent you after me?"

"Christ, no," he said.

"Who was the Public Works guy out there, directing me down here?"

"Donnie, my cousin. He owes me one, for something I did for

him last year . . . Christ, leave him out of it, okay? Don't want him to lose his job. 'Bout the only member of my family's got a reasonable job this year."

In the sharpness of what was going on, with the Italian-made pistol in my hand and with the two men in front of me, I suppose I should have been frightened, or stoked up, or angry. Instead, I almost felt sorry for them. "One more question," I said. "You tell me the truth, then we can all go home and forget this ever happened."

The guy on the right looked relieved, but then looked suspicious. "Suppose you don't think we're tellin' the truth?"

"Then you both better do a good job convincing me," I said.

"Go on," the first one said. "What do you want to know?"

"You heard what Joe said, back at the diner, about the shooting of Bronson Toles. Was that straight up?"

"What do you mean?" the second one asked.

The first one interrupted and said, "Yeah, that was straight up. Nobody knows nothing about that guy's shooting."

That was a double negative, but I wasn't going to press him. "Tell me more."

With hands still up in the air, he said, "When news got out about that shooting, Joe and his buddies on the council, they went ape shit. Said if it came out a union guy was involved, could croak the Falconer Unit Two deal for good. Said if a union guy did do it, best we give 'em up ourselves before the cops found out, try to salvage something. But nobody knew anything. Christ, let me tell you, somebody made a shot like that and got away with it . . . no way he could keep it quiet. He'd have to brag about it. Human nature. So yeah, Joe was straight up. Mister, I don't know who plugged that creep, but he wasn't a union guy."

I thought about that for a moment, then stepped over and kicked at the tire iron, so it fell into a nearby drainage ditch.

"You," I said, pointing to the chatty one. "Do the same to the baseball bat. Give it a swift kick."

His booted foot lashed out, and the bat spun around and went into the same ditch. I said, "This is how it's going to be. The two of you are going to walk around, in a wide berth, and climb into that Impala and drive off. You drive down that road until I can't see your taillights. Got it? Minute I don't see your taillights, then I'm out of here."

The second man started to move, and I said, "Wait, I'm not quite through yet. If I still see taillights, or if you try something funny like making a U-turn or anything else, then I'm going to shoot out the four tires in this pickup truck, and then for good measure, I'll put a round into the front and rear windshield and empty the rest of the clip into your engine. Think your insurance company will cover all of that?"

The first man shook his head. "No, they won't."

"Good. Now get moving, and as an extra bonus, I don't expect to see or hear from you ever again, unless you want me to tell Joe what fine fellows he has working for him and threatening people for a hobby."

They kept their mouths shut, and they walked out a bit in the road before getting into the Impala. The engine started up after three tries, and then the car slowly accelerated down the road. I waited, and then it went around a soft bend, and the taillights disappeared.

I took a deep breath, gently lowered the hammer on my Beretta, and got back into my Ford. I suppose I should have done the *muy macho* thing and demanded payment for the broken headlight, but I didn't want to push things with these guys on the edge, frantic about their futures, frantic about their jobs, and lashing out at the nearest target they had.

So I would consider the smashed headlight payment for the information I had just gotten.

Some payment. That broken headlight was going to end up costing me a lot more, and in a very short span of time.

I made a U-turn on the country road and went back up to Route 1, where the way was clear, and I made a right, heading back to New Hampshire. About two minutes' worth of driving later, I crossed over the border and was back in my home state, and in my mind, I was composing a story that I could send Denise's way about Joe Manzi and his point of view on the construction of Falconer Unit 2. It wouldn't be as sexy or as compelling as the previous demonstration story, but it would at least be something, and hopefully would keep her editorial demands satisfied.

This part of Route 1 was crowded with pawnshops, fried food outlets, gas stations, and convenience stores, plus the usual big box stores selling lumber or appliances. About ninety seconds back into my home state, it all went wrong, very quickly.

In my rearview mirror, flashing blue lights quickly filled my vision, and I pulled over, slowing down and putting my Ford into park, right next to a Kentucky Fried Chicken outlet. As I fumbled in my glove box for my registration, I knew instantly what had happened: An alert Falconer cop had seen me drive by with a busted headlight.

Damn. It meant that the bill for that broken headlight was going to be larger than I'd thought.

With registration in hand, I dug out my wallet, pulled out my license, and then placed both pieces of paper on the dashboard, and then put my hands on the steering wheel, at the ten o'clock and two o'clock positions, so they were both visible. In past talks with Diane Woods over a good meal or even better glass of wine, she had always told me that cops hate traffic stops more than anything else for the potential of bad things happening very quickly.

So I waited.

And waited.

Flashing blue lights still behind me, the headlights of the cruiser blinking off and on. So what the heck was going on back there? Traffic going up and down Route 1 slowed as it passed by me, and I was sure the passing drivers were wondering what crime I had committed.

The crime of being concerned, I thought, and then going down some odd paths to comfort someone I cared about.

I jumped in my seat as I heard a loud burst of static, and then a P.A. system in the parked police cruiser behind me kicked into action.

"Driver!" a metallic voice called out. "This is the police! Open your driver's side window at once! Do it now!"

I turned and looked back, wondering if this was some sort of joke. In Tyler . . . maybe, since I knew a number of the cops through my friendship with Diane. But Falconer? I knew a few of the cops and the police chief by sight, but none of them were my friends.

"Driver!" the voice came back. "Open your window, now!"

I didn't like it, but I did just that, powering down the window.

"Driver! Put both hands out of the window! Show me your hands!"

I was tasting something bitter and foul as I put my hands out of the window. The cop or cops back there were upset about me or something I had done, but I didn't know what. The two union hoys back there? Very unlikely. They were no doubt angry with me, but not angry enough to call the Falconer cops on me.

"Driver! Slowly and carefully, open your door! Do it now!"

I reached down with one hand, opened the door, and swung it wide. Another burst of static, and the unseen Falconer police officer called out, "Driver! Slowly leave the vehicle, hands up in the air, and stand with your back to me!"

My back started to itch as I got out, knowing that at least one cop back there had a weapon trained on me, so I was conscious of following their instructions. I was sure this was a mistake, but I wasn't going to give anyone a chance to escalate things, with a nervous finger twitching on a 10 mm Glock or something equally dangerous.

I stood still.

Waited.

Traffic was really slowing down as curious drivers watched this little drama unfolding before them.

"Driver! With your hands up in the air, slowly walk backward to the sound of my voice. Do not stop until I tell you!"

I walked backward, seeing the headlights pass me by, noting the shadows bouncing around me as the headlights and strobe lights flashed, and how everything had an odd bluish cast to it. I'd gone back about three yards when the voice interrupted me one more time.

"Driver! Kneel down, cross your ankles, and put your hands behind your head! Do it now!"

I knelt down on the pavement, wincing as a few shards of rock rubbed up against my knees, and I crossed my ankles and put my hands behind my head. I then heard someone approaching me, and I said, "Officer, I'm carrying a pistol, under my left arm, in a shoulder holster. I have a current concealed carry permit in my wallet."

The sound of the footsteps stopped, and I heard voices—so there were two cops back there—and one said, "All right. I'm going to reach in and take your weapon. You make a threatening move, hell, any move at all, and you're in serious shit trouble. Got it?"

"Yes, I do."

A hand came down, moved around, and I was relieved of my 9 mm Beretta. I kept still, the rocks digging into my knees.

"All right, stay there, you're going to be cuffed."

No point in arguing, no point in saying it was all a mistake; it had gone too far for that. So my hands were seized and brought down to my waist, and handcuffs were attached, and in another sixty seconds, I was placed in the rear of a Falconer police cruiser.

A car came by, some folks laughing and honking their horn, and then the two cops—a young man and woman—got in and drove me to the Falconer police station.

CHAPTER TWENTY

I was processed thoroughly and efficiently, after being driven to the rear of the white concrete building that was the Falconer police station. Like its neighbor up in Tyler, it was situated on the coast, since that's where most of the arrests take place, especially in the summer.

I was led into the booking room, where my treatment was brusque and to the point, and where I didn't bother asking any questions. The arresting officers and the booking officer were—and not in an unkind way—just following orders. Something was going on that marked a departure from a normal traffic stop, for a disabled headlight usually means either a warning or a ticket. Not a response more appropriate to a Charlestown armored car robber escaping north into New Hampshire.

Fingerprints and photos were taken, forms were filled out, and after being relieved of my cell phone, shoulder holster, belt, and shoes—along with my wallet and other personal items—I was deposited into a holding cell that had a stainless steel toilet and a concrete bunk with a dull green mattress that was just a shade softer than the supporting concrete. No blanket, no sheet, nothing else save for a drain in the center of the floor and light coming in from the corridor. I sat on the bed, folded my arms, and waited.

A heavyset woman came into view, wearing the uniform of the Falconer police department and dangling a heavy brass key in her manicured hands. She had short black hair and sharp black eyes, and she said, "Someone's here to see you, sweetie. My question to you is, will you be a gentleman and come out and see him with no fuss? Or do I need to put the cuffs on you?"

I remained seated. "I promise to be polite and quiet."

She jangled the key again. "You haven't been drinking or taking any drugs, now, have you?"

"No, ma'am," I said.

"Fair enough," she said. "Now, good-lookin', you stay there on your bunk. I'm gonna open up the cell door here, and then step aside. You're gonna come out nice and slow and walk out into the corridor, and then take a left. Just so there's no misunderstanding, sweetie, you do anything else at all, and I do mean anything, why, I'll break your balls so hard you'll be singing soprano even when Christmas rolls around. Savvy?"

"Every word," I said.

"Fantastic." There was a sharp clank as the lock was undone, and then she opened up the cell door, stepping back, keeping the metal bars and frame between her and me. I slowly got off of the bunk, the concrete cold against my stockinged feet, and I walked out and left. She slammed the cell door, staying behind me, and said, "Up there, last door on your left. You step in there and do what the man says."

"All right," I said.

"And thank you."

"For what? Being a gentleman?"

She laughed. "No. For calling me ma'am. Can't remember the last time anybody said that to me. There you go."

The last door on the left opened up, and I entered an interrogation room, seemingly ordered from some cop supply warehouse somewhere. It had a desk fastened to the floor, four chairs, a round eyebolt secured in the center of the table for those prisoners who weren't as gentlemanly as me, and the standard one-way mirror on one side of the room. I resisted the temptation to wave at whoever was behind the mirror. Instead, I took the chair just as the door behind me snapped shut and was locked.

So the wait continued.

I sat motionless in the chair, thinking about what I would do when I got home—a hot shower was first, second, and third on my list—and before long the door behind me was unlocked and a slim man walked in. He had the form of a long-distance runner, and had on black trousers, black shoes, a light blue shirt and red necktie, and fastened to the side of his belt was the gold shield of a Falconer police detective. His brown hair was short, and he had a prominent nose, and in his hands he carried a thick manila legal-sized envelope. He sat down across from me and didn't offer me his hand, and I wasn't offended.

"Mike Thornton, Falconer police," he said, taking a sheet of paper from inside the manila envelope. "Mr. Lewis Cole, you are in one world of hurt."

I looked around the small room, which smelled of fear, defeat, and tobacco. I knew that either from behind the one-way glass or someplace else, this entire conversation was being recorded. "Looks like the Falconer police station to me."

"Hah," he said. "Very funny. Let me know if you find any of this funny."

From the envelope, he pulled out a color photograph of a young man with curly black hair and merry eyes, wearing a Colby sweatshirt. My feet felt even colder. I now knew why I had been pulled over, why I was being treated like this. The broken headlight was just a good excuse.

"Recognize him?" he asked.

I knew who he was, but no, I didn't recognize him. "No."

"That's John Todd Thomas. A student from Colby College. A member of the Nuclear Freedom Front. Just a kid, in his twenties. Should be worrying about his grades, about his parents, about getting laid. But no. He's beyond worrying. And this is why."

I steeled myself for what was coming next. Another color photograph was slid across the dirty, scarred table. This one was of a body sprawled out faceup in a muddy ditch. He had on blue jeans, a dark sweater, and no shoes. The body was swollen, making the jeans bulge as if they were two sizes too small. The flesh on the hands and face was a ghastly ghost white, and the face didn't look quite human, since it had been in water for a while.

The face was disfigured and bulging as well, and another photo, in awful color, showed why. The head was rolled to one side, and a gloved hand was holding a ruler near where a good section of the rear of the head had been blown apart. There was bone, blood, brain and matted hair, all looking too real in the color photograph. I swallowed, looked up at Detective Thornton.

"Sad to see," I said.

"Yeah, and even sadder to have to make that phone call to a kid's parents, down there in Virginia. They think their boy's safe and sound, either up here in Maine or New Hampshire, where nothing ever happens, and I have to wake them up at three in the morning to tell them that somebody shot their sweet boy, their dream son, in the back of the head and dumped him in a swamp. You ever have to do something like that?"

"No, I haven't." I said.

"Lucky you."

"I guess."

"So here's the deal, Cole," he said. "One of the last times anyone ever saw John Todd Thomas alive was a couple of nights ago, when he was walking up Lafayette Road to meet up with a journalist. No names, but the journalist he was going to meet was driving a dark blue Ford Explorer and he was seen getting in the rear of the Ford.

"I do," I said, and I had the solid sense that my Ford was now being examined, inch by inch, for whatever forensic evidence in there could be used against me. No surprise there, but the fine detective before me had one more surprise for me. It wasn't up his sleeve but in that bulging manila envelope before him.

He slid out a plastic-wrapped package with red EVIDENCE stickers on the side, and he undid the plastic and displayed what was inside: a soaked wet reporter's notebook.

"Familiar?"

"Could be," I said.

With a pen, he moved the notebook around so I could see the stained cardboard cover, where my name, "*Shoreline* magazine," and my home telephone number were written.

"Looks like it belongs to you," he said.

"Well, it certainly looks like it has my name on it."

Thornton poked at the notebook again with his pen. "You're one careful person, Cole, I'll give you that—but sometimes even the most careful person can fuck up. Like leaving evidence behind. Evidence that can connect that most careful person to a homicide. So. Care to explain how your reporter's notebook was found not more than fifty yards away from the body of John Todd Thomas?"

"No," I said.

"No, what?"

"No, I don't care to explain how what appears to be my notebook was found fifty yards from the body of John Todd Thomas."

He stared at me and said, "You trying to be tough? Or a smart-ass?"

"I'm not very tough," I said, "and while I'm reasonably intelligent, I'm not that smart. Though I do admit to being an ass on occasion."

Then something came to me, and I said, "All right. I'll man up here for a second. Can I take a look at the notebook?"

"What for?" he asked.

"A deal," I said. "Let me look at that notebook for a minute, and then I'll tell you whether it's mine or not. How does that sound?"

"Why do you want to do that?"

I shrugged. "I like cops. Besides, I don't want you to think I'm a smart-ass."

Thornton seemed to think about that for a moment, and then he shoved the notebook over with the end of the pen. "All right. One minute. Not a second more."

I picked up the notebook, which smelled and was still damp, and I gently undid the pages until I found what I was looking for.

Then I closed the notebook and passed it back to Detective Thornton.

"That's my notebook," I said. "I've been covering the antinuclear demonstrations at the power plant, so obviously it fell out of my coat—but it didn't fall out of my coat because I was murdering John Todd Thomas."

He picked up the notebook and put it back in the plastic bag. "Here's the deal, Cole. We have your notebook near the crime scene. We have evidence that Mr. Thomas was on his way to see you when he disappeared and was murdered, and that's just the beginning."

I kept my mouth shut and looked at him, and Thornton said, "At this moment, a detective from the state police is coming this way. There's a good chance they will try to connect the murder of this young man with the murder of Bronson Toles, and the entire investigative force of Falconer and the State Police is going to turn on you, Lewis Cole. So before the state police arrive here, if you want to make a statement, make an explanation of what happened and how it happened, well . . . it would work out better for you to talk to me than the state police."

I said, "Is the state police detective Pete Renzi?"

"Yes," he said.

"Then I'll wait to talk to him."

Thornton's face colored. "One last chance, Cole."

"Nope," I said. "Renzi is who I'm going to talk to."

Thornton said, "I can make this—"

"Detective Thornton, you seem to be a fine young man, so let me explain this further. I'm only going to talk to Detective Renzi. You keep bugging me, and then I'll change my mind, and then I'll only talk to my attorney." I gestured to the one-way glass. "Later, unless some technical glitch strikes, you can rerun the tape and tell Renzi how you screwed it up so I wouldn't talk to him."

He glared at me for a few seconds, then got up and left. Then the heavyset police officer put me back in my cell, and after she locked the door, she said with a touch of sorrow in her voice, "You sure weren't a gentleman to Detective Thornton."

I said, "He didn't ask."

About an hour later, I was back in the interrogation room, with Detective Pete Renzi of the New Hampshire State Police. He didn't have a jumpsuit on like before but was wearing clean dungarees, a white shirt, a black necktie, and a dark brown jacket. He looked like he had averaged about four hours of sleep per night during the past few days, and he got right to it.

"I understand you were dicking around with Detective Thornton," he said.

"Am I under arrest?"

"What?"

"I said, am I under arrest?"

"Not at the present moment," he said, his eyes glaring at me, "but that might change in a big way, depending on how our little meeting here goes."

"Ask you a quick question?"

"Those are the best kind," he said.

"You smoke?"

"That's your question?" Renzi asked.

"That's the one," I said. "Do you smoke?"

"Yeah, I shouldn't, but I do."

"I could use a cigarette right around now," I said.

Renzi said, "You know how it is. No smoking anywhere in any public building."

"I know," I said. "So why don't we step outside?"

He stayed quiet for a moment, and I pressed him. "Come on.

What am I going to do? Make a break for it across the police station parking lot, with no shoes, holding up my pants so they don't fall around my ankles?"

Renzi kept still for another moment, then got up. "All right. Let's do it."

He led me out the other door to the interrogation room, and we went out down a small hallway and then back into the booking area. From here, he pushed an outside door and we went out into the nighttime. It was cold. My feet, covered in damp socks, quickly got chilled. He stood next to me on a set of concrete steps, sighed, and reached into his coat pocket, pulling out a pack of Marlboros. He tapped it and extended it to me, and I pulled out a cigarette. I examined it, said, "Thanks," and gave it back to him.

Renzi looked surprised. "What the hell is that all about?"

"I don't smoke," I said. "Never have, never will."

"You . . . you told me you smoked, you jerk."

"No, I didn't," I said, feeling a sharp breeze cut at me. "I said I needed a cigarette, and I did."

He looked at the cigarette, as if he were debating whether or not to light it and then shove it into my eyeball, and he put it back into the pack and returned the pack to his coat.

"You wanted out of the interrogation room," he said.

"That's right."

"So what we say will be private."

"Correct again, Detective," I said.

"So go on. You got your ass out of there—for as long as I'm interested in what you have to say. So make it interesting."

I rubbed my upper arms, trying to warm up. "If you've talked to Diane Woods, then she's made some statements about me, about who I am and what I do—and you must know, in your heart

220

of hearts, that I had nothing to do with the killing of that college kid."

"I must, must I?" he asked, voice sharp. "What, you're more than a magazine writer now, you know what's working inside of my head and heart?"

"Think about it," I said. "I don't know the kid, have no reason to hurt him, or to kill him. You've just got me here to shake things up, to get some information. So here we are, you and me, a couple of guys outside in a cold October night, so let's straighten it out."

Renzi said, "Okay. So. Did you have any kind of encounter with him, any at all?"

I thought for a moment, then said, "Maybe."

"What the fuck is this maybe?"

"Detective Thornton said a witness saw John Todd Thomas get into a Ford Explorer, a couple of nights back. All right. A couple of nights back, I was in Falconer, at the Laughing Bee doughnut shop. I was waiting for someone to escort me for an interview with the head of the Nuclear Freedom Front. Curt Chesak. While I was waiting there, somebody got in the backseat of my car. I couldn't see who he was."

"So what happened?"

"What happened is that this man guided me to a place on an unmarked road in Falconer. From there, I was taken out, hooded, and brought to a campsite in the woods. I had an interview with Chesak, I was brought out, and then somebody took over my departure. The man who brought me in first—who was called Todd, by the way, the kid's middle name—left. A little while later, I heard a gunshot. That's it."

"That's all you can tell me?"

I had already made up my mind when I looked at the cigarette what I was going to do next, and so I did it. "That's right. That's all I can tell you. I heard a single shot. I don't know who did the shooting. Along the way, I stumbled and fell, and that's when my notebook fell out. That's it."

Renzi stood there, rocked a bit on his heels, and then reached back in his pocket, took out a cigarette, and lit it up. He took a deep drag and said, "Damn, that tastes good."

I kept quiet.

He took two more deep puffs, then dropped it and ground it out with his foot. "I talked to Diane one more time before I came over here. She said you've done some tricky things in the past but that you're a stand-up guy. She would trust you with her life, and she says she has, and she said I could trust you as well." Then Renzi stared right at me. "That's very important to me, what she said. Because when she said her life, she meant more than her physical life, you know what I mean?"

Sure, I thought. *Her whole life, from her employment to her background to her sexuality.* Then I saw the steady gaze of Renzi and something clicked into place.

"So that's important to me," he repeated. "That she had that to say about you. So here's the deal. You're free to go, Lewis, but if I or any other law enforcement official determines that you had anything—anything at all—to do with that poor kid's shooting, then I'll hurt you. I'll hurt in places that won't show, that a doctor can't pinpoint, but you'll be one hurtin' puppy, and then you'll be arrested. Clear?"

"Clear as day," I said.

"Fine," he said, and his shoulders slumped a bit, as if he were so very tired, and his voice became slightly reflective. "Bad enough to deal with one homicide . . . especially a ball-buster like the shooting of Bronson Toles, and when you're on the edge, trying to do everything you can, another shooting pops up, in the same neighborhood, with this fucking demonstration and these fucking demonstrators all mixed in. Most homicides, it's easy to get a handle on it in two days or less. Love, money, jealousy, fear, or pure old craziness . . . but this one, man, you've got to dig and dig, and go beyond the surface, and then dig some more . . ." He turned to me. "Enough of my bullshitting you. Let's get you out of here."

About fifteen minutes later I was back to a close approximation of normal, and a tired Detective Renzi and a glum Detective Thornton watched me sign for my belongings. Thornton pushed over the keys to my Ford and said, "Get that headlight fixed as soon as you can," he said, "or you'll be pulled over again."

"Where's my Ford?"

He gestured. "In the rear parking lot. You'll be getting a bill next week for towing and storage."

"Gee," I said. "Why am I not surprised."

Renzi managed a small smile, and I looked again at my belongings and put my wallet in my back pocket, scooped up my change and ballpoint pen, and said, "My pistol?"

Renzi said, "What about it?"

"I'd like to have it back, please," I said. "I'm its rightful owner, and I'm licensed in the state to carry a concealed weapon."

The state police detective smiled a bit more. "We'd like to keep it for a while. Two, three days tops. You'll get it back, I promise."

"Why—oh," I said. "You want to do ballistics testing on it, make sure it really wasn't used to kill that college kid."

"That's right," Thornton said, and Renzi added, "Remember what Ronald Reagan used to say. 'Trust but verify.'"

I looked at them both and said, *"Davehr'yay, noh praver'yay."*

Both detectives seemed puzzled, which pleased me. I raised my Ford keys in a salute. "That's what Ronald Reagan also said, in Russian. Same phrase. And I know because I was there."

I walked out into the cold night air, as what passed for a free man.

CHAPTER TWENTY-ONE

At home, after stripping off the clothes that had the heavy scent of sweat and imprisonment, I showered up and then checked messages. There was just one message on my cell phone—from Denise Pichette-Volk, wondering when I was going to submit another piece, she was liking what I was doing, but could I make it shorter and edgier, please—and on my landline, three messages: Diane Woods, Paula Quinn, and my Annie Wynn.

I slumped back in my couch, the television on but the sound muted, as the Allies once again stormed the beaches of Normandy on D-Day. Some other time, some other life, I would have been thrilled to get phone calls in one evening from three separate women, but not tonight. I started dialing and decided to go in order.

At Diane's, the phone was picked up on the third try and Kara Miles answered. "Oh, she's gone out to gas up the Volkswagen and pick up a few things," Kara said. "She'll be back in about a half hour. You want me to have her call you?"

I looked at the nearest clock. "If all goes well, I plan to be asleep by then. It's been one of those days."

Kara said, "Tell me about it."

"How are you doing?"

She said, "Sore. Tired. Still trying to get the stink of tear gas and pepper gas out of my clothes—and, shit, water's boiling over on the stove. Gotta run, Lewis," and she hung up before I had a chance to say anything more. I had wanted to ask her how she really was doing, how Diane was, and why she had been having that violent argument back at the salt marsh the previous day, when the demonstrations had collapsed. That would all have to wait. I had two more calls to make.

At Paula Quinn's, I went to voice mail after six rings and left a quick message, and then I was left with just one lovely to call: my Annie Wynn. I called her on her cell phone, and it rang and rang and rang and then was picked up in a burst of static.

"Hello? Annie?"

Another burst of static, and then Annie's voice came through. "Wynn here, who's this?"

Voices, music, static, and I made another effort, and she said, "Lewis! I'm right in the middle of something! Are you okay?"

I thought about the past couple of days and whatever was going on, and instead of belaboring the point, I lied and said, "Sure, everything's fine."

Some voices grew louder. "Hey, can I call you back? Five minutes, promise!"

"Deal," I said, and hung up.

In the kitchen I rustled up some scrambled eggs with Parmesan cheese sprinkled in, and after eating and cleaning up and yawning, I went upstairs. It was late and I was tired and the phone hadn't rung. I had read once that a week is an eternity in politics, so I guess five minutes was considered an hour or two in that world. Upstairs I thought about writing something for Denise Pichette-Volk of *Shoreline,* but that thought lasted through one big yawn.

In my bedroom, I felt oddly out of place, and I knew why: My 9 mm Beretta was in the hands of the state police, being expertly tested to see if it had anything to do with the murder of John Todd Thomas, but that didn't bother me. What bothered me was that I was partially disarmed. I used to own a Ruger stainless steel .357 Magnum revolver, but due to a series of unfortunate circumstances some months ago, it was still in the possession of the Secret Service, and they were reluctant to tell either me or my attorney— an old-time friend of Felix Tinios—when it was coming back.

So I now had three weapons in my possession: a Remington 12-gauge pump-action shotgun under the bed, an 8 mm FN assault rifle in my office closet, and a Browning .32 downstairs in a kitchen drawer. No, I'm not a fetishist when it comes to firearms; I like having a full toolbox, and now it was being depleted thanks to various government officials and my own actions.

I yawned and went under the bed and dragged out my shotgun, which was resting on a foam pad. It was within easy reach, and on the nightstand was my portable phone. I crawled into bed. Usually I read before going to sleep, but sleep was going to win tonight. I looked at the clock, then went to sleep and never looked at anything more.

During the night I woke up, desperately thirsty for some reason, and I moved slowly into the kitchen, got a glass of water, and tried to think of what I had been dreaming about. It was that odd mix of dreams that makes no sense when you're awake, but makes plenty of sense when you're in the middle of the it. There were flashing snapshots of crowds, of smoke billowing, a child crying . . . and I had that melancholy sense that if I thought really, really hard, I could get to the beginning of everything and have it make sense.

When I was done with my drink, I went to the bedroom, looked out the windows to the east, saw and heard the ocean. Go to the beginning. Haleigh had mentioned that, the night she spent here in my home. The state police detective had said the same thing. That was a thought. That was a very good thought.

I went back to bed.

The next day, another phone call to Annie Wynn went right to voice mail, and again I had a quick breakfast date with Felix Tinios, who was in a hurry and who invited me to come visit him at his house, which was in North Tyler, on Rosemount Avenue. While my home was odd corners and two stories of history and creaking boards and drafty windows, his was a ranch dwelling with clean floors, Scandinavian-type furniture, and no dust bunnies. Dust bunnies knew better than to try to enter Felix's domain.

This morning he had on jeans and a dark green short-sleeve polo shirt, and around his broad shoulders he also had his own leather shoulder holster, with a 10 mm Glock hanging snugly inside. He made us both crepes and bacon, and as he cooked and chatted and made the strong coffee he prefers, the Glock was still there, exposed, like the proverbial bass drum in the bathtub.

When we were pretty much done, I said, "So, is this a game of 'show me yours, and I'll have to show you mine'?"

"Mmm?"

I said, "I think you've known me long enough to know that I'm not easily impressed or moved by the sight of a firearm. So you're going to have to do better."

He smiled, but I wasn't comforted by his sharp look. "Maybe I'm just softening up the opposition."

"Opposition? You've called me a number of things over the

years, but this is the first time I've ever been called that. So what happened, your union paymaster didn't appreciate my meeting?"

"Apparently so," Felix said.

"Thin-skinned guy, ain't he. I'm sure he's heard worse from other reporters, or union members, or attorney general types."

"Whatever types he's encountered, he didn't like you, and didn't like your questions about Bronson Toles. So do me a favor, will you? Stop with the questions, stop with the digging around Joe Manzi and his union. They don't need the publicity, especially at this time."

The coffee mug in my hand felt cool, and something was wrong in the kitchen, so that the fine hairs on the backs of my hands were tingling just a bit, as if an unexpected electrical charge had come close to me.

I said carefully, "Is this a threat, Felix?"

He stared at me and if it weren't for the history that we have together, I think the chances were more than even that I would have been leaving with a broken limb or two, at the least.

No answer from Felix. I said, "A threat?"

"Asking for a favor, that's all," he said slowly. "I'm in the employ of people who are in a delicate position, and they don't need you poking around and raising questions—and as a sweetener, Lewis, I can tell you that I see no indication that anyone connected with that union had anything to do with Bronson Toles's murder."

I waited just a little longer and tried a smile. "A favor?"

"That's right."

"How about a trade?"

He picked up a white coffee mug. "I'm open to a trade. What do you have in mind?"

I slowly reached into my pants pocket, took out a slip of paper, opened it up, and slid it across the countertop, past the coffee cups and breakfast dishes. "If you could trace this number for me, I'd appreciate it."

He picked up the paper, gave it a glance. "I thought you had . . . other resources available to do this for you."

"I do, but she's a busy woman, with a lot on her plate. Tell you what, do this favor for me, and Joe Manzi and his union brothers and sisters won't hear a thing from me. Deal?"

I could sense Felix's shoulders easing some, and the worrisome flickering on the backs of my hands went away as well. "Deal," he said. "Give me a minute."

He left the kitchen and went to his living room, and I heard a murmur as he made a phone call. I took a deep, satisfying breath. That had been close. Felix and I had a very long, somewhat complicated relationship, and I had no desire to make it even more complicated.

He came back to the kitchen and passed me the slip of paper with new writing on it. "There you go. Have fun . . . and I have no idea what you're after. You looking to expand your talent base or something?"

I looked at the paper, saw a name, business, and Boston address. "Or something."

"Good for you," he said, and then he started picking up the dishes. "You know, I'll be one happy *paisan* when these protesters pack up and go somewhere else. Like a coal plant. Or seal-clubbing ship. Or a factory farm."

"Getting tired of the attention?"

Felix looked at me. "Getting tired of it impacting things I do, places I go, people I know. You got it?"

"Got it," I said, getting up and heading for the door.

"Lewis? You still up to something?"

"Always," I said.

"Then take it from me," he said, looking somber. "When you

have thousands of people gathered together, full of anger, full of righteousness . . . then emotions and tempers rise up . . . and bad things happen—and even the good guys can get caught in the crosshairs."

"I'll try hard not to do that," I said.

Felix said, "Try harder, friend."

Two hours later I was outside a stretch of brick buildings that marked a built-up section of South Boston, with scores of years of history of blood feuds, criminals, Marine heroes, and other odds and ends of the Irish saga. In the past few years, businesses and people with disposable income had moved in, adding more spice to an already interesting mix. Where I ended up was one of these new office buildings, and where I went was to the law offices of one David Foster, on the second floor. It seemed to be a one-man firm, with a secretary in the outer area, which also held three chairs and a coffee table covered with that day's *Boston Globe*, *Wall Street Journal*, and *New York Times*, as well as copies of the *Hollywood Reporter* and *Variety*.

I went in unarmed, but through necessity, not choice. It's relatively easy for a New Hampshire resident to get a permit to carry a concealed weapon; pay a fee, submit a notarized form with the names and addresses of three state residents who agree to vouch for your good nature. In Massachusetts, among other things, if you're a resident, you need to bow and scrape before your local police chief to get the necessary permission, and if you're out of state, you'd have a better chance of being elected to the city council in Cambridge on the Carnivore and Conservative ticket than of getting a carry permit.

The secretary was an attractive full-figured woman in her early thirties with light brown hair, wearing a black knit dress that was buttoned all the way up to the scooped top, and given the way she was sitting, one hoped that the buttons were fastened by industrial-strength thread. Gold jewelry was around her neck and wrists, and she bit her lower lip when I told her that I wanted to see her boss.

She flipped through a large calendar book, her fingernails shiny and maroon, and said, "Oh, I'm so sorry, but the earliest Mr. Foster can see you is . . . two weeks from next Tuesday."

I nodded and passed over my business card identifying me as a writer from *Shoreline* magazine. "I'd like to see Mr. Foster now, and tell him I want to see him concerning the Stone Chapel in Tyler, New Hampshire."

I'm not sure if it got her attention, but it did result in her getting up from behind her clear desk and going into another office. There was a moment, and she came back out and said, with a surprised look on her face, "Mr. Foster will see you now."

"Thanks," I said, giving her my best smile.

Inside Mr. Foster's office there was one wall covered with a bookcase that looked to have a complete set of the state laws for Massachusetts, and another wall with framed certificates and such. From behind a wide wooden desk, the man I had seen last week at the memorial service stood up, wearing black trousers, red suspenders, and a light blue shirt with a white collar and a red necktie. His thick blond hair was cut and styled expertly, and he had a thick gold ring on each pinkie finger. I shook an extended hand, and he said, "Mr. Cole, I only have a few minutes, so let's make this productive."

"I agree," I said. "Let's."

We both sat down, and he leaned back in his chair and put his hands behind his head. "A magazine writer. So ask your questions."

"What can you tell me about your connection with Laura Glynn Toles and the Stone Chapel?"

"I'm sorry, that's privileged information."

"Are you representing her and the facility?"

"I'm sorry, that's privileged information."

"What kind of law are you an expert in?"

He said, "Are you hiring me?"

"No," I said.

His smile grew larger. "Then that's privileged information as well, Mr. Cole."

So this little dance went on for another ten minutes or so, with every question I asked him being tossed back at me with the same nonresponse response. Not once during our formalized conversation did I bother taking a note, and when I had run out of things to ask him, I said, "Mr. Foster, I appreciate your time. I'm afraid I've run out of questions."

He stood up and so did I, and after another round of handshaking, he said, "Sorry it turned out to be a waste of time for you."

I gathered my notebook and headed out the door. "Mr. Foster, it was anything but a waste of time."

I was pleased to see the surprised look on his face as I closed the door behind me.

CHAPTER TWENTY-TWO

Outside in the cool air of South Boston, I knew I was about two blocks away from the *Shoreline* magazine offices. It would take about five minutes to go in there and pay a surprise visit to my new boss, maybe impress her with my thoughtfulness and thoroughness, and maybe build a few bridges between us, so she wouldn't be so snappy with me and I wouldn't feel like I was working for the female version of a crazed Colonel McCormick of the old *Chicago Tribune* days. Sure. I could do that.

I got into my Ford, started her up, and headed north.

About a half hour into my trip, on a long stretch of Interstate 95 near Beverly, my cell phone rang, and I flipped it open and said, "Hello, this is Lewis."

"I know," came the voice of my editor, Denise. "I wasn't calling the damn White House, now, was I?"

The proverbial They say you should pull over while making a cell phone call, to avoid distractions, which is what I did. I pulled over to the side of the four-lane highway and thought about distractions, like tossing the cell phone out the window and running it over. I also thought it was ironic that I had been in her neighborhood less than a half hour ago. Maybe she had sensed me nearby and decided to check in.

I said, "Not sure if the White House would take your call. What's up, Denise?"

"You didn't file yesterday," she said.

"I was kind of busy."

"Well, I was kind of being an editor who needs copy submitted, to send out. So hear me well. I need some more copy today—and make sure you add something about that college kid getting shot. Readers love that stuff."

"They do, do they?"

"Christ, yes. Haven't you ever heard that expression, if it bleeds, it leads?"

"I thought that was just for newspapers or television."

"What's the difference now, hunh? Get that copy to me, Lewis."

Then she hung up.

I remained in park, on the side of a busy highway, still a bit distracted, and then I got going and resumed my trek north.

About an hour later I was in Durham, the home of the University of New Hampshire, several thousand students, a couple hundred professors and administrators, and one Haleigh Miller. Without knowing where she lived—whether on campus or off, or in which dormitory or housing development—but with the keen insight that comes from years of poking around and paying attention, I went to the Memorial Union Building, a squat, somewhat modern-looking place on the top of a hill, which housed most of the college's student organizations, including UNH Students for Safe Energy. The office was on the bottom floor of the building, down a long, narrow corridor that held the offices for the radio station, the group responsible for bringing speakers and musicians to campus, the yearbook, the student-run video organization, and the student newspaper, which seemed to attract a number of eager types that Paula Quinn could probably out-report and out-write before having her first cup of coffee in the morning.

The Safe Energy office was in a room about the size of my home office, and it was crowded with students, denim, wool sweaters, bumper stickers, pamphlets, and about a ton of attitude. There were about a half dozen young men and women in there, and I could see their mental antennas quiver as I passed through the door, and almost as one, they gave me a suspicious look as I stepped in. Could hardly blame them, for I was of a certain age and was dressed in a certain way.

I gave the closest bearded male my best nonthreatening smile and said, "I'm looking for Haleigh Miller. Do you expect her around?"

"Depends," he said, rocking back and forth slowly in a swivel chair that looked like it was kept together by chants and duct tape. "Who's asking?"

"I'm from Greenpeace," I said, hating to lie but knowing this was all for some greater good. Or something like that. I went on. "I want to talk to her about a possible internship at our D.C. office."

Saying I was from Greenpeace was like going into a high school choir group and announcing I was from a Broadway talent agency. Immediately they all wanted to be my new best friend, and I smiled again and held up my hand and said, "Guys, I'm sorry, I really need to speak to Haleigh. Time is of the essence—and if I can't talk to her soon, the internship will go to somebody else."

My new best friends came up with suggestions, possibilities, and after a few more minutes of corrupting our youth, I went back out to the campus.

According to the members of UNH Students for Safe Energy—who should have known better than to give me the information they did, for I could have been involved in about a half dozen separate criminal enterprises—Haleigh lived in a dormitory called Congreve Hall, set in the middle of the campus. I walked in without much difficulty; the signs at the entryway informed me the admissions desk was manned only during the early evening hours. There were a number of posters and stickers on her dormitory door, all involving either the antinuclear cause or some other movement, but no answer from behind it.

So I went outside and sat on a stone wall and waited. Around me students went back and forth, laughing, talking, most of them carrying book bags or knapsacks, and I'm sure they thought they were the best, brightest, and most committed of any college generation, and in a way, they would be right. Except, of course, the fact that my college generation, and the one before that, and the one before that, all thought the same thing—probably all the way back to medieval times.

So I waited, and I thought about my visit to Boston, and how the good attorney down there thought he hadn't told me a thing, when, in fact, he had by his constant refusal to tell me anything. If Attorney Foster had told me he had no idea what I was talking about concerning him and the Stone Chapel, then so be it. Instead, even though his appointment calendar was supposedly full, he had seen me instantly when I mentioned the name of the Stone Chapel, and any additional question was met by "privileged information." Over and over again.

Which meant there was some serious connection between him and Laura Glynn Toles and the Stone Chapel.

There. Walking down a cement sidewalk, wearing jeans and a navy blue sweatshirt, looking down at her feet, a light red knapsack on her back. I got up and met her on the sidewalk, and she looked up, startled.

"Oh, Lewis," she said. "What are you doing here?"

"Hoping I could ask you a few questions."

She looked over at her dorm. "I . . . I'm really behind in my classwork, since the demonstrations. I really don't have that much time."

I gently grasped her upper arm. "Just a few, and then I'll be on my way. Promise."

I knew I was treading in some potentially dangerous territory, and I was wary. If she pulled away or made a scene, I'd leave: Campus cops can be very unforgiving of males of any age harassing a student.

Haleigh just shook her head and came back with me to the stone wall that I had been occupying for a while.

"Before I start, I just want to know how you're doing," I said.

She pulled back at her hair. "It's . . . it's strange. That's all I can really say. When I was in Falconer, I was part of a community, you know? People who shared food with you, blankets, water . . . helped you if you got knocked down by the cops or got pepper-sprayed. There was just . . . a sense of unity, of being part of something bigger . . . and then it collapsed . . . and now I'm back here in Durham . . . and my classmates and people in my dorm, they don't care. They don't care at all. It's all about who's hooking up, who's getting ready for midterms, who's got a lead on a great internship this summer." Her face looked pale as she glanced over at me. "So you feel like . . . is that it? Is that all there is? When we were leaving Falconer, some of the organizers tried to say it had been a success, that we had been building spirit, showing defiance . . . and I cried. Because we failed. Look at it realistically. We failed."

"What about the other group, the Nuclear Freedom Front? They're trying again."

She shivered. "You saw what the cops did to peaceful protesters. Imagine what they'll do to protesters who don't rule out using violence."

"I see."

"Lewis . . . please, what are your damn questions. I don't have that much time."

"It's about the Stone Chapel, and Bronson Toles."

"Cripes," she said. "Can't you journalists stop playing with his corpse?"

"Never said I was a journalist," I said, "and I'm not playing with his corpse. I need to follow up on some information that somebody told me about Bronson."

She sighed. "Go on."

"Did Bronson . . . did he ever have . . . well, did he ever have an unhealthy interest in his employees?"

Haleigh's gaze sharpened. "Don't dance around it. You're asking me if he fooled around with the help."

"In so many words, yes."

"No."

"That was a pretty quick answer."

"Because it's a pretty accurate answer," she shot back. "I worked there weekends, nights and into the early morning. I never saw anything or heard anything about him fooling around. It never happened."

"So if somebody told me that the reason he only hired females is because he wanted to be around them, and have the occasional relationship, then that somebody would be wrong?"

"No," she said calmly. "That someone would be lying. You want to know why he only hired women?"

"Sure," I said.

"Because he believed the deck was stacked against women, right from the beginning, that men had an advantage when it came to jobs and to learning, and he was going to do what he could to level the playing field. That's all. He did something gracious and noble, and now you tell me somebody's using that against him. Disgusting."

"So no chance of an upset father or boyfriend picking up a rifle to take his revenge on Bronson."

"Oh, Christ, no, Lewis. That sounds like a bad movie."

"All right, enough of that," I said. "About the Stone Chapel. The musical groups that Bronson hired to bring in—any disputes from anyone? Did they feel they got treated unfairly? Paid too little? Not promoted enough?"

She shook her head and stood up. "You really don't know Bronson, and you really don't know the Stone Chapel. Bronson always treated them fairly, like members of the family, and he gave a lot of musical groups their first break, and some of them became famous because of it—and there are groups and performers who practically fight for the chance to come to the Stone Chapel. So if you think some disgruntled musician killed Bronson over some contract dispute, you're wrong."

"So who do you think killed him, then?"

Haleigh had tears in her eyes when she said, "Enough, okay, enough."

Then she ran into her dorm.

I sat for a few minutes longer and then, feeling older than when I began my questioning, I got up and left.

I drove the half hour or so from Durham to Tyler Beach, thinking I would go home, regroup, get something to eat, and then write something to satisfy my editor's unceasing demands, but as I entered the outskirts of Tyler, just before passing over I-95—the interstate that divides the state's seacoast into two unequal lumps—my cell phone rang again. It was Diane Woods, and her message was short and to the point, and I quickly sped up my drive, exceeding the speed limit by at least twenty miles an hour.

CHAPTER TWENTY-THREE

I pulled up to the condo complex on High Street where Paula Quinn lived, about a five-minute drive from Tyler Beach. Three green and white Tyler police cruisers were parked haphazardly in the adjacent lot, lights flashing, and yellow crime scene tape was already unfurled. A cluster of neighbors watched as one Tyler cop entered the woods to the rear of the white two-story building, a barking German shepherd leading him on. There was also an unmarked dark blue Ford LTD with lights flashing in its radiator grille, and I slammed my Ford to a halt behind it and got out.

I walked quickly over to the crime scene tape where a young Tyler officer, serious-looking in his dark green uniform, was keeping tabs on the spectators. I know most of the Tyler cops, but I didn't know this one. He must have been a recent hire. His name tag read LAMONTAGNE, and I said, "Officer, I'm here to see Detective Sergeant Woods."

He shook his head. "Sorry. She's busy."

"She'll see me," I said. "She just called."

Officer Lamontagne stared at me with his light brown eyes and said, "Name?"

"Lewis Cole."

With that, he toggled a radio microphone dangling from his shoulder and said, "Tyler Twenty-two to Tyler D-One."

From his radio I heard the slightly distorted voice of Diane. "Tyler D-One, go."

"Detective, I have a Mr. Cole here to see you."

A faint crackle of static. "He's clear. Send him in."

Officer Lamontagne looked slightly impressed. "All right, sir," he said, lifting the crime scene tape. "If you go in and—"

"That's fine," I said, impatient, "I know the way."

I brushed past him and trotted across the parking lot, to the open door of the condo complex, and up a set of stairs. The door to Paula Quinn's unit was open, and a young female officer was there, clipboard in hand, writing down everyone who entered and left Paula's residence, and as I passed this second checkpoint, I got a sharp jolt as I saw Diane and other police officers in Paula's living room. I had been here on several occasions—none lately, but not much had changed in the intervening time—but there was something so wrong about seeing law enforcement officers among her furniture, her books, the piles of Tyler *Chronicle* newspapers on the carpeted floor.

"Tell me she's okay," I said.

"We think so," Diane said, a metal clipboard in her hands.

"What do you mean?"

She pointed to the kitchen area, off to my left, where a window over the sink was shattered. The window overlooked a rear lawn and the woods. Another Tyler cop was going into the trees, wearing body armor and carrying a shotgun.

Diane said, "What we know is that someone took a shot at her, missed, and the bullet ended up over there." She pointed her pen to the opposite wall of the living room, where a Tyler cop in a dark green jumpsuit was measuring a hole in the plaster. "That's the first bit of good news, that we'll have a bullet to recover and examine, to get this son of a bitch."

"Tell me there's more good news."

She gestured to the tile floor of the kitchen and the light tan of the living room rug. "No blood. Nothing at all. When she called dispatch to report the shooting, she didn't say she was hurt. She just said she'd been shot at—and even though the dispatcher told her to wait for the first units to arrive, she didn't."

"Her car gone?"

Diane shook her head. "Car keys still here. Her cell phone, too. We've searched the complex, the neighboring buildings. Nothing."

"Her boyfriend, Mark Spencer, the town counsel. Could she be there?"

"He lives on the other side of town, but we have another unit going over, just to check. He's in Concord today, but he's coming back. Lewis . . . what can you tell me?"

I knew Diane and I knew the look on her face. No evasions on my part. "Ever since Bronson Toles got shot, she's been scared.

She's been obsessed with thinking that the shooter was coming after her next."

"Doesn't make sense."

"I know it doesn't, but there's that damn bullet hole."

We both looked over at the broken window. "Can't be a coincidence," she said. "Bronson Toles being shot and killed, and then a woman standing next to him . . . almost killed a few days later. So where's the connection? Was she working on anything about Bronson Toles?"

"No," I said. "Her stories were just about the antinuclear demonstrations. She didn't want to have anything to do with Bronson or his murder. The whole thing . . . it really spooked her."

We stood quiet there for a moment, and then I spoke up. "Me. I'm the connection."

"Go on."

I motioned her into the kitchen and lowered my voice. "You know . . . you know what I've been up to."

Another look from her. "Yeah, I know your methods. You're the one that's been digging into Bronson Toles—not Paula—and I've been in touch with Peter Renzi, trying to make a stand for your good character. So I know you've been doing your usual poking and prodding."

"True enough, and anyone out there, it wouldn't take much work to know that Paula and I are friends. So the shot here is a warning to back off, or something more."

"What about you? Anything dark sent your way?"

"No gunshots through my kitchen window, if that's what you mean."

"It's not. I mean anything, Lewis."

I spoke calmly, though I was choosing my words carefully. "Out on the marshes, during the demonstrations . . . a couple of times I was assaulted by a male. Nothing too serious. I'm still here."

"So you are. Do you know who did the assaulting?"

I shook my head. "Once I was literally in the dark, and the second time, I was in the middle of a tear gas cloud when someone came after me with a large stick—someone wearing a bandanna over his face."

"I see," she said. "Anything else?"

"Two threatening phone calls."

"What did they say?"

"Usual stuff about how I was next, I should stop doing whatever it is I'm doing, crap like that."

"Glad to see that didn't drive you off."

I said, "You really mean that?"

"Hell, no, you should have told me."

"Right," I said, "and maybe a story comes out, that someone who was caught up in that nonsense during the primary and connected to the campaign of Senator Jackson Hale was also caught up in another shooting. Didn't want that story being made public, Diane."

She said, "So that's what it's about? Protecting your Annie?"

"Among other things."

Diane said, "So who gave you the burden to protect all the women in your life?"

I thought about that and said, "Me. Just me."

She opened up her clipboard. "Then be careful. Someone's gunning for you, and Paula—and I need to know one more thing."

"What's that?"

"You find something, something that's a good solid lead—you tell me, okay? This isn't white knight time. There's a smart guy out there, a hunter who's on the scent, on the trail, and I don't want you messing with him."

I said, "All right. You get the call."

"Thanks," she said. "Now if you don't mind, I got a hell of a lot of work to do—plus I get to return to Falconer tomorrow afternoon for the latest installment of idiots on parade."

I looked out, saw that the Tyler policeman in the jumpsuit had left. It was now just me and Diane. "How goes it with Kara?"

Oh, it was a pleasure to see her grin. "Better. Definitely getting better. I'll have a story to tell you, when I can—but not now."

"Fine," I said, and then I left one of my best friends to her job.

Back in my Ford Explorer I started up the engine and waited, thinking about Paula. Thinking about her being in her home, her comfort zone, after a long day as assistant editor at the *Chronicle*. Maybe she's thinking of dinner plans. Maybe she's thinking about her beau, the town attorney looking to run for state senate. Or maybe she's just thinking about what to catch on late afternoon television.

Then it's all shattered, in an instant, with the sound of a rifle shot echoing right after a bullet smashes through the kitchen window and buries itself in the living room wall. In that split second, all of your fears are realized. You're no longer paranoid. There really is someone out to kill you.

So you call the cops and get the hell out. Moving so fast you leave your car keys and your cell phone behind.

So where do you go? I looked out at the woods behind the condo unit, where the cop with the German shepherd kept on hunting.

Hunting.

Like the shooter, trying to hunt down Paula, and most likely trying to hunt me down as well.

Hunting.

Damn, I thought, *damn, damn, damn.*

244

I thought as well of what Diane had just told me, about being a white knight. I was nowhere near being a white knight. Just a guy trying to do his best for a woman he cared for, a woman he had shared some special moments and times with a while ago.

So if back to Diane one goes . . . what then?

Conference call. Planning session. Finding a judge for a possible warrant. Based on what, Your Honor? Oh, based on what a writer from *Shoreline* just brought to us, a writer who wants to keep his name out of the process to protect his woman trying to elect the senior senator from Georgia as our next president.

I backed the Explorer out onto High Street and got right to work.

I pulled into the empty expanse that was the parking lot for the Stone Chapel, and I backed up my Ford so I was close to the main entrance. I also kept the keys in the ignition. If things went badly in a very quick way, I didn't want to waste precious seconds looking for my SUV's keys. I got out and walked up to the main entrance of the Stone Chapel. Found it locked. A handwritten sign dangling from a red firebox next to the door read: TO OUR FANS AND FAMILY, THE STONE CHAPEL IS CLOSED UNTIL FURTHER NOTICE.

I pulled at the door once and then peered through a window. Just seats and the tall windows and the stage. I went around to the side door, the one that had been used by us media types during the memorial service for Bronson Toles. Locked as well.

I kept on walking to the rear of the chapel, which had an attached two-story wooden cottage. There were two sets of bay windows and another door, which had a doorbell, which I pressed, and then pressed again.

I waited. I didn't like where I was. My Ford was too far away for comfort. Maybe I should move it.

Maybe.

It was too late.

The door opened up, and there was Victor Toles. He had on sneakers, jeans, and a shapeless blue sweater.

"Vic Toles?"

"Yeah," he said.

"I'm Lewis Cole, from *Shoreline* magazine," I said. "We met during your stepdad's memorial service. Remember?"

He nodded slowly. "Yeah . . . I remember you. What's going on?"

"I was wondering if I could talk for a few minutes with you and your mom."

He glanced behind himself, then turned back to me. "I don't know . . . we're kinda busy."

"Only a couple of minutes," I said. "Promise—and it's very important. Urgent."

Vic's hand was still on the doorknob, and I thought about what I would do if he were to close the door suddenly, but he shrugged and opened the door wider.

"Come on in," he said, and I did just that.

I followed Vic into a large entryway. To the right was a set of concrete stairs leading to a basement, and at the top of the stairs was a pile of athletic equipment—softballs, baseball bats, and gloves—and to the left was a wood-paneled hallway. Vic led the way, and I kept up with him. On each wall there were framed photos of Bronson with political types, local community leaders, and musical groups. There was an opening to the left that led to a large living room and attached kitchen, and to the right, an open door.

"Mom?" Vic asked, standing in the doorway. "There's someone here who wants to talk to us."

Inside the room was a windowless office, with Laura Glynn Toles sitting behind a cluttered desk. The desk held papers, file folders, receipts, and an adding machine with a long loop of white paper running to the carpeted floor. There were four three-drawer gray metal filing cabinets and the consistent trophy photos of her dead husband. There was also a green and white ecology flag and a host of NO NUKES bumper stickers. Laura looked tired, her usual black ponytail undone. She was wearing a gray cardigan.

"Yes?" she asked. "Who is it?"

I stepped in. "My name is Lewis Cole, Mrs. Toles. I'm a writer for *Shoreline* magazine. I know you're busy, and I'll be as quick as I can."

She yawned and said, "Oh, God, excuse me, will you? The past couple of weeks . . . With the protests, with Bronson, with us putting the Stone Chapel up for sale . . . do sit down, will you? Vic, how about a cup of tea for all of us? Would you like a cup of tea with honey, Mr. Cole?"

Not particularly, but I was going to be as gracious as I could, considering the circumstances, and I took a folding wooden chair in front of the gunmetal gray desk. Vic went out, and she looked back at the papers and said, "The amount of paperwork . . . it's unbelievable. Are we putting the Stone Chapel up for sale, or the place and the name that goes with it? Is the sound equipment part of the deal? How about doing an inventory of the food and drink? My word, it's amazing that anything gets done when property is sold."

"So the sale is going forward?"

She nodded. "It's too much. It's just too much. I was hoping that some group of concerned folks might get together and buy the place, but I don't think that's going to happen. The value of property in Tyler is way too high—which is another reason we have to sell. The property tax bills . . . twice a year, my hair almost turns gray when we get the town's property tax bill."

Vic came back in with a tray bearing three teacups and a steaming pot, and Laura smiled. "My second cup of the day. Do join us, won't you?"

So I did. There was a brief ceremony of tea pouring and honey dispensing and the *clink-clink* of spoons, and then Laura took a slow sip and said, "What are you looking for?"

"Some information, that's all—but it's vital."

She smiled at her son. "Vital? My, that sounds urgent. What's it about?"

I opened my new notebook, though I knew I wasn't going to need a pen and paper to remember whatever answers I was about to receive. I kept my notebook in one hand and the offered teacup in the other. "Do you know Ron Shelton?"

Vic smirked, and his mother said, "Of course. The spokesman—or spokesweasel—for that damn power plant. I swear, I don't know how that man can sleep at night, or look at himself in the mirror every day, knowing he's working for such an evil entity that will turn this seacoast into one giant deadly cove."

"Are you familiar with his sister?"

Laura shook her head. "No. Why should I?"

"His sister is Clara Shelton. Do you know that name?"

"I don't," Laura said. "Vic, do you?"

My cell phone suddenly rang, making me jump, and without looking, I reached down, opened it up, and toggled it off.

Vic said, "No. I can't say that I do. Where is this going, Mr. Cole?"

"Ron's sister, Clara. She's a singer. She's sung at a number of clubs and local venues. Ron's very proud of her, but he says she never got the break she deserved. That certain . . . club owners took advantage of her. Do either of you remember anything like that happening?"

Vic seemed stone-faced, his teacup gingerly held by both hands, and Laura said, "This is all news to me . . . so why are you bringing it up?"

"I was wondering if there was any legal action being brought against you by Ron's sister, or by Ron on behalf of his sister, if she thought she was being treated unfairly by the Stone Chapel."

"No, not at all," Laura said. "We've never had problems like that. I still don't understand what this has to do with us."

I put my teacup on Laura's desk. "Mrs. Toles, it's like this. Ron Shelton is an avid hunter. You have secured the services of a prominent entertainment lawyer in Boston. David Foster. I believe there's a connection, especially if someone who has performed here has brought a legal action against you and—"

Vic spoke up. "Wait just a minute. David Foster. How did you find out about David Foster?"

I said, "In doing research—and in talking to him."

Laura's face turned red, and Vic said, his voice rising, "You talked to him? You talked to David Foster? What did he say?"

Laura tried to smooth things over. "Vic, calm down. I'm sure it'll be fine."

Vic turned to her, his face mottled white and red, his voice rising. "Mom! Did you hear what he said? He talked to that snake Foster! Cole talked to him! I told you we couldn't trust that bastard!"

Laura held out a hand to her son. "Victor Henry Toles, you calm down, now . . . you calm down . . ."

That rising voice.

I had heard it before.

In the woods. With a hood over my head.

Victor Henry Toles . . .

John Todd Thomas . . .

Calling each other by their middle names as some sort of code.

Victor Henry Toles.

Who grew up living off the land in a commune in Vermont.

I looked at Laura, who seemed angry, trapped, and upset that something important was slipping away, and I looked at her son, and his cold, dead-eyed gaze chilled me to the bone.

I grabbed my cup of tea, threw it at him, and got up and ran out as Laura screamed and Vic shouted.

CHAPTER TWENTY-FOUR

I ran down the hallway, heading to the entryway and from there to the door and a sprint out to the parking lot to my Ford with the keys inside and a quick call to Diane Woods and—

I threw open the door.

Haleigh Miller stood there, face red, crying.

"Oh, I'm so sorry, Lewis," she said, and from behind her back, she produced a softball bat and slammed it across my forehead.

I fell back, fell back, and then tumbled down the set of stairs as loud voices approached from up above. The cement stairs were hard and sharp against my spine and the back of my head, and I stopped tumbling at the bottom, everything aching. I forced myself to my knees and looked up at the top of the stairs, where Haleigh shouted, "Hurry up! He's down here!"

A flash of memory. A pink ribbon tied onto my knapsack, back at the demonstration—to mark me as a target. Not a mark of friendship. To my right and rear were blank walls. To my left was an open door. I got up with some effort and went through the door and slammed it shut behind me.

It was dark. No windows. No openings. I felt around with my outstretched hand, thankfully touched a light switch. I flicked it on and the room lit up and came into focus. A low basement with a concrete floor, and overhead, beams and planks. Some old wooden church pews stacked on one side of the room. Boxes. Trays. Tables. Chairs.

From the other side of the door, feet clumping down the concrete steps. I turned and locked the door, and for good measure threw a bolt. Then I stepped back, took a breath.

The doorknob wiggled. I heard the slippery metal sound of a key being inserted, and then the doorknob rotated, but the door wouldn't budge. A couple of thumps as the person on the other side—Vic Toles, I'm sure—threw his weight against the door.

I looked around. Boxes and boxes in front of me. The basement stretched out to the other side and ended with shelves and boxes and industrial-sized cans and bottles of food and drink.

No windows. Nothing. Just the door I had just come through, the door I had locked, and on the other side, one young and very cold-blooded killer.

I felt at my side, sighed with relief at finding my cell phone. One quick phone call and this would end quickly, and end well.

I brought the cell phone up, flipped open the cover, looked at the screen, and—

Capital letters in the center of the screen:

SEARCHING FOR SERVICE.

Damn.

All this thick wood, thick concrete, and metal around me . . .

251

I was certainly stuck.

Another thump from the other side of the door.

"Cole!" Vic shouted. "Come on, give it up!"

I looked some more, hoping that Vic kept his firearms in a locker down in this part of the building, but I was out of luck. Off to the right was a pile of kitchen gear that went with their catering business: tablecloths, chafing dishes, silverware, and glassware.

No shotguns, rifles, or pistols.

"Cole!" Vic shouted. "Come on out!"

I couldn't help myself. "Why? So you can shoot me out there, like you shot your stepdad, and John Thomas, and Paula Quinn?"

He laughed. "Missed that bitch, didn't I. I was hoping to splatter her brains over her kitchen so you'd do something else besides sniff at me and my mom—but she dropped something on the floor just as I pulled the trigger."

I kicked at the nearest cardboard box in frustration and the box burst open, spilling reels and reels of old-fashioned tape recordings, brown tapes that rolled out onto the dirty concrete floor. There were dozens of these boxes carefully stacked up, with names and dates written on the outside with black marker. Seeing those tapes, something suddenly made sense to me so quickly that it almost made me dizzy. These weren't just tapes. They were gold. They were diamonds. They were silver.

"That's why you killed Bronson, isn't it," I shouted back at Vic. "Because of all these tapes! He had the rights to recordings made by rock and folk groups before they got famous, tapes that could be worth millions of dollars—and now you and your mom own them! What happened, was he too greedy? Didn't want to share?"

Even through the door I could sense the anger and frustration in his voice. "Greedy? Greedy? I wish that goody-two-shoes bastard was greedy—because he'd still be alive. Those tapes are worth tons of money, and you know what he wanted to do with all that money? Save the fucking rain forest. Save the polar bears. Save the shoreline. What about me? What about Mom? Years and years of living on food stamps, shivering in the cold, shitting in a cold outhouse—we had the chance to get away from it all and live like royalty but that fucking moron wouldn't do it." He banged against the door one more time. "No more talking, Cole. Your last chance. Come out or I'm coming in."

"Come out and face what?"

He laughed. "My good nature, what else? But if I have to come in—only one of us will be going back up those stairs."

I looked around the basement again. "What are you going to use to get in? A super key?"

"Yeah," he said. "A fucking Remington loaded with twelve-gauge buckshot. It'll take care of that lock in under a second, and will take care of you in just under two. See ya."

I heard him running back up the stairs. I took out my cell phone again. Still looking for a signal. Good luck with that. I went over to the boxes of tapes, recognized some of the names inked on the side. Poor old Bronson Toles. Kept these tapes over all these years, finally found out that they were worth money . . . and then you're killed because of what you want to do with it.

Precious.

These tapes were precious.

I went over to the catering gear, started looking, hands shaking, wondering how long it would take for Vic to grab his shotgun, load it up, and come back down. A minute. Two? Maybe three if I was lucky.

There. Tablecloth. Silverware. Took a knife, tore some strips from the tablecloth.

Some chafing dishes fell over with a crash that startled me. *Come on,* I thought, *come on . . .* there.

Matches.

Nice blue box of matches.

Over there.

Some six-packs of India Pale Ale, in tall bottles. Grabbed a bottle, twisted the top off, laid it on the floor, let it drain while I searched the other catering stuff, looking, kicking with my feet, this part of the room smelling of beer, and—

Thank you.

A little cardboard box with four bottles inside.

"Hey, Cole!" came the voice from the other side of the door. "Your last chance. What do you say?"

I shouted back, "Can you give me another minute?"

"How about no for an answer? How does that sound?"

Plastic bottle in one shaking hand, pouring its contents into a glass bottle with another shaking hand, overfilling it and then putting it on the floor. Stuffing the torn bits of the white tablecloth into the glass bottle.

Grabbing the matches, picking up the bottle, and back to the door.

"All right," I said, throwing the bolt open. "I'm coming out!"

With the matches, I tried to light the cloth.

The match head crumbled as I dragged it across the side of the box.

Damn.

Again.

The matchstick broke in half.

My chest was heavy and thumping, and Vic shouted, "That door handle better be moving in five seconds, or I'm opening fire!"

Another match . . . a scrape . . . a little hiss, and it blossomed into flame. I held it underneath the white rags until they caught fire, and then took the doorknob in my free hand and pushed the door open. It opened just fine, and I ducked my head around the opening, holding the lit bottle in my hand, and Vic was there, his mom standing behind him. Vic's shotgun was pointed at the door, and he was grinning.

"What are you going to do, scorch my eyebrows or something?"

"Or something," I said, and I turned and tossed my homemade Molotov cocktail at the priceless collection of tapes.

The bottle shattered itself on the concrete floor with a very satisfying noise, and then a *whoomph* of burning lamp oil flared out into the open box of tapes, and the flammable tapes caught fire instantly, curling up and exploding in a beautiful blossom of flames and smoke. Vic and Laura both yelled, and Vic burst into the room, looking at the burning tapes, and I grabbed the shotgun with one hand and punched him on the side of the head with the other. He might have put up more of a fight, but the tapes . . . the tapes were everything. His mother ran in and picked up a tablecloth and started battling the flames.

"Water!" Laura screamed. "Get some water!"

With shotgun in hand, I swung it around and caught him in his chest, and he fell back on his butt with an audible *oomph!* I got out of the room, still holding the shotgun, slammed the door, and ran upstairs and—

Haleigh Miller was there just outside the door, trembling, face pale, holding her hands together in a tight fist. No softball bat in sight.

"Go," I said.

"What?"

"Go, run for it. I'll tell the cops somebody slugged me and I didn't see a thing. So get out of here. Now!"

Haleigh turned and started, then stopped, turned again. "I . . . I was in love with Vic. That's all. I didn't mean to hurt you. I was in love with Vic and—"

"For God's sake, stop talking and get moving! The cops and firefighters will be here in a couple of minutes."

She wiped at her tear-filled eyes. "You . . . you're doing this for me?"

"No, you silly girl," I said, shifting the shotgun from one tired hand to the other. "I'm doing it for your dad."

"I don't understand . . . you don't even know my dad!"

"I know enough. Your poor overworked dad, stationed overseas on behalf of a grateful nation that's not too sure why he's there, getting paid crap, working eighty or so hours a week, open to being blown up at any time . . . I don't know your dad, but I know he doesn't need to have his daughter arrested. So get moving . . . now!"

No more talking from her. She turned once more and started walking, then trotting and running, across the parking lot.

I looked back to the Stone Chapel. Smoke was rolling up the stairway to the basement, hugging the top of the slanted ceiling. A person with sympathy and empathy would probably make his way back to the cellar, open up the door, and free Laura and Vic.

Instead, using the shotgun as a cane, I went along the side of the Stone Chapel to the closed entrance, tore the sign down from the fire call box and popped it open, and tugged down on the white handle.

Then I limped back to my Ford, opened up the door, and sat down and waited to hear the sirens.

CHAPTER TWENTY-FIVE

Hours later, I drove down the bumpy driveway to my beach house, body aching and head spinning, as if it had been pumped with nitrogen. My forehead also throbbed with a deep burning feeling, after being whacked by the softball bat wielded by a young woman in love. Earlier, after I'd pulled the fire call box, it took less than five minutes for the firefighters from the uptown Tyler fire station to get to the Stone Chapel, followed by one and then two and then several police cruisers, including the unmarked one belonging to Detective Sergeant Diane Woods and a dark green one belonging to State Police Detective Pete Renzi.

Ambulances arrived as well, and after the fire was knocked down, stretchers were dispatched, and after talking and retalking to both Detective Woods and Detective Renzi, it was time to go home.

Home was where I wanted to be.

I pulled into the shed that served as a garage and walked over to the front of the house, hearing the reassuring sound of the Atlantic rolling in and out. I went up to the front door, grabbed the knob, and—

It spun open.

It was unlocked.

I pushed the door open and heard the low murmur of a television, and lights were on, and I called out, "Annie?"

"Not quite," came the reply.

I stepped into the living room, and a question I had earlier, of where Paula Quinn had gone after being shot at, was answered.

She had come to my home.

I went back and closed the door and returned to the living room. Paula was curled up on my couch, a blue comforter wrapped around her, and she had a weak smile on her face. "You don't like answering your cell phone, do you?"

I pulled my cell phone out, flipped it open, and saw three voice mails. I remembered the call that had come in when I had been talking to Laura Toles.

"Been busy," I said.

"I guess," she said, burrowing deeper into the comforter. "What happened to you? It looks like you've got a hell of a bruise starting up on your forehead."

"Ran into a baseball bat," I said.

"Want to tell me more about that?"

"Not at the moment," I said.

"Fair enough," Paula replied. "My friend, you really should move your spare key to another place. I could have been anybody you know, especially somebody with a bad intention."

I said, "Only a very few people know where that key is. And everyone of them I trust."

Her smile got wider. "Glad to know that."

I went over and sat down on the couch, and she moved her legs to give me room. Her right hand was on top of the comforter, and I softly took her hand in mine and said, "It's over."

"What?"

"It's over. The man who shot Bronson Toles and the Colby College student and who took a shot at you earlier today—he's been arrested. Done. You're safe. Nothing more to be afraid of."

She squeezed my hand tight and closed her eyes. "Tell me more."

"It was Vic Toles. The stepson. He was working with his mom."

"My God. What the hell was going on?"

"What was going on was that Bronson had the rights to years of tapes he had recorded, of musical and comedy groups that had their start at the Stone Chapel, and those tapes were worth millions of dollars. Bronson wanted to spend the money for a variety of causes, and his wife and stepson wanted to take a break from the causes and to see how the other half lives."

"And the college student? And me?"

I squeezed her hand. "He tried to kill me in the marshes after I interviewed Curt Chesak, and that poor John Thomas—he was the only witness to me and Vic being together, just before my supposed murder."

Her voice lowered to a whisper. "And me?"

"I was pushing around, asking too many questions, and he thought that by . . . by causing you harm, I'd step away."

Paula said, "I guess he doesn't know you that well."

"You guess right." I looked around my small living room. "You been here long?"

"Long enough," she said.

"How are you doing?"

She sighed and sank back into the couch. "Much, much better since you came through that door and brought me that news. Lewis, I can't thank you enough, and—"

"How was it, back at your condo?"

Paula looked over my shoulder, at a distant point, and she started talking, in one long breath, as if whatever was inside had to come out, and had to come out quick.

"I was in my living room. It had been a long day. I was just tired . . . felt empty, like all the stories I had written since the gunshot had just drained and drained me. I went to the bathroom . . . my mouth felt foul and I was brushing my teeth, and then I went out to the kitchen to see what I might have for dinner . . . and I dropped my toothbrush . . ." Tears were rolling down Paula's cheeks, but her voice didn't quaver. "So I bent down . . . and the noise all sort of blended together . . . that glass breaking, the bang of the rifle being fired, and so many thoughts went through me, all at once . . . thinking I was hallucinating about what had happened at the Falconer campground, maybe I was sleeping and this was all a bad dream . . . but I hit the floor and knew it was real . . . knew he was out there, trying to kill me . . . I called the police by pulling my phone down off the wall . . . and then I scooted out, like a scared little girl . . . and I ran and ran to the east . . . to the beach . . . and I knew I had to be someplace safe . . . and this is where I ended up, Lewis . . . this is where I ended up . . ."

I squeezed her hand. "You're safe. It's over."

Now she looked at me, tears still in her eyes and rolling down her cheeks. "You're sure? You're absolutely sure?"

"He's in state police custody," I said. "He's being charged with two first-degree murder counts, plus a host of other charges, including the shot at you this morning. Vic Toles is never going to see the free light of day, ever again. This isn't Massachusetts, this isn't New York. If he's very, very lucky, he won't face the death penalty. Paula, he can't hurt you, or attempt to hurt you. Ever again."

Now she smiled and wiped at her nose. "You did it, didn't you. You made it happen."

"I was lucky."

Paula shook her head. "No. You told me you would take care of it, that you would make me safe, and by God you did it. You can do anything, can't you?"

"Not on most days."

She laughed and rearranged the comforter around her. "So those tapes, those million-dollar tapes that caused all these deaths and shootings. Who gets them now?"

"Nobody, I guess," I said. "Most of them don't exist anymore."

"Why's that?"

"Because I torched them, that's why."

She looked at me, gauging, I think, whether I was joking, and then burst out laughing. "Oh, crap, Lewis, that is so funny . . . that is so very precious . . . really? You burned them all?"

"Most of them," I said.

"Why?"

"Extenuating circumstances. I was trying to save my butt."

She smiled. "Such a cute butt it is."

"It holds up my legs," I said.

Then she stopped talking, and her face flushed, and she reached over and took my hand in both of hers and said, "Thank you. Thank you so very much . . . I . . . I really depended on you, Lewis, and you came through. Thank you."

"I was glad to do it."

Her hands didn't leave mine. "Lewis . . ."

"Yes?"

"I have to tell you something."

"Go right ahead."

It was like having my head thunked for the second time that day, for she looked right at me with her bright eyes and teary smile and said, "Lewis, I love you. I've always loved you . . . and this . . . this has just made it that much clearer to me."

What to say to something like that? I looked at those eyes and felt the flash of muscle memory, of the times a few years back when we had been lovers and something very sweet and special, and when I opened my mouth to say something, there was a heavy knock at my door.

I squeezed her hands and got up, and leaned down and kissed

her briefly on the top of her head, and walked to the door. When I opened it up, the surprises kept on coming: It was Mark Spencer, town counsel, state senate candidate, and Paula's supposed boyfriend. He was wearing a dark gray wool coat that fell to his knees and was probably worth more than all of my coats put together.

"Is Paula here?" he asked briskly. He looked pressed for time. "I got her call just a couple of minutes ago."

I opened the door wider. "Come on in. I think she's been waiting for you."

He brushed past me and went into my living room, where Paula was standing up, a tentative smile on her face. They hugged, and he said words of concern and comfort, which I did my best to ignore, and in a manner of seconds, the two of them were leaving. Paula caught my eye and said, "Later?"

"Absolutely," I said. "Later."

Mark led Paula out into the darkness, where his SUV sat, engine grumbling, lights on.

Much later I was in bed and trying to get to sleep after everything that had gone on during this day, and before I started dozing off, I remembered something: those unanswered calls to my cell phone made to me when I was stuck in the basement of the Stone Chapel. I stumbled out of bed and padded downstairs to the kitchen counter, where my cell phone was patiently charging up.

I switched on a kitchen light and, with bare feet on the cold floor, dialed up my voice mail account. There were three messages waiting for me: The first two were from Paula; both were tearful, both were asking where was I and could I please come home as soon as possible. After listening to them both, I deleted them.

The third message was from Annie Wynn. "Lewis, old man, sorry I've been playing phone tag with you . . . okay, you've been playing phone tag, and I've been playing campaign bitch on wheels. Look . . . I'm getting on a plane here in fifteen minutes and I'm going to . . . Christ, where am I going? Let me look at my boarding pass . . . Detroit. I'm off to Detroit . . . and I'll try to call you when I land. . . . Hope you're doing well . . . and friend . . . maybe it's the campaign or that time of the month, but I need to know something important from you . . . about where we're going after the first Tuesday in November . . . and I'm not looking for a commitment . . . but I'm looking for a commitment that this is going to be settled. . . . Damn, my flight's being called. . . . Later, sweetie . . ."

I paused, thinking about what I had just heard. My mind felt like it was surrounded by fog. I pressed the numeral on the keypad that saved the message and went back upstairs to bed, and it took a long time for sleep to come.

CHAPTER TWENTY-SIX

The day was cold and overcast, with rain predicted for later, and I couldn't stop yawning. I was back at the Falconer nuclear power plant site, and I had been cleared to return with a phone call to Ron Shelton that had been accepted with quick professionalism. With me on the same knoll of land as before was Detective Sergeant Diane Woods in black fatigues and wearing a riot helmet with the plastic visor up.

She said, "You look like shit."

"Thanks for the vote of support," I said. "How are you doing?"

"Waiting for this last day of nonsense to end, that's how I'm doing," she said. Out on the salt marsh, beyond the fence line, protesters were gathering in ragged bunches. These weren't the larger groups from the past few days; these people were from the hardcore Nuclear Freedom Front, and it didn't look like there was much hardcore left in anyone.

Even the cops seemed more relaxed, and the National Guard troops were missing as well. I said something about that, and Diane said, "The governor and the legislature don't want to spend a nickel more on this circus than they have to, and so it's up to us cops. Doesn't look like it's going to be much of a problem."

"Looks like you're right," I said.

"Speaking of problems—kudos on what you did on the Toles case. How's your head?"

"Doing fine."

"Hell of a bruise there. What did you do, run into a door?"

"Something like that."

"Hah. I guess we all have our reasons. I suppose Paula Quinn is doing better."

"Yep."

She looked at me, and I looked at her, and my oldest friend laughed. "Go on. You know you can't keep secrets from your Auntie Diane. What's going on with your Paula Quinn?"

"Not sure if she's my Paula Quinn . . . but she's something. You see, after Vic Toles shot at her, she had a number of choices where to go."

"So she ended up at your house."

"Yeah. When I got there later, she was on my couch. We were having a nice little chat and then, just about one minute before her boyfriend showed up, the honorable town counsel from Tyler, she looked up at me and told me that she loved me."

"Loves you like one loves chocolate, or something more meaningful?"

"The second."

"Oh, my poor boy. What did you say to her?"

"With her supposed boyfriend rolling through my front door, not much. Just said we'd talk later. To make things even more interesting, I got a phone message from Annie Wynn, saying it was time for me to man up or something. She wants a commitment for us to discuss what happens next."

"She talking marriage?"

From the salt marsh I could make out some halfhearted chants and jeers. "Not necessarily. It looks like she's going to be in D.C. when the election is over, win or lose, and she wants to know whether I'm going to D.C. or not."

"Your old stomping grounds."

"Didn't particularly like it at the time, and I think I'd like it less if I went back. Even with Annie there, keeping the home fires burning. Or something."

Diane smiled and gently tapped me on the shoulder. "Sweet old Lewis. Women problems, up and down the line. What's a guy to do?"

"I don't know," I said. "I was planning to ask you."

"Advice? Advice on women? My dear boy, that's a mystery I'll never be able to solve. Even if I do pee sitting down along with billions of my sisters."

Her attitude was bright and cheerful, and something came to me. "All right, now it's time to talk to Uncle Lewis. What's going on with you and Kara?"

The smile was so bright it was almost blinding. Then she raised her left hand and wiggled the fingers at me. Light flickered on a diamond ring I had never seen before.

"True?"

"Oh, very true, Lewis."

"You two set a wedding date yet?"

"First day of summer, next year. Which is the anniversary of our first date. Can you believe it?"

I hoped my smile matched hers. "Diane, that's great, great news."

"So you better be there that June day, my friend, or it's going to be dangerous driving in Tyler for the rest of your life."

"Wouldn't miss it for anything."

"Glad to hear that, because you're going to be part of the ceremony—and no excuses. I want you to stand with me when I get married."

"Diane, I'd be honored."

She was still smiling, even as her eyes moistened. "Thanks it's been a long, long haul—and who can believe that this quirky little state will give Kara and me marriage rites. Oh, such a long haul . . ."

"Are you finally coming out of the closet?"

"I've been half in and half out for the past few years, Lewis, but I'm going to be so hard and fast out of the closet its door is going to be orbiting Jupiter."

I remembered something and said, "You know, during the last day of the regular demonstrations, I saw Kara in the crowds. And when the demo was over for the day, I saw her arguing with a couple of her fellow marchers. Any connection?"

"Very perceptive, Mr. Cole. She told me all about it later that night. Three members of her affinity group were giving her a hard time about the police response. Calling me a jackbooted thug, fascist, member of the corporate party state. That sort of thing. Kara didn't like it very much, they got into a shouting match, and that was that."

"She out of the antinuclear movement?"

Diane looked over at the rest of the cops. "She's still against nuclear power, but she's finally decided that she's for me a bit more. What a life, eh?"

"I guess. How about your end-of-the-season sail run on the *Miranda*?"

"Still on for this Saturday, weather permitting," she said, looking up at the clouds. "Tell you what, you want to come along?"

"You sure?"

"Of course I'm sure. You, me, and Kara." She looked around, lowered her voice. "But if you're expecting a threesome, buddy, forget it."

That drew a fresh smile from me. "Maybe the two of you can figure things out for me instead."

"Lewis, you're a smart fellow, I'm sure you can figure it out on your own."

I kept quiet. Her expression changed from Diane my best friend to Diane the police detective sergeant. "Lewis . . . what's going on?"

I looked at that serious face. "What's going on is that I think Paula Quinn was acting entirely out of emotion. Ever since the shooting, her life has been in turmoil. She knows I've been working the matter. And when that shot came through her window, she went to the nearest place that offered sanctuary. My home."

Diane nodded. "And?"

"And when I got there and told her that she was safe, that the shooter was under arrest, I think her emotions got ahold of her. She blurted out things that might have made sense at the time, but maybe not down the road."

"Nice analysis there, pal. So, your Annie Wynn?"

"She's being serious, she's being forward-looking. She's working in an environment that's daily chaos, everything depending on polls, pundits, and the voters. She's looking for something solid to hold on to, and she's wondering if that's going to be me."

"You're two for two, Lewis. So what, then?"

"Am I the solid one for her? Still thinking it through."

Now Diane the detective sergeant was back to Diane my oldest friend. "Don't think it through too long. The ones who offer themselves, who offer their love and devotion . . . they are hard to find. Don't let this one slip through your fingers."

"Thanks for the advice."

"Only good advice if you take it."

From the line of cops someone blew a whistle, and Diane frowned. "Time to get back to the playground. You take care . . . and thanks for everything—and I mean everything."

"Just doing my job, ma'am."

Standing there, with her riot helmet, her black jumpsuit and heavy boots, her equipment belt with nightstick, gas mask, and handcuffs, my friend suddenly looked very vulnerable. "No, my dear. You're being you. Loyal, trustworthy, all that Boy Scout stuff. Plus being a pain in the ass and sometimes on the outer limits of the law."

"Sounds good to me," I said.

"Later, Lewis."

"Later."

Before she rejoined her fellow police officers, she did something I will always remember.

She reached over and touched my cheek with her gloved hand.

Diane touched me.

Then she was gone.

CHAPTER TWENTY-SEVEN

The protesters approached in a ragged line, carrying wooden staves and plywood shields with the Nuclear Freedom Front logo spray-painted on the front. They wore bandannas or balaclavas over their faces, and some wore hockey helmets. Unlike the other group of demonstrators, they had no happy balloons, papier-mâché puppets, or banners. Just the lines of NFF members approaching, banging their staves on the shields. I was standing with a few reporters, including television crews from the Boston channels and Manchester. Usually television crews and reporters are a cynical and wisecracking lot, able to make jokes at bloody traffic accidents and beach drownings, but they watched in silence as the protesters came up to the fence. There was no joy, no singing, no chanting from those approaching the power plant. Just the marchers and the rhythmic pounding of the staves on the plywood shields.

"Pretty pathetic, don't you think?" came a male voice. Next to me was Ron Shelton, the power plant's spokesman. He was dressed sharp from his hard hat to new work boots, but his arms were folded and his face was drawn from exhaustion.

"Some would say they're just exercising their constitutional rights," I said.

"No doubt—but you know what else they're doing out there? They're damaging the same environment they claim they love so much. For the past several days, there's been thousands of people out there trampling on the salt marsh, tearing up and tromping on rare vegetation, digging fire pits, shitting and pissing in the woods—have you seen a single chemical toilet out there?—and leaving mounds of trash behind. Us? This whole complex is built on granite bedrock. We had to put up barriers to protect the salt marsh from any runoff, and we had to file thousands of pages of environmental impact statements. Those clowns? Not a fucking thing."

His face was sharp, and I said, "For what it's worth, everything you've just said has been off the record."

"Thanks."

"But one quick question."

"That's my job. Go ahead."

"Your sister, is she still singing?"

He looked surprised. "Yeah. She is. Why do you ask?"

"She sounds like a talent. I'd like to hear her sometime."

"If you don't mind going to temple, sure, I'll let you know."

"Thanks," I said.

Ron looked at the ragged group approaching, shook his head, and walked off.

A light drizzle started falling.

My cell phone rang, and I looked at the incoming call. Boston—but not Annie.

I flipped it open and said, "Go ahead, Denise."

"Where are you?"

"In Tahiti. You?"

"In Boston, still looking for that elusive sense of humor I'm supposed to have. Look, is that demonstration under way yet?"

"Sort of," I said. "The cops are on one side of the fence, the antinuclear folks are on the other side of the fence. Whether the twain shall meet we'll see."

"Fine," Denise said. "Give me another thousand words at the

end of the day—and make it good. We're on the verge of getting some venture capital investing to take *Shoreline* digital and high-tech, and your pieces over the past several days are one of the reasons we're getting there."

"That sounds nice," I said. "Does it mean I get a raise?"

"It means you keep your job," she snapped back, and then she hung up.

With the other journalists, I tagged along behind the police officers, marching up to the fence, moving in a straight line the best they could over the rough terrain. From where I stood, the line looked pretty thin, and I wondered if the governor's decision to pull away the National Guard had been the right one.

The drizzle was coming down harder.

"Lewis? Lewis Cole?"

A young woman reporter moved over to me, wearing a light blue knit cap over short blond hair. She had on a black wool coat and blue jeans, and she looked like she could be Paula Quinn's younger sister.

"That's right," I said, "and you must be Melanie, the stringer for the *Chronicle*."

"The former stringer for the *Chronicle*," she said, smiling. "Thanks to Paula, I'm now a full-time reporter."

"Good for you," I said. "I hope it works out."

"I hope so, too. I have a message for you, from Paula. She's taking a few days off—understandable, right?"

"Right," I said. "What's the message?"

"A simple one," Melanie said. "Just 'thanks.'"

"Just 'thanks,'" I repeated. "Appreciate you passing it along."

"No problem," she said. She looked over at the fence and the two opposing lines, and she said, "What's going to happen?"

"The protesters are going to try to occupy the plant site. The police are going to try to keep them away. Good chance it's going to get nasty, and quite soon."

"So much for peaceful protests."

"The NFF makes no bones about what they plan to do, and if it takes violence, so be it."

She looked again. "I wonder where their leader is—that Chesak fellow."

I took off my small knapsack and retrieved a set of binoculars. I brought them up to my face and scanned the approaching crowds. I looked twice more and handed the binoculars over to Melanie. "Doesn't look like he's there. Quite the surprise."

She took the glasses, gave the crowd a good look. "Yes, quite a surprise."

Not the last one for the day.

Melanie went closer, and I stayed back, watching half of the protesters break away from the crowd and move to the left, moving quickly, coming to the fence. Some carried ladders and propped them up against the chain-link fence. Cheers broke out as three protesters scaled the ladders and reached the top of the fence, but they were knocked sprawling as police officers up against the fence poked through the openings with their nightsticks, pushing the ladders back. The other group—a ready reserve, it looked like—hung back, cheering on their comrades.

Other police officers stood by the fence as well, squirting pepper spray. Some of the antinuclear activists turned away, but some wearing gas masks or goggles managed to stay there, working at the fence.

More shouts, more pounding of the staves against the shields. The crowds were falling back. The number of people seemed smaller than what I recalled from the other day. Raindrops splattered against my coat. A wind picked up from the east. It looked like the protest was faltering. If it ended in the next half hour or so, I could get home, write my column, and make a very important phone call to Annie Wynn. Then maybe to Diane Woods as well.

It was time for decisions, and all I needed was the proper time and place.

Then it all went wrong.

To the right, about fifty yards away from the place where the police and the protesters were battling, seven or eight young men suddenly stood up, wearing coverings with leaves, twigs, and vegetation about them. Ghillie suits, what snipers use to come up close to their prey.

The men trotted to the fence line, each carrying a length of rope. They clipped the ends of the rope to the fence, and as one, they tugged.

The fence fell.

"I'll be damned," I whispered.

Sometime during the night, they must have crept up to the fence and quietly sabotaged it, cutting through the supporting wires and frames. Then, at the proper time, this hidden crew had broken a lengthy section of fence. There was a large open space leading right into the power plant property.

The group of protesters that I thought had been waiting and killing time as some sort of ready reserve started running to the opening, moving fast, shields and staves at the ready.

A diversion, that's all the fence climbing with the ladders was. It was just a diversion.

With shouts and yells of triumph, the NFF members ran into

the plant property. From the left, a line of police officers was running to the fence opening as well, and in another minute or two, they collided.

Fighting broke out, a confusing mass of police officers and pro-testers, wrestling, punching, flailing. I tried to keep track of it all and failed. Three demonstrators ran past me, hooting and laugh-ing, hollering, "We did it, we did it, we did it!" Somewhere horns blew. There were whistles as well. The protesters moved against some of the police officers, and there was fighting among them all, nightsticks against wooden staves, against shields, against raised arms.

Near me was a construction trailer, and smoke billowed out as flames burst through broken windows. On the cement wall of a building, a solitary demonstrator was spray-painting FUCK NUKES. Two dark gray pickup trucks came in from the plant site, screech-ing to a halt. Security officers from the power plant tumbled out, shotguns up. I looked around, looked around. More shouting. Two police officers were nearly surrounded by protesters, re-treating up on a small rise of land near the burning trailer. One officer fell. The protesters ignored him. They kept on pushing and pushing at the solitary police officer.

Leading the charge was a man I recognized, even with a ban-danna over his face: the previously missing Curt Chesak. He was shouting something I couldn't make out, but he was also carrying a length of metal pipe, which he swung back and forth at the po-lice officer holding a nightstick, reaching for a weapon, the police officer stumbling . . .

It was Diane Woods.

I started running.

Someone tripped me. I fell, scraping my knees and hands. I

got up and ran again, and Diane was on the ground, curled on one side, as Curt stood over her, hitting her again and again and again with the length of pipe. He then bent down and tugged at something, and with a whoop and yell of triumph, he held up her riot helmet.

"Diane!" I yelled, getting back to my feet, and there was a *pop pop pop* as tear gas canisters exploded in the crowd. Some of the police officers tugged on their gas masks, but I kept on running, pushing, shoving, and then I was there. The ground was stone and gravel with some tufts of grass, and blood. There was sprayed blood. Diane was on her side. Her hair was matted on one side. Blood streamed from her mouth and nose. Her eyes were closed. I gently rolled her onto her back. My hands were shaking. Rain started pouring down. I touched her skin. It was cold and clammy.

Loud reports, coming from behind me. Gunshots. Not more tear gas. Gunshots.

I put my hand at her throat, feeling and looking for a pulse.

I couldn't feel a thing.

Couldn't feel a thing.

CHAPTER TWENTY-EIGHT

I was grabbed from behind, thrown to the ground. Sirens wailed, and I got up and was kicked in the head and fell back. Long seconds seemed to pass. I got up again in the rain. An ambulance from the nuclear power plant was parked near the rise of land, and a folding gurney was being pushed in, a still shape wearing a Tyler police officer's jumpsuit aboard, a blanket pulled up, the head secured in a pink foam collar. Four or five police officers were helping put the gurney in. The door was slammed, and the ambulance roared off, siren sounding.

Two other ambulances were parked nearby. A fire engine was by the trailer, and firefighters in yellow turnout gear were wetting down the structure. I got up, legs shaking. Some semblance of order seemed to be restored in the driving rain. Police officers with shotguns were standing guard over a seated assembly of protesters, their hands behind their heads. Another line of police was standing by the opening in the fence. Between them was a pile of wooden staves and plywood signs with the NFF logo. Two more gurneys were being loaded onto ambulances. On paved ground near a collection of pipes and valves, two bodies were stretched out, and police officers there were taking photos, measuring, talking to each other, hands moving a lot. Little triangular signs with letters on them were set up around the bodies, marking evidence.

I swallowed. My mouth was very dry, and my hands and knees hurt where I had fallen onto the dirt and gravel. A helicopter roared overhead, followed by another, both from Boston television stations. There were loud voices coming from somewhere, and I saw Ron Shelton standing on a cement block, being besieged by reporters. I moved over and caught snatches of his conversation, as Ron tried his best.

". . . we abhor violence, of course we do, but this was not a peaceful organization . . ."

". . . we can't make a comment yet on these deaths, until we have the full facts from the investigating authorities . . ."

". . . we believe our security force responded appropriately to the threatening actions posed by these trespassers . . ."

I elbowed my way through the reporters frantically taking photos and shouting questions, and I yelled out, the best I could, "Ron, can I get an escort to leave the plant site?"

I had to shout twice more before he responded. His face was quite red, and his hands were trembling. "No," he said. "No one's leaving until the police and our security organization complete their preliminary investigation. I'm sure you understand that."

I was going to say something else, but I saw two security officers from the Falconer nuclear plant standing warily behind Ron, watching us members of the Fourth Estate at work, and I just nodded and slipped out from the crowd.

I walked away from the news gaggle, took out my notebook, made sure my press pass was fluttering publicly in the breeze. I knew I was being watched, and I had an idea of what to do. I walked slowly and then stopped, making notes in my notebook, trying to shield it from the rain, so it looked like I was trying to reconstruct what had just happened. There were more sirens sounding out in the distance, meaning reinforcements were on their way, so I didn't have time to waste.

So I didn't waste any. I ambled slowly away from the ambulances, the bodies, the police, the security force, the firefighters, and the helicopters overhead, and from that bloody rise of land where one Chris Chesak had pummeled my best friend, Diane.

In a few minutes, unescorted and by myself, I reached the main parking lot, where my Ford Explorer was parked. About twenty feet away, there was a news van from the ABC affiliate in New Hampshire, and a young, attractive woman dressed in a red cloth coat whom I recognized from the 6:00 P.M. newscasts was screaming at two plant security officers, her face the color of her coat, using language that would make a U.S. marine blush.

I quietly got into the Ford, started up the engine, and slowly backed out of the parking lot and went out to the main access road, where I halted at a stop sign. Ron had said the plant was closed down, which meant that the gates at the north and south ends were closed and guarded.

I shifted into drive. I knew there were other ways out of the plant site.

I felt the urge to slam the accelerator down and get going, but I kept things under control as I made a turn onto a bumpy dirt road, and kept my speed limit at about fifteen miles an hour, passing underneath the huge transmission lines that led out to the rest of the state. It was a short but difficult drive, because in my mind's eye, I kept on seeing the form of Diane on the ground, the gleeful joy that Chris Chesak took in battering her, and I also remembered the cold touch of her skin, and my frantic search for a pulse.

There. The Stony Creek Road gate. Last time I was here, it was locked and unguarded. Today, in the driving rain, it was still locked.

Locked and guarded.

I drove up a bit and glanced over at the gate. A pickup truck from the Falconer security force was parked at the side, and two security officers were standing outside, in light brown rain slickers, weapons over their shoulders, watching me. I gave a cheery wave, then stopped the Explorer, then put the gearshift into reverse. I slowly backed into a turn, as if I had gone down the wrong road and was lost.

I backed down a few yards toward the gate and waited, looked out the rain-streaked windshield, watched the moving wiper blades, and then looked up at the rearview mirror. The security officers were talking and didn't seem too concerned, and again I saw the bloody shape of Diane on the ground.

I slammed my foot down on the accelerator.

Still in reverse, the Explorer quickly barreled its way down the dirt road, right up to the gate, and the guards seemed shocked, and I braced myself for the impact as I roared right by them and the rear bumper of the Explorer struck the fence hard. The jolt of the collision rattled my teeth, and my hands flew off the steering wheel, and the Explorer fishtailed and went off the side of the road, and the rear hatchback window was shattered, but in front of me was a splintered and open gate.

Two very angry security officers were running toward me, one shrugging off his shotgun, the other frantically talking into a handheld radio.

I gave them another wave, punched the Explorer into drive, made a muddy and violent U-turn, and got the hell out of there.

The trip from Falconer to Exonia takes about twenty minutes.

I got there in twelve.

As on my last visit to the hospital after a violent incident, the parking lot was crowded, with cars parked everywhere, another news helicopter overhead, and a television crew doing a live stand-up outside of the emergency room entrance, the harsh lights from the camera making everything look unreal in the driving rain. I found an empty spot at a parking lot a hundred yards or so away, and backed in my Ford so the broken rear window wasn't visible. If the security people at Falconer had put out an alert to local law enforcement about a Ford Explorer with a shattered rear window, I didn't want to make it easy for the Exonia cops to track me down.

I trotted up a slight hill to the emergency room and was out of breath when I got in, and I was so fortunate as to see Kara Miles standing by herself, sobbing. When she threw herself at me I hugged her hard and said, "How is she? What do you know? How is she?"

Through the sobs she gasped out that she wasn't sure, that Diane had gone straight into surgery, that she was promised an update as soon as one was made available, and for God's sake, will you stay with me?

"Yes," I said, still holding her tight. "By God I will."

We found a place to sit just outside of the emergency room entrance, in a short hallway, and she held my hand and said, "Thank God I got the call . . . there's a secretary at the police station, she knows about me and Diane . . . when she got word about her being hurt, she called me . . . and bless the people here, Lewis, there's none of this bullshit about me not being a family member or a relative . . . so here I am . . ."

She had on a pair of dark blue sweats and a dungaree jacket, and her eyes were swollen and weepy. Her nose looked raw as she sniffled. "Lewis . . . you're bleeding. Your lower lip."

I touched my lip, and my fingers came away bloody. I put a handkerchief to my lip. "Had a bit of a problem getting out of the plant site. How long have you been here?"

"Not that long . . . damn it, did you see Diane before the fighting broke out? Did you talk to her?"

"Yes, I did," I said, "and she told me the good news about you two. I'm happy . . . real happy."

Kara drew a forearm across her nose, wiping it. "Some fucking happy good news . . . I gave her a hard time, I delayed and delayed, all because I was such a tight ass about fighting for some cause . . . instead of fighting for the woman I love . . . and look where I am. Shit, Lewis, tell me . . . how bad is it? Did you see what happened?"

I couldn't say anything else. "She was cornered by a couple of the violent ones. She put up a fight. She fell. They beat her up pretty bad, Kara . . . I saw a lot of blood . . . but this is a good place. They'll do their very best."

She sobbed some more, and as the minutes and minutes dragged on, more police officers from the Tyler Police Department came in, most of them in civilian clothes, as the usual efficient cop telegraph got to work, alerting everyone that a fellow officer had been hurt. While they came in, a few nodded at Kara, but they clustered together as a wounded tribe as Kara held my hand tight and talked about the trips she and Diane had taken over the years to Northampton and Provincetown and Key West, and lots of islands in the Caribbean, where Diane would often rent a sailboat so they could go island hopping, and how they had planned a trip after Christmas to the British Virgin Islands to celebrate their engagement, and—

A short, plump woman in surgical scrubs came out through a set of swinging doors that had HOSPITAL STAFF ONLY posted on them, and then she spotted Kara and came toward us. Kara squeezed my hand so hard I could feel my muscles ache, and she whispered, "Oh Christ, what will I do if I'm a widow before I get married, oh, Lewis, what will I do?"

The doctor smiled weakly and said, "Let's go somewhere private, all right?"

The two of us got up and made the very, very long walk to a private reception room that was about five feet away.

The doctor's name was Hanratty and she got right to it. "The good news is that she's alive. She's made it through surgery. However, she's suffered some severe injuries to her face and skull."

The doctor went on, talking about fractures and abscesses and broken orbital sockets and nose, and stitches and such. I felt like

I was going to float out of the chair. Diane was alive. She was alive. I knew her well. She was so very strong, and—

Then I came back hard to the chair.

"Excuse me, could you say that again?" I asked. "I didn't quite hear it."

The doctor looked to Kara and then at me. "What I said is that she's in recovery, but so far, she's not responsive. It appears that she suffered some severe trauma to the head . . . and as of this moment, she's in a coma."

Kara's voice was bleak. "How long?"

Dr. Hanratty said, "We just don't know. It could be a day or two. Or more than that. If it goes on beyond a week . . . we'll be very, very concerned, and we'll be looking at other options."

"What other options?" Kara demanded.

"Options that we don't need to discuss at the moment," she said, but I knew what those options were going to be: an eventual transfer to a long-term-care rehabilitation facility, as whatever passed for Diane Woods in the recesses of her brain flickered and died, and her strong body withered and curled up and looked like an adult fetus, staying alive year after year through tubes and humming machinery.

"Can we see her?" I asked.

The doctor shook her head. "Not right now. She's in recovery, and will be there for a few hours. Then she'll be transferred to the intensive care unit. Your best bet will be to come back sometime tomorrow—but your visit will have to be a short one, you understand."

I'm sure Kara understood, but her face was set, tears streaming down her cheeks. Dr. Hanratty got up and passed over a business card. "We're doing all that we can . . . and I'm sorry, right now I have to brief the Tyler police chief. She went through surgery better than we anticipated . . . so keep that in mind."

Kara nodded, and Dr. Hanratty walked out, and I stayed with Kara as she cried some more.

Later we ate something in the hospital's cafeteria, and Kara said, "I called my brother. He's coming up here to be with me . . . and I don't plan to leave this place. I mean, what if she wakes up and asks for me?"

I wasn't going to crush her illusion, so I said, "I hate to do this, Kara, but I've got to leave. I don't want to, but there are things going on."

She stared right through me and said, "I think I understand. I really do. So go and do what has to be done . . . and thanks, Lewis. Thanks for being here."

I got up from the cafeteria table. "I couldn't be anywhere else."

CHAPTER TWENTY-NINE

After making an ATM run in Exonia and traveling as fast as I could without being pulled over, I was in a small motel on the outskirts of Concord, New Hampshire's capital, where I paid in cash and registered as Kelly Smith. Earlier I had made a quick stop at a nearby Walmart and had taped up the rear opening the best I could with duct tape and plastic sheeting. Now I was lying on top of the motel's lumpy bed, a McDonald's plain cheese-burger and fries balanced on my chest as I watched and rewatched the news coverage of the day's disaster from the three Boston channels, the Manchester channel, and the small but proud New England Cable News Network.

I ate without tasting a damn thing as I kept track of the coverage. The current numbers showed nearly fifty protesters arrested, two dead, and several injured. There were also a half dozen officers injured, one critically, said officer being Diane Woods. Ron Shelton, the plant spokesman, looked about as calm as a French noble approaching a wooden wheeled cart in 1795 in Paris, and there was some controversy over how the two protesters—a young man from Maine and another young man from Pennsylvania— had been shot and killed, since some of the arrested protesters were found to be carrying firearms.

There was also an alert to locate and arrest one Curt Chesak, of the Nuclear Freedom Front, for trespass, assault, and incitement to riot. Only one television news camera had caught Diane's beating from Curt, but that one camera did enough: I saw that video about a half dozen times that evening, and seeing it didn't help me get to sleep at all.

Neither did seeing one other thing on the video: a shape in the foreground, not moving, who looked an awful lot like me, and who didn't do anything to help out his beaten friend.

With lights and my cell phone off, I spent most of the next several hours staring up at the ceiling, thinking and planning a lot.

At 9:01 A.M. the next day, I presented myself at the headquarters of the New Hampshire State Police in Concord, located in a collection of state office buildings on Hazen Drive. Among the roadways and parking lots, there were a number of wooded areas. I went into the lobby, found the offices of the Major Crime Unit, and told the accommodating secretary that I wanted to see Detective Pete Renzi. I took an elevator up to the third floor and met Renzi right outside the elevator doors. He was a bit better dressed than the last time I saw him, but not by much. His hair was still cut short and his skin was still light olive, and he said, "How's Diane?"

"Not good," I said. "In critical condition. Look, you got a minute?"

"Sure," he said, gesturing with an arm. "Come on back to my office."

"I could really use a cigarette," I said.

His gaze was steady. "All right. A cigarette it is."

We took the elevator to the ground floor in silence, and we walked across the parking lot to a grove of trees. He turned and said, "Here we go."

"Not having a smoke?"

"Trying to quit for the sixth time this year. Now go on. What's up?"

"Curt Chesak. What can you tell me about him?"

Renzi said, "Not much. Seemed to come out of nowhere a year ago, hooked up with the Nuclear Freedom Front, which at the time was about a half dozen college students, former anarchists who thought fighting for safe energy was the way to go."

"Anything else?"

"Not sure what you're driving at, Lewis."

I said, "Diane is my oldest and best friend. I want to know everything I can about Curt Chesak."

That seemed to get his attention. We stood there among the big old tall pines, and he reached into his coat, pulled out a pack of Marlboros, and lit one up. "Shit. Off the wagon again." He took a deep puff, let it out, and said, "Based on what you did with the Bronson Toles matter, I suppose this shouldn't come as any surprise—but are you sure?"

"Very sure," I said.

Another deep drag. "I told you earlier that I know Diane.

Know her very well. In fact . . . you could say we travel in similar circles. So I've trusted her for a very, very long time. So you have that going for you. You were lucky with the Toles case; you could have ended up in a swamp somewhere, with your brain matter being picked over by seagulls. So what I need to know is this: Are you going to do the right thing with any information I give you?"

"Meaning what?"

"Meaning that there's no blowback, nothing to connect you with me or the New Hampshire State Police. Because by talking to you right here, I've crossed a line, and I'm trusting you to make sure that nobody else knows that this line has been crossed."

"Nobody will. Guaranteed."

Another puff of the cigarette. "This Chesak character . . . like I said, not much known about him. Came out of the darkness and took over the NFF and built it right up, in a matter of months. The only lead we have is that he's associated with a college professor in Boston, a history teacher at B.U., but that history professor, a sharp guy, won't say one goddamn thing. So there you go."

"That's it?"

Renzi said, "Stay here a couple of minutes, and I'll come back out with a few sheets of paper that contain all we have on that squirrelly bastard. So you mind sticking around?"

"Not at all."

He lifted up a foot, carefully stubbed out the cigarette on the sole of his shoe, and went back into the office building. I stayed there in the trees, waiting. I could hear the hum of traffic from the nearby I-393. Just another workday for lots of people, but not for me. Renzi came back a couple of minutes later and passed over a thin brown envelope. I took it, and he said, "Anything else?"

"Yeah," I said. "I think the Falconer police and the security folks at the power plant are looking for me. Any chance you could intervene, get them off my back for a while?"

"What did you do?"

"Left the power plant property without proper permission."

"Doesn't sound like much."

I said, "I seem to have destroyed a chain-link fence gate along the way."

"Oh," Renzi said. "Yeah, that'll piss off some people. Sure, I'll make a couple of phone calls. That detective in Falconer, Thornton, he's a good guy. I'll . . . I'll talk to him, maybe share a cigarette or two. The Falconer power plant folks, I don't know . . . I don't know how long I can hold them off for. Maybe a day or two."

I held up the envelope to him in a salute. "That will be plenty of time. I won't be around in a day or two."

On the drive back to the seacoast on Route 101, the two-lane highway stretching from the ocean to Vermont, I switched on my cell phone, and like magic, it started ringing. I answered the phone and was immediately rewarded by a blast of irritated woman, so loud it was like she was in my backseat and not in Boston.

"Lewis!" Denise shouted. "Where in hell is that copy you owe me? Remember? A thousand words last night about the demo?"

"Guess it slipped my mind," I said.

I know it's not nice to say a woman screeched when her voice reaches a certain level, but it was certainly the case with Denise, who went on and said, "A major demonstration! Protesters shot! Cops beaten up! The plant terrorized! And you didn't file a goddamn thing—even though I told you how important it was, for the magazine's future, and the venture capitalists who are—"

"Denise?"

"What?"

"Can I say something here?"

"If it's another one of your lame apologies or goddamn jokes, then no, you can't say anything, because—"

"Denise," I said. "I quit."

There was some static on the other end, and I thought maybe she had hung up or the line had gone dead. I passed a truck hauling a Walmart trailer and said, "You still there, Denise?"

"Lewis—"

"I quit, I resign, I depart, I am now leaving the employ of *Shoreline* magazine. Have I made that clear enough?"

"Don't you dare."

"I just did."

"Then I'll come after you," she said. "For back wages. For getting paid by us illegally when you should have been paid by the government. For defrauding the magazine. What do you think of that?"

I passed another Walmart truck. I briefly wondered if they were hiring. "Gee, that sounds awful," I said, "and you know what? Fine by me. I still quit."

Then I hung up, switched off the phone, and tossed it to the seat beside me.

CHAPTER THIRTY

At home I made a list and started working my way down, packing things, getting the utilities paid in advance, and a bunch of other little irritating details. I made a phone call to another friend and was very pleased that I wasn't interrogated at length: I was just asked one question, about time and place, which I answered. Then

I had to drive out to the Tyler Post Office—still bravely stuck in the nineteenth century, I couldn't get my mail held without going there in person—and when I got back home, I found something on my concrete doorstep: a small cardboard shoe box from Timberland, with nothing on the outside as a message.

Inside, though, were two messages. One was with two typed words on a plain piece of white paper: Good luck.

The other message was my 9 mm Beretta, returned after being taken into custody by Detective Mike Thornton of the Falconer Police Department.

Later that night, my list, which had grown as the night progressed, ended up with only one item left, and after a series of unanswered phone calls, the phone was finally answered at 1:00 A.M. as I sat on the couch and watched a Discovery Channel program about crab fishermen.

"Lewis," she said.

"Annie," I said.

"Late night for you," she said.

"You, too?"

She yawned. "I have a staff meeting in thirty minutes, so what do you think?"

"I think this campaign has gone on too long for you, me, and the rest of Western civilization. That's what I think."

"No argument here. What's going on?"

On the television screen the crab fishermen were exhausted and nearly frozen, ice-water spray dunking them over and over again as they hauled in pots weighing hundreds of pounds. Right about now, from where I was, it looked like a lot of fun.

"Your last message, you said you were looking for something

from me. A commitment . . . as to whether a commitment was going to be made."

I waited. No reply. I said, "Something's come up . . . and it can go a number of ways, and if it goes bad, I want you to be able to say with a clear conscience that you had no idea what I was up to. In a few hours I'm leaving Tyler, and I don't know how and when I'm coming back . . . but in the meantime, I want to ensure that there's nothing going on that connects you with me . . . as I do this thing."

Her voice had no emotion. "Can it wait?"

"No."

"Lewis, you know what I have facing me in these next few days. You can't delay this . . . secret mission of yours to help me out?"

"Again, I'm sorry, no."

I heard a deep breath from her side of the phone. "I don't want to get into an argument . . . a discussion . . . or pleading . . . it's just that for a moment, I thought we had something special, something we could build on . . . and I see I was wrong."

"You weren't wrong, Annie. It's the circumstances that were wrong. That's all."

"So you're asking me to wait?"

"I am. You're . . . you're the best thing that's ever happened to me, in a very long time . . . and something this special . . . it has to be protected . . . but at the same time . . ."

"Duty calls, eh?"

"Yes, it does."

A long silence. "Then you be damn careful, all right? And if you don't come back and tell me everything that has gone on, and then talk to me about where we go from here, then I'll break your arms."

"Deal," I said.

"Don't think I'm joking. In this campaign—I've gotten to know people."

"I know you have."

There was a *click-click* sound, and she said, "Shit, another call coming in. I'll have to call you back."

"Sure," I said, and I hung up and stretched out on the couch, knowing Annie, and knowing that call would never come.

The morning October air was cool as I walked up my dirt driveway carrying two zippered black duffel bags. I looked back at my solitary house and the cove from where it kept view, and maybe it was the cold or what had gone on before, but that normal happy sight seemed empty to me, like a barren cove, void of joy and happiness.

In the parking lot of the Lafayette House, Felix Tinios waited for me, in a black Cadillac Escalade SUV. He helped me put in my luggage, and I got into the warm front seat.

"Not your usual wheels," I said.

Felix had on a nice gray wool coat, black trousers, and a white turtleneck. His own luggage and gear were in the rear. He drove us out to Atlantic Avenue and said, "Got it from a friend of a friend . . . not traceable to you or me. Where to?"

"Boston, eventually," I said, "but first, Exonia."

"All right."

At the Exonia Hospital, the intensive care unit was on the third floor, and I was admitted into the room only after promising to stay just five minutes and not say or do a damn thing. Outside the ICU, on a long couch, Kara Miles had been sleeping, and I let her be. In the ICU room I didn't sit down; I just stood there and watched, and remembered.

I had first met Diane Woods when she had been the sole police detective for Tyler and I had moved to New Hampshire after my career at the Department of Defense had come to an early and disastrous end. While working through my long recovery in Tyler, I found an urge, a quest, to get involved and do things, and make them right when I could. When that process had started, I had at first bumped heads with Diane, until we had gotten to know each other when she realized I would try so very hard never to put her into jeopardy, or to betray her.

Over the years there had been ski trips, many meals in places from hot dog stands at Tyler Beach to five-star restaurants in Boston, tips given from her and cases solved from me, sailing trips on her boat, and just a deep, strong, and devoted friendship between us, a friendship that had weathered a lot of things along the way.

Now she was silent, in a bed, a ventilator tube breathing for her. Her face was swollen and had no resemblance to her usual appearance. Both eyes were blackened, her head was covered in bandages, and a drain was running out of one side. Her hands and arms were still, and IV tubes ran out from both of them to bags of fluid hanging from metal poles. Overhead were monitors that beeped and whirred, and I just stood there, watching her chest slowly rise up and then come down. Over and over again. There were two empty chairs in the room, and a locker, and a window that gave a view of some oak trees, their leaves bright red and orange.

I knew time was slipping away, and I knew I had to leave, but it was like I was frozen to the shiny clean floor. I wanted her to stir. I wanted her eyes to flicker open. I wanted her to yank out the ventilator tube and look to me and say, "Lewis, what the hell is going on here?"

Nothing happened.

The machinery clicked and whirred. Her chest rose up and down.

I squeezed her hand, kissed her where I could, and then left.

In the parking lot of the hospital, I rejoined Felix and wiped at my eyes. "Thanks," I said. "I appreciate it."

"No problem."

He drove us out of the parking lot, and I said, "No, Felix. I mean . . . this is taking you away from your paying union gig and who knows what else."

Felix laughed. "I was getting tired of that union job, to tell you the truth. Too much skulking around, too many times I had to sit still and hear about the problems of the working class while Joe Manzi had plans on expanding his Aruba condo stuck in his briefcase. Besides, this sounds like it's going to be . . . interesting, and I've been bored lately."

"Glad I could help you out."

In a few minutes we were out of Exonia and were briefly back in Tyler as we took I 95 south to Boston. Felix said, "All right, all I ask is two things. Okay?"

"What's that?"

"First is, my assistance here is never acknowledged publicly or privately to anyone else. Word gets around that I'm helping you in connection with a police detective, even one as fair as Diane Woods, who's arrested me at least three times, well, it would look bad."

"Fine, that's easy," I said. "What's the other demand?"

Even in the flowing traffic, he looked right at me. "That there's no bullshit here, okay? We're off on a trip here that's going to have some serious consequences, so I need to know, in what way am I helping you? Okay? You've got me here, and this is a job, but I need to know up front what you have planned."

Inside the Cadillac, it was warm, and safe, and so very comfortable.

"Fair enough," I said. "Felix, I want to find out who this Curt Chesak is, and I want to track him down."

"All right, and what happens after that?"

"Felix," I said, the dark words coming out but sounding so very right, "after I find him, I'm going to talk to him so he knows who I am and why I'm there."

A slight pause. Felix asked, "Then what?"

"Then I'm going to kill him," I said as we made our way south.